REAP

RED RIDGE SINNERS

CAITLYN DARE

Edited by Pinpoint Editing

Proofread by Proofreading by Sisters Get Lit(erary) Author Services

1

RIVER

"**W**hat the fuck did you do?"

Terror slams into me as blood seeps from Zach's shoulder.

"Relax." My brother tucks his gun into the waistband of his jeans. "It's just a surface graze."

"You shot me." Zach winces, trying to stem the bleeding. "You crazy fucking asshole shot me."

"Yeah, well, you touched my sister."

Rhett at least has the balls to look apologetic.

"I hate you," I shriek. "I hate you. I hate you. I hate—"

"Deal with that, would you?" Rhett says to Diesel, who's still holding me. He tries to whisper soothing words in my ear, but all I can see is Rhett—my big brother, my everything—pointing a gun at Zach and pulling the goddamn trigger.

People swarm the roof. Crank and Dane and a couple of the other guys. They take one look at Zach and both start yelling at Rhett. Crank attends to Zach, saying something about him needing sutures. Kat appears next, her gasp audible.

"River, oh my God, what happened? What—"

"I said stay the fuck down there." Crank pins her with a dark look.

"Fuck you, Killian. She's my best friend. I wasn't just gonna—"

"Fuck, that hurts."

"Oh my God. Zach." A fresh wave of terror fills me and I sob harder. "You could have killed him, Rhett. You could have fucking killed him."

Everyone looks at me, frowning at the pain in my voice.

"Does someone want to tell me what the hell happened up here?" Dane looks between us. Me and Rhett. Then me and Zach.

"Ask Stone." Rhett spits, his expression still murderous. "He was pawing all over her, like she... fuck. *Fuck!*"

"So you... shot him?" Disbelief coats Dane's words, but Rhett only snorts.

"Like you wouldn't act first and ask questions later if it was your baby fucking sister."

"Okay, okay, let's just all calm the fuck down. Crank, go see to him. Preferably inside, where we're not all just sitting ducks."

"Yeah, come on, man." Crank slips his arm around Zach and leads him toward the emergency access ladder.

Zach doesn't look at me.

Not even a glance.

Not that I blame him. I got him shot.

Shot.

Oh my God.

But he knows—he knows the truth about what

2

happened that night with Henry and his friends. If he tells them... If he tells Rhett...

Crap.

"Riv, talk to me." Kat stares at me with a worried expression. "What the hell happened?"

"I..."

Before I can beg Zach not to spill my secrets, he disappears. Letting out a heavy sigh, I look over to where it went down, and my gaze collides with Diesel's.

His expression is flat, and realization slams into me.

He saw me too.

He saw me and Zach... together.

Guilt coils around my heart. I don't regret what happened with Zach, I can't, but I do regret that Diesel found us like that.

He looks away first, following the rest of the guys off the roof, leaving me with Kat.

"Rhett shot Zach?"

"He... God, Kat, I messed up. I think I really messed up."

"Come on, let's sit. Whatever it is, it can't be that bad."

"They found us," I whisper-hiss. "My brother and Diesel turned up right as Zach and I were..."

I can't get the words out over the giant lump in my throat.

"Oh shit, that's... wow. You're right, I'm not sure there's any coming back from that."

"Helpful, thanks." I glower at her.

"Joke." She nudges my shoulder. "I'm joking. Rhett will get over it. You're not his kid sister anymore."

"I'll always be his kid sister," I point out.

"You know what I mean."

3

"Kat, he literally saw Zach... you know."

"Fucking you?"

"Oh God." I bury my face in my hands.

How embarrassing.

I'll never be able to look Rhett in the eyes again, let alone talk to him.

"Still, shooting Zach... that's pretty badass."

"There is something very wrong with you." I shake my head, and she smirks.

"What? It's hot."

"We should probably go down there, make sure they aren't killing each other."

"Crank and Diesel will keep the peace." I frown and she adds, "River, what aren't you telling me?"

"You promise to keep this to yourself? It's not something I want everyone knowing. Not yet, at least."

Unless Zach opens his big mouth before I have a chance to tell him not to.

"Sure, you can trust me."

I nod, trying to find the words. But then Sadie Ray's voice cuts through the air.

"River? Oh my God, Riv." She swings her leg over the edge of the roof and practically runs for me. "What happened? What the hell happened?"

"Rhett shot Zach," Kat says as if it's nothing.

As if my brother didn't pull out his gun, aim it at Zach, and clip him with a bullet.

"I got the short story. But what I haven't yet worked out is why." She arches her brow at me.

"I..." I glance at Kat, and she holds up her hands.

"Oh no, this is all on you."

"Thanks," I mutter before expelling a shaky breath. "Rhett and Diesel found me and Zach... you know."

"Fucking. He found them fucking."

I shoot Kat a 'what the hell' look and she shrugs.

"Holy shit, you and Zach? But he's so... and you're..."

"Gee, thanks."

"No, no, I don't mean it like that. I'm just surprised." Her expression softens, but hurt glitters in her eyes. "You never said anything."

"It's been a confusing time."

"Do you... like him?"

"It's complicated."

"Complicated how?"

"Because she likes my brother too."

"*Kat!*"

"Shit, sorry. I'm no good at this. I should go. I'll be in the clubhouse." Kat takes off, leaving me with Sadie Ray.

She watches me intently, willing me to look at her, but I don't know what to say.

She's the one person who might know how it feels to be in my predicament, yet I can't bring myself to say anything.

"River, come on." She squeezes my arm. "Talk to me, please."

Slowly lifting my head, I offer her a weak smile. "I don't even know where to start."

"How about the beginning?" she suggests.

Maybe it's time. Maybe talking about it will help.

Maybe.

Maybe.

Maybe.

But how can I talk to anyone about it when I haven't even figured out where I stand with each of them first? There isn't an *us* yet, there's a me and three guys I can't let go no matter how much I try.

"River?"

I blink at Sadie, hardening my resolve. "I'm fine," I say.

"You're not going to tell me, are you?"

"I'm not ready." I stand. "We should probably go down there."

Before I cause any more damage.

———————

The second we step into the clubhouse, the tension hits me.

Sadie Ray didn't push when I told her I wasn't ready to talk about it, but I can tell she's pissed at me.

She can get in line.

"Stop squirming like a little bitch and let me see to it."

Dane and Crank have Zach pinned in a chair as Crank attempts to clean the graze on his shoulder.

"It stings."

"You're lucky I didn't leave you with a hole," Rhett grunts.

"I warned you, brother." Dane pins my brother with a heavy stare. "If you can't cool it, then you can't be here. We need to get this taken care of."

"Quit fussing Stray, it's nothing more than a surface graze."

"You shot him, asshole. You're lucky he isn't on his way to the hospital right now."

"I didn't shoot to kill." Rhett shrugs.

"I swear to God, Savage. Quit it or—"

"Why doesn't everyone just relax?" Sadie wraps herself around my brother and demands his full attention, the two of them communicating with nothing but heated looks. It must work, because Rhett visibly relaxes and drops his antagonistic bullshit.

"Okay, now I'm going to suture it." Crank opens the suture kit and begins laying out all the contents. "It'll probably hurt. You'll want a shot of whiskey."

"Nah, I can handle it." Zach finds me across the room, finally looking at me.

"Get your fucking eyes off her, now."

"Rhett." Sadie grips his arm.

"Guess baby Savage is all grown up," Dane chuckles.

I roll my eyes, joining Kat over at our usual booth.

"Hey, listen," she says. "Sorry about before."

"Forget it."

"Shit, River, I..."

"Kat, I said it doesn't matter."

Guilt flashes in her eyes, but she doesn't say anything. Instead, we just sit there, watching Crank stitch Zach up.

"How's that feel?" Crank asks.

"Yeah, it feels okay." Zach stands, rotating his shoulder a couple of times. "Thanks, man."

Crank runs a hand through his hair, glancing between Zach and my brother. "Figure we got some shit to work through."

"Yeah, like how you've been lying through your fucking teeth to everyone about who Zach really is."

A ripple goes through the air, and everyone stops what they're doing.

"You got somethin' you wanna say to me, Savage?" Crank steps up to Rhett, and I don't miss the way he's actively putting himself between the two of them—Zach and my brother.

"I don't know what game you're playing, but she's my

sister—my fucking family—and you didn't think to fill me in?"

"Rhett, what are you talking about?" Sadie asks. When he doesn't answer her, she pins Dane with a worried look.

"Don't look at me, princess. I'm as in the dark as you are."

Diesel moves closer to them. He lays a hand on my brother's shoulder. "Rhett, man, why don't we just cool down, yeah? It seems we all need to talk."

"Talk?" Rhett spits. "It's a bit late for that, Walker. He"—he jabs his finger toward Zach—"was all over my sister. I can't unsee that. I can never—"

"Stop. Just stop."

I don't realize I've spoken until everyone is looking at me.

"You don't understand," I say.

"River," Diesel says. "You don't have to do this. You don't—"

"He shot him. What if he'd, he'd..." A shudder goes through me as I think of how differently tonight could have ended.

"Riv, you gotta see it from my point of view. I—"

"You messed up, Rhett." I stare at my brother, the guy who's always protected me, with hate in my eyes. "I'll never forgive you for this." The words are out before I can stop them.

Before I can process what they mean.

Pain flashes across his face, but his expression quickly darkens. "You don't mea—"

"Okay, okay," Dane says. "Why don't we all just take a breath? You two," he says, jabbing a finger at both Rhett and Zach, "my office. Now." Then he looks at Crank and

Diesel. "I'm guessing this is a conversation you should probably be there for as well."

Crank scrubs his jaw, nodding, and the four of them disappear down the hall.

Dane looks back at me with a small smile that doesn't reach his eyes. "We'll get this shit sorted, little Savage. You'll see."

He takes off after them, leaving me standing there.

Wishing I could believe him.

2

DIESEL

"What the fuck is going on?" Stray barks the second he swings the door closed behind us, making his office feel smaller than it's ever been.

"Don't fucking look at me," Rhett hisses, glaring between me and Crank.

"Fuck. How'd you find out?" I ask.

"Does it matter? What matters is that the two of you have been lying to two fucking clubs about who"—he jabs his finger in Zach's direction—"that asshole is."

"Rhett," Dane snaps before walking over to his desk and dropping down into the chair behind it. "Shut the fuck up, yeah?"

Crossing his arms over his chest, Rhett sulks while Dane turns to his VP.

"Wanna start talking?" he hisses at Crank.

"Zach isn't just our cousin," he starts. It might not be common knowledge around the club, but the reason we helped Zach in the first place was because he's family. Something we didn't make public outside of this office for fear of people looking too hard into his past. "He's family. Family who needed help," Crank emphasizes, knowing that Dane will understand.

"I fucking get that, man. But did you really think I didn't need all the fucking details?"

"We were hoping to keep it on the down low," I mutter.

"How's that working out for you?" Rhett mutters.

"You just fucking shot one of our brothers. Be glad I haven't sent you the fuck home," Dane booms, much to Rhett's surprise. "What? This club is mine, Savage, and I won't have anyone running around with a fucking gun getting trigger happy. Even you."

Rhett's jaw tics as he grinds his teeth, but he doesn't respond for long seconds.

"Get the truth. Then you might feel differently. This club might be yours, but I guarantee there's a girl out there looking after him that you'd lay your fucking life down for. And while he's here, she's in danger."

Dane's body jolts as if Rhett just pulled his piece again.

"Exactly," Rhett says, smugness laced through his voice.

"Who is he?"

"He came from the Colton Night Crawlers," I confess.

"WHAT?" Dane barks. "Are you fucking serious?"

"It gets worse," Crank adds.

"Of course it does," Dane mutters, rubbing at his temples.

"He's on the run because he killed their second."

"Great, so not only are we harboring a fucking Night Crawler, but he's also in fucking hiding from the boss?

Don't you both think we've seen enough trouble over the past few months?"

"He's family," I sigh, knowing it's the only angle Dane will understand.

"I know, and I fucking get that—" His eyes move from mine to Zach when he shuffles in the corner, his hand clamped over the wound on his shoulder. "Sit the fuck down, Zach," he demands.

Zach looks at the couch where Rhett is sprawled out and then to the one remaining empty chair I'm yet to sit in.

"Fine," he mutters, stalking to the seat beside Crank and lowering his ass down.

"Tell me you had a really good fucking reason for wiping out the Night Crawlers' second," Dane begs, staring Zach dead in the eyes.

"Because he was a cunt," Zach scoffs, clearly not wanting to tell his story.

"Truth, Zach," I tell him. He's not going to get out of this room without it.

"He was abusing my mom," he confesses quietly. "He'd been controlling her for years, but one day I came home and... I'd put a bullet through his head before I even knew I'd pulled my gun." He shrugs like it was nothing, as if he regrets nothing. And I must admit, after hearing the whole story from Mom, I'm pretty sure I'd be feeling the same.

"And you ran?"

"Yes and no. Mom got me out, set me up here. Evelyn is my dad's sister. She thought it would be safe here."

"You didn't want to come," Dane correctly guesses.

"The fuck I did. I want to be in Colton, protecting Mom," he spits, his fists curling on the arms of the chair.

12

"Jesus fucking Christ. So basically, we're expecting the Night Crawlers on our doorstep any moment, ready to enact revenge on this motherfucker?" Dane summarizes.

"They won't come here," Zach says, although there's not much confidence in his voice.

"You killed their VP. You don't just walk away from that."

"Unless your mom is paying the price," Rhett chips in, making Zach's entire body still. "She is, isn't she? How is she protecting you, Stone?"

"It doesn't matter," he hisses, forcing the words out through clenched teeth as the skin of his knuckles turns white with the tightness of his fists.

"She's shacked up with the boss," Crank explains.

"Ah, distracting him with blow jobs," Rhett announces with a smirk.

"Shut the fuck up," Dane barks, knowing his brother well enough to know he's taunting Zach into another fight.

"What matters is that Zach is safe here," Crank says. "And if the worst happens, then we've got his back, right? He's our brother now."

I agree, while Rhett glowers at all of us. Dane just looks like we've steamrolled him into a corner.

"I guess there's not much else we can do, is there?" Resting his elbows on his desk, he leans forward, glaring at all of us.

A ripple of anticipation goes around the room. Dane might be young—many would probably say too young to be our prez, to take charge of this club—but age doesn't matter to us. It's just a number.

A fact that makes me wince internally, seeing as it's

the excuse I've used time and time again when it comes to River.

He's the boss, plain and simple. And what he says goes, because no matter how he landed the role, it's his. We stand by our leader until the end.

"Does anyone else have anything they need to tell me?" he asks, a clear warning in his tone.

Silence rings around his office.

"Okay," he says, pushing his chair out behind him and resting his palms on the old walnut top. "From here on out, I want to know every detail when it comes to this. No matter how fucking small. I will not allow this club to be ambushed by the fucking Crawlers."

His eyes focus on Zach, and something passes between them. "D is right. We look after our own. And you're one of us now. So anything happens, you tell us. We've got your back."

Zach nods, but he doesn't say anything.

"The four of you need to sort this out. And I need a fucking drink."

He storms from the room, leaving only the echo of the slamming door in his wake.

"Fuck this," Zach barks, pushing from the chair as if he's about to bolt, but Rhett soon puts a stop to that when he stands and gets right in his face once again.

"Rhett, chill the fuck out, man," Crank sighs, stepping forward, ready to get in the middle of the two of them.

I, however, stay where I am with my back resting against the wall, silently hoping Rhett takes a swing at the asshole.

The image we stumbled upon on the roof is burned into my fucking brain.

Seeing him with his hands all over River. Watching

him stare down at her like she was his. Knowing that he was taking exactly what I wanted.

What I still want.

My fists curl with my need to storm over there myself and take a swing.

She deserves better than him.

Better than any of us.

My chest heaves right along with theirs as they stare each other down.

"You need to stay the fuck away from River," Rhett finally seethes, his voice almost inaudible with his barely-contained rage.

"And you need to let River make her own choices," Zach counters.

"No fucking chance when her choices involve fucking stupid ones, like going anywhere near the likes of you," he spits.

"You really don't know her at all, do you?" Zach tells him, his voice steady and deadly serious.

"She's my sister," Rhett booms, his voice echoing off the walls around us. But despite the volume, Zach doesn't so much as flinch. "I know everything about her."

"Do you?" Zach taunts. "Do you really?"

"Yeah, and I know she's too good for a fucking scumbag like you. She's good. Pure. A fucking angel. She—"

Zach's laughter rings through the air, cutting off Rhett's rant. "Bro, you're a fucking idiot," he manages through his amusement.

Rhett has his hand around Zach's throat and him pinned back against Dane's desk faster than either Crank or I expect.

"I'm fucking warning you, Stone. If I hear of you

putting any part of your fucking body anywhere near my sister again, I'll make sure my next shot is fired to kill."

Not wanting things to escalate again, Crank pulls Rhett off Zach, leaving him gasping for breath.

"Let's go and cool off. You're embarrassing yourself."

Rhett's eyes find mine, and he begs for me to back him up. There's a part of me that wants to. I've got a little sister, and fuck if I want any of the guys around here touching her. And I can't deny the fact that if I'd walked in on what we did not so long ago and discovered Kat in that position, I may have reacted similarly. But I also can't forget that we're not talking about Kat, we're talking about River, and agreeing with Rhett right now would be nothing but hypocritical.

Reaching out, I open the door, refusing to comment on the situation for fear that Rhett will discover something else which will send him even more psycho where River is concerned. He just caught Zach between her thighs—he really doesn't need to know I've also had my face down there.

"I thought you'd have my fucking back, D," Rhett seethes.

My lips part to say something, fuck knows what, but thankfully, it's not necessary, because Zach's voice fills the room instead.

"You need to talk to River, Savage. Find out who she really is, what her life in Colton was really like."

Rhett stills, and Crank's grip on his shoulders tightens, ready to stop him from doubling back and taking Zach to the floor.

"Keep walking, man." Crank pushes him forward and lets the door swing closed behind them.

My eyes hold Zach's as his hand drops from rubbing at his throat.

"What?" he snaps.

"I don't know what you think you know about River, but Rhett's right. She's too good for you."

He barks a laugh, shaking his head at me. "You're only saying that because you want her to yourself."

"That's not—"

"Don't fucking lie to me, cous. I see it in your eyes every time you look at her. I felt it the night you hit me after discovering I was the one who roughed her up. You want her just as badly as I do, but just like Rhett, you're totally fucking naïve as to who she really is."

"And you're not?" I ask, ignoring all his other points, because I can't exactly argue with them.

"I know exactly who River is. And she's not the sweet, little, innocent flower you've all pegged her as."

"Explain," I demand, finally pushing from the wall and closing the space between us with my fists curled.

"No," he states simply.

"No?"

"Exactly. If River wanted you to know, then she'd have told you herself by now, don't you think? You want the truth about your 'pretty girl,'" he mocks, making me see red, "then you need to ask her yourself."

"Fucking asshole," I grunt before swinging my fist and knocking him back down on the desk.

I shouldn't have done it, but fuck. I can't deny that I don't feel a little better as pain radiates up my arm and wipes out that image of him about to push inside her that's still so vivid in my mind.

3

RIVER

"Hey," Jax says with a hesitant smile. "What's going on?"

"I... long story," I reply right as Kat blurts out, "Rhett shot Zach, and now they're all in Dane's office—"

"Kat, seriously?"

"Sorry." She shoots me an apologetic smile.

"Rhett shot Zach?" The blood drains from Jax's face as he frowns at me. "Did he—"

I shake my head, mouthing, "Not here," and flick my gaze to Kat.

"Oh, oh." She darts up. "I just remembered, I have to... do some homework. I'll be going, but you two should stay, talk."

"I... uh... are you okay?" Jax asks her, and I stifle a chuckle.

"Yep, fine. I'm fine. But you two should..." She wags her finger between us and practically runs out of the clubhouse.

"She's discreet, huh?" My cheeks flush as Jax slides into the booth.

"So Rhett shot Zach? Do I even want to know?"

"Probably not."

"Oh." His expression falls.

"It's complicated."

"Tell me about it," he murmurs. "But you're okay? That's got to be... intense."

"It was awful. I thought he was going to kill him."

"They don't say your brother is Savage by name, Savage by nature for no reason."

"I guess." I peek up at him.

Things feel weird between us. We haven't talked since the other night at the motel.

"How are you... I mean, after what happened—"

"River, you don't have to explain. It was a wild night."

"I want you to know, I didn't know Zach had planned that. I didn't know..."

"Hey." He reaches over, his hand hovering over me as if he's torn between comforting me and not. "It's okay." His hand covers mine, and warmth spreads through me. "So the two of you are what, exactly?"

"Like I said, it's complicated."

"And you and D?"

"Jesus, Jax." I snatch my hand away. "I don't know, okay? There's been a lot going on."

"Sorry, I didn't mean to upset you."

I let out a heavy sigh, feeling it settle in my stomach. "It's not you. It's everything. Rhett shot him, Jax. He pointed his gun at Zach and pulled the trigger. That's not normal."

"He just wants to protect your honor."

"Yeah well, it's a bit late for that."

"A bit late for what?"

I startle at the sound of Rhett's voice. He's leaning against the doorjamb, watching. He still looks murderous, his eyes dark and stormy.

The rest of the guys barge past him and I search for Zach. But he's nowhere to be seen.

Oh God.

Did he tell them?

Did Zach tell them all the truth about me? About that night?

My stomach churns as Rhett stalks toward us.

"Can we go somewhere? Talk?"

"I..." I gulp.

"Please, Riv. We need this."

"You should go," Jax says, and I shoot him glare.

"Fine." I stand.

"Come on, let's take a walk." Rhett motions for me to go ahead and I do, not bothering to wait for him.

I don't want to do this. Not now. Not tonight.

But he's right, we do need to talk.

Especially if Zach told him everything.

Dread snakes through me. I've always been Rhett's sweet, innocent, little sister. I don't want him to look at me and see me differently.

I don't want him to be disgusted with me.

But I'm also so sick of being treated like a kid.

The silence is thick between us as we make our way outside.

"Come on." Rhett beckons me to follow him past the shop. Unlike the Savage Falls compound, Red Ridge's land doesn't back onto the river, but its far border is a line of dense trees. There's a small woodshed and a couple of benches. We sit at one.

"I owe you an apology," he says.

"You do?"

"Yeah. I shouldn't have gone off like that. But shit, Riv, when I saw that fucker on you, I lost it." His fist clenches against his thigh.

"Lost it?" I let out a bitter laugh. "You shot him, Rhett. What the hell were you thinking?"

"It was barely a—"

"I swear to God, if you say it was only a surface graze, I will lose my shit."

"Fuck, when did you get so... grown up?" He stares at me as if he doesn't recognize me, and I hate it.

I hate the distance between us lately.

He's always been my big brother. My protector. But somewhere along the line, things changed.

"I'm not a kid, Rhett. In a few months, I'll be eighteen."

"Don't remind me."

"So... what did you guys talk about?"

His brows knit as he scrubs a hand down his face. "Stuff."

"Stuff." The pit in my stomach churns wider. "You talked about *stuff*?"

"You want to know what Stone told me?"

"I want to know that you didn't try to kill him again."

"Shit, Riv. He was practically fucking you into—"

"Please, don't." I hold up my hand, flinching at his harsh tone. "I was there, remember?"

"But of all people... why him? Are you lashing out? Is it some kind of way to piss me off?"

"Oh my God, Rhett. Has it ever occurred to you that this isn't about you? It's about me."

"What the fuck is that supposed to mean?" He gawks

at me. "I spent years, *years* keeping you away from this world. Do you know why? Because you're good, Riv. You're too fucking good for this life, for guys like me. Like Stone."

"But my life is the club now, Rhett. You can't expect me to live with one foot in and one foot out. It doesn't work like that."

"But Stone? He's a fucking moron."

"You don't even know him."

"And you do? Is that it? Does he have a side he doesn't let anyone else see but you? Because that's some fucked-up bullshit right there."

"You mean like you and Sadie Ray?" My brow lifts.

"It's not the same," he huffs.

"Isn't it? You're not exactly a warm person, Rhett. The two of you hated each other when I first moved here."

"I guess I don't really have an argument there."

"No, you don't."

Silence descends over us, thick and oppressive as Rhett considers my words. I know he only wants the best for me, but it hurts that he doesn't think I'm capable of making my own decisions.

"You deserve better, Riv. I'm sorry... but you do."

"You don't understand," I whisper, unsure if I feel relief that Rhett doesn't know the whole truth, or disappointed that now I have to be the one who tells him.

Because he needs to know.

If I ever want him to forgive Zach—and it's a long shot that he will—Rhett needs to know the truth.

"So talk to me, tell me what's been going on with you. You can always come to me, River, with anything."

"You say that, but you've barely been around lately."

"Riv, that's not—" Rhett stops himself, guilt shining in his dark eyes.

He knows I'm right. How can he not? Since he moved in with Sadie and the guys, they've been living in their little bubble of happiness, leaving the rest of us—me mostly—to fend for ourselves.

"You're right, I've been wrapped up in Sadie, the house... the club."

"I get it, I do. But she moved out and it's like... it's like I'm back in Colton again. Alone."

"Colton? What does Colton have to do with this?" His expression darkens. "What's going on, River? Stone said—"

"What did Zach say?" I rush out, fear racing up my spine.

"He said I should talk to you, that I had you all wrong. There's something I'm missing here, isn't there? About Colton. About whatever's going on with you and Stone."

"We met in Colton."

"What?" He stares at me as if I've grown a second head.

"Remember Henry? Henry Parsons?"

"The spoiled rich prick from school?"

Of course Rhett would call him that. He didn't know just how close the two of us got.

"Yeah." I swallow down the rush of bile up my throat. "We were friends... actually, we were more than friends. Kind of."

"Kind of? What the fuck does that mean? And why the hell am I only just hearing about this?"

I inhale a shaky breath. "Rhett... you're not making this easy. Maybe that's the reason I've never talked to you about this before."

23

He grumbles something inaudible, and I roll my eyes.

"I had a major crush on Henry, and in tenth grade, he finally returned my... interest." I cringe. This is harder than I thought.

"Was he your boyfriend or something?"

"I wanted him to be. But Henry was... rich, spoiled, used to getting what he wanted."

"I know the type." Rhett scoffed.

"Yeah, well. I didn't. We were friends first. I trusted him, I didn't think he would..." I drop my eyes, unable to look my big brother in the eye.

"Didn't think he would what, River?" His anger is palpable, rippling through the air like a wake current.

"There was a party. He wanted to take me as his girl. I was so excited, Rhett. You don't understand, I was desperately lonely. I struggled to make girlfriends because I didn't fit into their perfect world. But Henry never cared about that stuff. He was nice to me. Kind.

"I snuck out that night. You were in Savage Falls as usual, and Mom was... well, she was checked out. I'd saved up all my allowance to buy a new dress. I was so excited. I really thought it was the night Henry was going to tell me he wanted to go steady."

"What happened, River?" His voice is a low growl.

"It was a cruel trick. He didn't want me. He wanted to toy with me. Use me. He got me drunk. It was silly, I know, but I was so nervous. I thought the beer would help... I thought it would make it easier to talk to people.

"Henry told me he wanted to take me somewhere more private, away from the crowd. We went to a room." A shudder goes through me, and I have to take a second to calm my racing heart. "But we weren't alone. All his friends were there, waiting."

24

"No, fuck no." Rhett inhales a thin breath. "Did they—"

"N-no," I rush out, "it didn't get that far. At first, I didn't understand. Didn't understand why they were all leering at me, laughing and pointing. Henry grabbed me and kissed my neck, whispering how hot I got him. How much he wanted me to please him. Before I understood what was happening, he... he pushed me to my knees and then he..."

Silent tears roll down my cheeks. "He undid his jeans and wound his fist in my hair while his friends all laughed and looked on. I was so scared, Rhett. But more than that, I was heartbroken. I'd spent months following him around, hoping that one day he would return my affections... and it was all a joke. It was all—"

"He touched you?"

"I—I..."

"Did he touch you?" Rhett roars, making me flinch, and I smother a whimper. "Shit, River... fuck. *Fuck.*" His fist slams against the bench, cracking the wood.

"Nothing happened because Zach saved me. He saved me, Rhett." I stare him dead in the eye. "If he hadn't turned up when he did, I... I don't know what might have happened."

"I'll kill him." Rhett shoots up. "I'll fucking kill him."

"W-what?" I scramble to my feet, grabbing his arm. "What are you talking about?"

"That fucker Henry is a dead man walking."

4

ZACH

"Rhett, no, please," River begs, rushing after her brother as he tries to storm away.

I'd told the guys I was going to my room to change. D wanted to argue, I could see it in his eyes. He was worried I was about to go and do something stupid. And I guess he was right to some extent, because while I might have headed toward my room, instead of going inside, I slipped out the back door and went in search of River and Rhett.

I knew he wouldn't hurt her. He loves her more than life, that much is obvious, but he's angry, and I know all too well how anger can overtake any rational thought. That's pretty much how I found myself here in the first place.

I acted before my brain could catch up with me, and by the time I registered what was happening, there was a naked man bleeding out at my feet.

Moving around the tree I'm hiding behind, I watch as they both move, River clinging to Rhett's arm in a hopeless attempt to stop him from doing something about the twisted fuck who tried to ruin her that night.

The need for vengeance, for that fucker's blood burns through my veins almost as hot as it did the night I found her surrounded by that cunt and his little gang of douchebags.

I shudder as I remember the way they were looking at her, the things they were saying to her while she knelt there, utterly terrified. But they were getting off on that. They were feeding on her fear, and it was fucking sick.

"Okay, fine," Rhett snaps, dragging me from the nightmare of that night and the guilt that floods me every time I think about it. "Fine," he snaps, tugging his arm free of her grasp.

"Do you really mean that?" River asks, her voice weak and shaky as if she's balancing right on the edge of keeping her shit together over all this.

The air crackles between them as Rhett stares at her, clearly not wanting to agree to this insanity. And for probably the first, and possibly the last time, I can't help but be on his side.

Henry needs dealing with.

It should have happened that night, but I couldn't do it.

Now, though... Now, I've got nothing to lose.

"Yeah, Riv. I mean it," he tells her, forcing his voice to soften a little.

Her body immediately relaxes, and she falls into him, wrapping her arms around his big frame.

She looks so tiny, so vulnerable. My muscles ache to be the one feeling her warmth, although I'm not sure I'd be satisfied with a fucking cuddle right now.

Sweet little River owes me one, and after tonight, I fully intend on cashing that in. Soon.

"River?" a soft, familiar voice calls, and she pulls back from her brother's embrace to respond.

"Down by the woodshed," she shouts back, her voice sounding stronger.

Kat emerges from around the corner of one of the storage buildings and steps up to the two of them. I can't hear what they discuss, and my need to know almost forces me out of hiding. But I lock it down.

After a few minutes, Kat takes River's hand and together they walk back around the building, leaving Rhett alone. His hands go to his head before he tips his face up to the sky as if he's praying for some fucking strength.

Twigs snap beneath my boots as I emerge from the shadows. If Rhett hears it, he doesn't react. Well, not until I speak.

"Do not tell me you really meant what you just said," I say.

His eyes find mine, hardening instantly. "You were fucking listening?" he spits.

Ignoring his question, I keep our conversation on track. "You're not really going to let that sick fuck get away with this, are you?"

Rhett scoffs, turning his back on me, ready to walk away.

"Hey, asshole. I asked you a fucking question."

He pauses, his body locking up, his shoulders tensing. "Why haven't you already done it? Why is he still breathing after laying a fucking finger on her?"

"Because—" I swallow, regret and guilt twisting in my

stomach. "Because I couldn't do it. Henry is connected. If I so much as touched him then—"

"It's a bit fucking late for that now, don't you think? You've already been cast aside. Beating up some fucking rapist scumbag would be nothing compared to killing the second in your stupid fucking gang."

"My stupid gang?" I drawl, lifting my hand and gesturing toward the compound. "Are we really going to stand here and argue over stupid fucking gangs?"

"The club isn't a gang. It's a lifestyle, a family. The Colton Night Crawlers are fucking scum and you know it. They don't blood you in for no reason."

I jolt like he just took another shot at me.

"And they don't just let you fucking get away, either," he seethes, his hard eyes narrowing.

"They'll find me one day. And they'll kill me," I state with a shrug. It's a reality that I came to terms with the night I ran. Something I wouldn't have done if it weren't for Mom.

"And you brought that to our fucking door? To my sister's doorstep?"

"I don't want to be here as much as you don't want me here, I can assure you of that."

"Then why are you fucking here?" he barks.

"For Mom. For family," I add, knowing it'll hit a soft spot. "She's got in bed with the devil over this, and I fully intend on getting her out. I just need to figure some stuff out."

"Fucking hell," he mutters, kicking at the ground beneath us, sending a cloud of dust into the air.

His eyes hold mine, searching, trying to find the lies in my words. But he won't. There are none there. My mom is the single most important person in my life, and I'll happily give mine in return for hers if that's where this needs to go. It's not like I'm worth much to anyone. She deserves it more than me.

"No," Rhett finally says, confusing the shit out of me.

"W-what?"

"No, I'm not going to let that motherfucker get away with laying a fucking finger on my sister." His face morphs into the monster that was glaring pure death at me on the rooftop.

"Good. I'll be right fucking beside you."

His lips part to respond, but he quickly changes his mind about what he was going to say.

"Not here," he hisses. "Come on."

E very single member of the club turns to look at us when we march back into the clubhouse. D and Crank are immediately on their feet as they look between the two of us.

"Chill out. We haven't killed each other... yet," Rhett mutters, marching toward the bar and demanding an entire bottle of whiskey from Bones.

"Same," I mutter, dropping my ass to one of the barstools.

The second the bottle appears in front of me, I twist the top and lift it to my lips, swallowing down nearly a quarter of it in one go.

A shadow falls over me, and when I glance back, I'm hardly surprised to find D standing there, looking concerned. Although there's a harsh edge to his expression, and I know why.

He almost witnessed me taking exactly what he wants.

That shit must have stung.

Making a snap decision, I stand, taking the bottle with me, and turn away. "D, you're going to want to be involved in this," I tell him, quietly enough so only Rhett hears.

He shoots me a concerned look, but I wave it off.

If anyone else is going to be gunning for this asshole, then it's going to be D.

"Savage," Stray calls before he gets to follow us, and when I look back, Rhett nods for us to continue without him.

"What the fuck is going on?" D asks the second we're away from prying ears.

I ignore the question until we're inside my room with the door closed behind us.

"There's something I never told you about River." His eyes widen in curiosity. "And Rhett and I need your help with a rat."

"Keep talking," he says, dropping down onto my couch while I give him the CliffsNotes about Henry.

His body morphs from being pretty much chilled to buzzing with barely restrained anger right before my eyes.

The transformation is actually pretty beautiful.

Until he came at me the night he figured out I'd fucked River raw, I wondered if he really had what it took to be Stray's Sergeant. But that night, I saw the devil hiding behind his protective big brother façade. Couple that with the look on his face right now, and I know he's got what it fucking takes.

I also know just how deeply he feels about River, too.

31

"When are we doing this?" he asks, not needing to hear any more to be convinced that he needs to be a part of it.

"Well, if Savage would get his ass in—" As if my saying his name summoned him, the door swings open and in walks the man himself.

His eyes immediately find Diesel. "You told him." It's not a question. He can see the fury swirling in Diesel's eyes.

"He'd want in," I tell Rhett, praying he doesn't lose his shit all over again when he realizes D wants River just as much, hell, probably more than I do.

"If this were Kat, I know you'd have my back, man," Diesel says cleverly.

"Yeah," Rhett mutters, rubbing at the back of his neck.

He's really not buying this shit, but fuck it. If he wants this done, then the more of us the better.

"What's the plan then, Stone? You're the one who can find this prick."

Taking a long pull from my bottle of whiskey, I drop onto the edge of my bed and start relaying everything that's been swirling around my head since that night.

We've almost got a solid idea of what to do when a knock sounds out on my door. The three of us look at each other before I call out to tell whoever it is to come in.

My eyes widen the second Jax steps into the room with his head held high and determination written all over his face. His eyes hold mine as the tension in the room mounts to almost unbearable levels.

"What's going on?" Jax finally demands, sounding like an entirely different person to the guy I was with in that motel room not so long ago.

When none of us offer him any answer, he continues. "Kat's taken River home," he informs us, "and I can't help feeling like I'm missing something fucking big about all of this."

D's eyes find mine, a silent question passing between us.

"I think you'd better sit down, Jaxy boy," I say. "What we've got to tell you is probably going to hurt."

His lips part, but after pushing his hair back from his brow, he rests back against the wall and nods.

If I thought he looked wrecked, watching River as I got her off right in front of him the other night, then I really underestimated the level of wounded puppy his face was capable of. Because right now, he looks like someone just told him the world has ended.

"When?" he asks simply, not even needing to hear the plan.

"Tomorrow night. No cuts. Nothing that can identify us. We go in darkness, teach this motherfucker a lesson, and come back like nothing ever happened."

"Get a fucking alibi," Rhett adds.

"And River is to know nothing about this," Diesel warns.

"You got it," he says, cracking his knuckles, already gunning for this cunt's blood.

"Great. Well, if that's sorted. I'm going to leave the three of you to your pajama party," Rhett says, taking what's left of his bottle and marching toward the door. "And if tonight has taught you fuckers anything, then you'll stay away from my fucking sister." His simmering anger almost bubbles over once more as he pins each of us with a warning look before blowing out of the room.

"We'll see," I mutter the second the door slams behind

33

him. My eyes connect with Jax's and then Diesel's, all of us feeling whatever's crackling between us.

5

RIVER

Kat offers to stay with me, but I decline. I need some space. It's been a crazy few hours.

Rhett was so angry about Henry that for a second, I thought he was going to get on his bike and go straight to Colton to look for him.

It's exactly why I didn't tell him when it happened. That and I was desperately ashamed.

I'd always been the outsider at school, but Henry made me feel included. He made me feel like my childhood, my upbringing, and my mom's addiction didn't matter. He was my friend, and I wanted—*hoped*—he would be my boyfriend.

But it was all a lie. A cruel, sick game to use and degrade the club whore. That's what they called me that night. I left that part out when I confessed everything to Rhett. I didn't need to stoke the fire.

Moving to Savage Falls, although hard, was the best thing that could have happened to me. I didn't see it at the time, but I fit in better here than I ever did in Henry's world. But my secret has made it hard for me to truly belong.

Now that Rhett knows, maybe I'll feel differently. Maybe things will change.

I grab a bottle of water from the refrigerator and head to my room. Ray and Victoria must still be at the compound, because there's no sign of them.

But I welcome the silence.

Watching my brother shoot Zach will haunt me for a long time. I just hope it doesn't cause too many problems for the club. My cell phone vibrates and I check my messages, surprised to see Zach's name.

Zach: We need to talk

Me: Not tonight. I need some space...

Me: I'm really sorry... about everything

Worrying my bottom lip, I await his answer, but it never comes. Guess he didn't need to talk that much, after all. If he knows what's good for him, Zach will stay away from me. But something tells me a guy like Zach Stone won't appreciate being told who he can and can't see. And I can't deny a part of me wants him to disobey Rhett's order. I want him to come after me.

For once, I want to be worth more than my name or my connections or my past.

I want someone to want *me*.

Ugh. I flounce down on my bed, clutching my cell phone, willing him to reply. I need to speak to Diesel too, to explain... but that's a conversation that will have to wait.

I close my eyes and let out a steady breath, replaying the moment Rhett shot Zach over and over in my head. I love my brother, but he drew a line tonight. Him on one side. Me on the other.

But the jury is out on which side Zach will stand.

The next morning, I wake feeling like I've been hit by a truck. Part of me thought Zach might turn up to talk. But he didn't.

I guess I shouldn't be surprised after everything that happened. It still hurts, though.

Hurts to think that he might not believe I'm worth the fight. If he decides I'm not, it's only going to prove Rhett right. The thought irritates me. Because I defended Zach, I defended him... and—

The doorbell startles me and I climb out of bed, pulling on a hoodie. Ray's bedroom door is closed, so he and Victoria must have eventually made it home.

Unlatching the lock, I open the door slightly, surprised to find Diesel standing there.

"Hey," he says. "I know it's early, but I couldn't wait any longer. Can we talk?"

"I..." My eyes drop down my body. "Breakfast?"

"Sure. Shall I uh... wait by the car? Or..."

"Yeah, Ray and Vic are still sleeping. I'll be out soon."

He nods, taking off down the driveway.

I fly into action, quickly washing up and pulling on some clean clothes. I leave Ray a note on the refrigerator saying I've gone out to get breakfast with a friend. I'm sure he'll have questions, but right now, I have bigger problems to deal with.

Like the fact that Diesel wants to talk. After he saw Zach about to fuck me on the roof of his club.

Inhaling a sharp breath, I grab my keys and slip out of the house. Diesel offers me a tight smile that makes the knot in my stomach twist.

"That was quick," he says as I climb inside the car.

"I'm hungry." I'm not, but he doesn't need to know that. "How are you?"

"Jesus, Riv, you can't—" He stops himself. "Let's just get to the diner, then we'll talk."

I nod, feeling like a child caught with their hand in the cookie jar. His disappointment lingers in the air around us.

"I never meant to hurt you," I whisper, staring at my hands.

"Yeah, well... shit happens."

Diesel is quiet as we arrive outside the diner.

Too quiet.

"Come on," he says before I can suggest that maybe this is a bad idea, that maybe we should go somewhere more private.

But he doesn't wait for me, unfolding his body out of the car and stalking toward the diner.

It's the same one he brought me to before. When things were less complicated between us.

Or maybe they've always been complicated.

I've always felt a connection to Diesel. I thought he could help me move on from Jax. I thought he was the guy to mend my broken heart. But I was wrong. And now, I have all these feelings for three guys.

Three different, complicated guys.

Diesel holds the door open for me and I slip inside.

"Morning, kids. Grab a table and I'll be right over," an older woman calls, and I wince at her use of the word 'kids.'

As if Diesel needs any more reminders of our age difference.

I choose the booth we sat at last time and study the menu, anything to keep myself distracted from the stifling tension swirling around us.

"River," he says softly, "look at me."

I lift my eyes.

"How are you?"

"I... I'm sorry. I'm so sorry, I never meant for you to see—"

"Stop, just stop." He lays his hand on mine, glancing around the diner to make sure we have privacy. "You have nothing to apologize for."

"We both know that's not true."

"You're your own person, River. If Zach is who you want—"

"It's not... that's not..." I let out an exasperated breath. "It's more complicated than that."

"Yeah, I know." He scrubs a hand over his jaw. "If I'd have known... I would have kept Rhett off the roof."

"Why? Why would you do that?"

"Because I care about you, and the last thing I want is for you to get hurt."

"It's funny." A strangled laugh bubbles in my chest. "Jax broke my heart. You refused to fix it... and then Zach came along, and everything is different now."

"Sometimes it takes losing something to realize how much you want it." His eyes bore into mine with an intensity that steals my breath.

"That's not fair, D, and you know it."

He gives me a sad smile. "Doesn't make it any less true."

"We should order," I say, glancing back down at the menu. I can't think with him looking at me like that. Silently telling me things I've been desperate to hear.

Does he want me to choose him?

Choose him when he's made me no promises, even after everything that's happened between us?

Because I can't do it. I can't choose.

I won't.

"Shit, Riv, I didn't mean... I brought you here to check if you were okay, not to make things worse. You know I care about you."

"I care about you too, D." I peek up at him.

"So we're good?"

"We're good. Although, I'm worried about what Rhett might do."

"Do? What do you mean..."

"I..." Crap, why did I say that? "To Zach, I mean." I quickly cover my slip.

"Well, he already shot him, so I'm not sure it can get any worse." Diesel smiles, but I only grimace. "Too soon?" he adds.

I nod.

"Sorry, I was just trying to lighten the mood."

"Will you promise me something?"

"Anything."

"Don't let Rhett do anything stupid, okay? I know I don't have any right to ask, but I trust you, Diesel."

"You don't need to worry about Rhett going after Zach, I promise."

His words should settle some of the unease fluttering in my chest, but there's something about his expression that confuses me.

"What is—"

"Good morning, what can I get for you?" The server chooses that moment to look over at us.

Diesel starts reeling off his order, and I take the opportunity to study him. He seems lighter, like a weight's been lifted. But I can't forget the flash of guilt I'm sure I just saw in his eyes.

I only wish I could read his mind to know what it means.

After breakfast with Diesel, he takes me back to his house because 'Kat wants to see with her own eyes that you're okay.' His words, not mine.

He doesn't stick around, and I can't help but feel like he's trying to avoid the unfinished conversation we had at the diner.

"Thank God." Kat pulls me into the house. "I've been worried."

"I'm okay."

"How was breakfast?" Her brow lifts.

"It was... breakfast."

"You know, just because it's my brother, you don't have to spare me the details. Well, some details." She shudders. "But you can talk to me about him."

"What do you want me to say?" I follow her into the kitchen and perch at the counter.

"I don't know. Whatever you want to share with me."

"Kat..." I sigh.

"Fine. Fine." She holds up her hands in defeat. "You're not ready to admit it."

"I'm... can we not do this right now? I have bigger things to worry about."

"Like what?"

"Like my brother doing something stupid."

"He already shot Zach, Riv. I'm not sure it gets more stupid than that."

"I'm not talking about Zach, Kat."

Her brows furrow. "I don't understand. What else—"

"I need to tell you something."

"I'm listening."

"Something happened to me, before the summer. Before I moved to Savage Falls."

"Okaaaay..."

So I tell her.

I tell her all about Henry and our friendship, the way he led me to believe that we could be more, that he wanted me the same way I wanted him. I tell her about that night, how confused and scared I was. How Zach saved me, but I didn't remember until recently.

By the time I'm done, she's gawking at me, the color drained from her face.

"What a piece of shit. I hope Rhett and the guys go break his legs. Or at least chop his tiny dick off."

"Kat!"

"What?" She shrugs. "He deserves it."

"I don't want Rhett to do anything. Henry is well connected in Colton." But I pause, her words reverberating through my skull, and I ask, "What do you mean, Rhett and the guys? He wouldn't tell them."

No way.

It's my secret.

My business.

Kat shoots me an apologetic look. "Babe, if you think Rhett and Zach aren't plotting ways to make that asshole pay, then you clearly haven't been paying attention." Her expression falls. "The Sinners look out for their own, River. And you, girl, are practically Sinners royalty."

6

DIESEL

Guilt still sits heavy in my stomach as I walk into the clubhouse after my morning with River. I'm not really sure what I was hoping to achieve by taking her out for breakfast. Obviously, I wanted to know that she was okay after the fallout of yesterday. I guess a part of me wanted her to confide in me, to tell me the truth about what brought her and Zach together. But I'm also not surprised she kept it quiet. There's a reason no one aside from the two of them knew it happened before last night.

Anger and the need for vengeance for the girl who's turned my world upside down burn through me.

I hate that I lied to her.

But she can't really expect us not to do anything about the pathetic cunt who abused her like that.

If Zach weren't there that night... a shudder rips through my body.

Fuck. What he was going to do would have irrevocably changed her. And although I might want to follow Rhett's lead and put a fucking bullet through his

44

skull for treating her as roughly as he has, I can't help but be grateful that Zach was there when she needed him most.

If he weren't, then the girl I would have met all those months ago would probably be an entirely different person.

I take a seat at the bar, asking for a black coffee when Tank steps up to me. He quickly disappears again before a shadow falls over me.

I don't bother looking over my shoulder. If someone wants to talk to me, then they're going to have to come to me.

"Have a fun morning?" a smug-as-fuck voice asks before Zach drops onto the stool beside me.

My lips part in shock before they close again while he smiles at me.

"How the fuck do you know what I did this morning?"

He shrugs innocently, although he's anything fucking but. "Call it a sixth sense."

One of my brows lifts in question.

"I might have gone to her this morning too," he admits, "but you beat me to it."

I try to fight it, I really do but a smug grin appears on my lips, knowing that I might have won this round.

It's pathetic and the kind of thing that should be reserved for school, but I can't help it.

"How is she?" he asks, looking genuinely concerned about her.

"Embarrassed. Scared. She thinks Rhett is going to do something to you that he'll regret."

His eyes brighten at that. "She's worried about me?"

"Uh..." I rub at my rough jaw. "I mean, yeah, I'm sure

that's part of it. But that was just a cover to tell me she's worried about him going to Colton."

His shoulders slump a little, and I feel like an asshole for popping his bubble. Although I can't deny that there's a part of me dancing for joy.

I push him aside, though. We all need to be on the same team for what we have planned for tonight.

Our issues—jealousy—over River are going to have to wait until we've dealt with the motherfucker who hurt her.

"She knows him well," he mutters, slamming his indifferent mask back on.

"Yeah, she's going to be pissed when she finds out."

"So? Is that going to stop you?"

"Hell no," I state as Jax appears, carrying two mugs. He lowers one in front of me and sips at his own.

"Everything still in place?" he asks quietly, cutting off our previous conversation.

"Sure is. Seven pm sharp," Zach says.

"I'll be ready."

He holds both our eyes for a beat before turning his back and heading across the clubhouse toward the main doors.

"You think he's good for this?" I ask Zach.

"Yeah, I think he is. Whatever his issues are with River and whatever else, it's not going to stop him fighting for her."

I stare at him as he watches Jax walk across the lot toward the shop. "He talked to you?"

"Yes and no. I gave him a bit of a push to try to force his hand like I promised. Didn't fucking go to plan, but I had fun."

My brows lift, wanting him to elaborate.

"Anyway," he says, standing and walking around the stool. "I'd better go polish my brass knuckles for tonight. I can't wait to party." He winks and disappears before I can argue, leaving me waiting for the time to tick around until we can go and pay this cunt a visit he won't forget.

A fter what has felt like the longest day of my fucking life, I finally emerge from my room, dressed head to toe in black with both my gun and knife strapped to my body, ready to give this Henry motherfucker the lesson of his life.

Three dark shadows linger by the truck, and bloodlust like I haven't felt for a while surges through me. Fury burns red hot in my stomach as I think about this faceless, pointless fucker who thought he could hurt one of us.

If he knew who River was, then he should have known better. And he should have spent his life since that night looking over his fucking shoulder.

"You good to go, bro?" Rhett asks darkly, death and vengeance swirling in his eyes.

"Yeah. Let's do this." I clap him on the shoulder before pulling open the back door and climbing in, allowing him and Zach to sit up front.

We made our plan before leaving Zach's room last night, all of us agreeing that he needed to be the driver and the lookout after he confessed that we'd probably end up with the Night Crawlers sniffing around the second Henry figured out who he was.

He looked anything but happy about the plan, but he also couldn't really argue, because he knew we were right.

Really, he should have been staying behind, acting as a decoy, distracting River—not that I really want to allocate him that job. But I fear that the second she realizes what we've done, she's going to lose her shit with all of us.

The drive to Colton is pretty much in silence, all of us too lost in what we're going to do tonight, in the memories of what River herself and Zach explained to us about the night in question.

I don't know about the others, but I've heard all I need to know that we're about to do the right thing.

Zach pulls the truck to a stop around the corner to keep it out of view and kills the engine.

"His little gang of pretentious dickheads aren't Night Crawlers, but they're in their back pocket. The second they get wind of something going on, they're going to come running," Zach tells us, as if he hasn't already explained all of this.

"Henry is always the last to leave. His family owns the building, so he locks up after they pray to Satan, or whatever fucked-up shit their elite little club does in there on a Saturday night before they head out to party."

The second he says that final word, a rush of adrenaline surges through me.

We're now all aware of how he and his boys like to party, and with a bit of luck, we're going to put a stop to some poor, unsuspecting girl's life being ruined tonight.

"Slip inside once everyone else has left and go to fucking town. If you don't come back covered in blood, telling me that he's barely breathing, then you're not getting back in this fucking truck."

"We've got it, Stone," Rhett barks, clearly unimpressed with the pep talk. "We have actually done this kind of shit before. It's not only the Crawlers who can fuck up assholes who wrong them."

"All right," Zach says, holding his hands up in surrender. "Fuck off, then."

Rhett and Jax immediately climb from the truck, but I pause when Zach's eyes lock on mine in the mirror. Reaching forward, I wrap my hand around his shoulder.

"We've got this. Justice will be served."

He nods once, but his lips remain firmly closed.

Tugging my hood up, I slip from the car and the three of us make our way toward the building and the entrance Zach described to us.

We step into an alcove between two buildings and wait.

"It's time. Where the fuck are they?" Rhett snaps, looking at his watch for the millionth time since we came to a stop. "If he's fucking playing us, I'll—"

"Look," I hiss as a group of guys finally emerge from the building.

"Seven of them," Jax says, confirming what Zach told us about their little elite boys club.

"Sweet. Let's go."

Rhett surges forward, and Jax and I quickly fall into step behind him.

Everything is exactly as Zach described. The door is unlocked, and the second we step inside we find an ornate staircase that leads to a basement.

Perfect. Less chance of anyone hearing the cunt screaming and begging for his life.

Silently, the three of us descend the stairs, the creepy-ass classical fucking music from below making my skin erupt with goose bumps.

My eyes widen when we emerge in the barely-lit basement.

Fuck me.

Zach really wasn't joking about them praying to Satan. There are crosses, skulls and flickering candles on every wall and surface. Makes me wonder if this little rich boy club is really a fucking cult.

"What the hell?" Jax breathes, clearly as shocked as I am.

"Shut up," Rhett barks as movement in the corner of the room catches my eye.

Excitement explodes in my stomach as he backs toward us, completely unaware that he's about to walk right into hell.

"Henry Parsons. It's so nice to fucking meet you."

A gasp rips from our new friend before he turns around, his eyes widening at the three dark-hooded figures before him.

"Looks like it's your turn to meet the devil," Rhett mutters before lunging forward, his fist connecting with Henry's jaw with a force that makes his head snap to the side.

"What do you want?" the pussy cries.

The laugh that comes from Rhett makes even my blood run cold as he grabs the twisted fuck by the throat and pins him to the wall.

Henry's face turns beet red, and he claws at Rhett's forearm.

"What do we want?" Rhett echoes. "We want you to fucking pray for your life, motherfucker, before we carve you up like the sick fucking rapist that you are."

"No, please. I haven't done anything. You've got the wrong person." His panic is laughable.

"So you're not Henry Parsons?" Jax confirms.

He pales before a body surges past me, knocking Rhett out of the way a second later and laying into Henry himself.

A flash of light catches on the brass on his knuckles, and I know instantly that Zach's bloodlust has got the better of him.

"What the fuck are you doing?" Rhett snaps.

"Sorry, bro. Couldn't do it," Zach confesses, before kicking Henry so hard I swear I hear ribs crack over the bone-chilling music that's still playing around us.

"Get him fucking out of here," Rhett demands before I reach forward, grabbing Zach's arm to pull him back from Henry and into the shadows before the stupid fuck gives himself away.

But I quickly discover that it's probably too late when I shove Zach into the corner and realize his hood is lowered as he scowls at Henry over my shoulder. When I look back, I find Henry staring right back at him before Rhett's boot connects with his stomach.

7
———

RIVER

"Why do you keep checking your phone?" I ask Kat as the opening credits to another Channing Tatum film start rolling.

When Diesel brought me here earlier, I didn't realize I'd end up spending the day. But Kat was hellbent on us spending some time together, and Evelyn insisted we all hang out.

So the day has been filled with baking cookies, watching old reruns of *Friends*, and topped off with the hottie that is Channing.

"I don't," she says, dropping it like a hot potato. "Just scrolling."

My brows furrow. Kat isn't fooling anyone. Least of all me.

"Is it Styx?"

"No! Why would you even think that?"

I roll my eyes, and Kat grabs a handful of popcorn and throws it at me.

"Don't waste it," I complain, picking a piece off my sweater and popping it into my mouth. "Mmm, so good."

But Kat isn't listening—she's looking at her cell phone. Again.

"Seriously? That's it, hand it over." I hold out my hand dramatically. "If you can't be trusted not to keep looking at it, I'm confiscating it."

"It's just habit, a bad one at that. I'm watching the film, I swear. It should be illegal to look that good." She lets out a breathy sigh.

"What's your brother up to?" I ask.

"Diesel? Uh, how should I know?"

"Unless you have another brother... Why are you acting so weird?"

"I'm not... you are."

That has my attention. She won't look at me, and she's fidgeting like a child who knows something she shouldn't.

Sitting up straighter, I pin her with a hard look. "What aren't you telling me?"

"I... nothing. I don't know anything."

My eyes narrow. "But you know something."

A trickle of unease slides down my spine.

And then it hits me.

"I don't, I swear. I'm just... I'm waiting for a text, all right?"

"Why didn't you just say?"

She shrugs, barely meeting my gaze. "Because it's weird. It's Styx..."

"So?"

"So, I'm not supposed to like him."

"When has that ever stopped you before?"

"True." A smirk traces her lips. "But I don't know, this is different. He's my brother's ex-best friend. You know they fell out over a girl... Well, it was bad, babe. Really bad. Diesel loved—"

My heart sinks, and Kat blanches.

"Shit." She claps a hand over her mouth. "Pretend I didn't say that. D would murder me if he knew I was spilling all his secrets."

"That's... I don't really know what to say to that." My stomach twists.

"He doesn't speak about her, like ever. He thought they were the real deal."

"Yeah. You should probably stop talking," I say, trying to focus on the film.

The last thing I need is to hear about another one of Diesel's exes. Although this one sounds a lot more serious than Lucy ever was.

We watch the rest of the film in comfortable silence. Kat is constantly checking her cell phone, but I let it go. I know all too well how it feels to be strung tight over a guy.

When the end credits start to roll, I gather my things.

"You're leaving?" she asks, jumping to her feet.

"Yeah. I want my own bed."

"You can stay here, take D's room. I'm sure he wouldn't mind."

"No, I'm going to go. But I'll call you tomorrow."

"At least let me give you a ride."

"Kat, seriously, I'll get a cab. It's fine."

"No, let me—"

"Kat, Katrina, a little help please, baby."

"Shit, that's Mom." Panic washes over her. "Let me see to her and then I'll give you a ride. Please."

"Your mom needs you, and I'll be perfectly fine getting home. Now go."

Hesitation lingers in her eyes, but when her mom cries out, Kat takes off.

I slip out of the Walkers' house without so much as a

goodbye. My heart aches to hear her mom crying out in pain, and I know if I were Kat, I wouldn't want an audience around to witness it.

Crossing the street, I hitch my bag up my shoulder and start the short walk to the Red Ridge compound.

Diesel might be avoiding me, but he isn't the only guy I want to talk to.

And I know exactly where to find Zach.

I sneak into the compound undetected. It's amazing what you can learn when you watch the people around you closely.

Dagger is supposed to be watching the gate tonight, but Dagger also enjoys the odd double scotch. I've seen him napping on the job more than once, and tonight is no different. I slipped my hand through the hole in the steel, unlatched the lock, and snuck inside before Dagger had even opened his eyes.

Sticking to the perimeter, I move around the side of the building and enter through the fire exit. The same one the guys come and go from for a smoke. It sounds awfully quiet for a Saturday night, but it doesn't matter, because I didn't come to hang out. I came to talk to Zach.

When I reach his room, I inhale a steadying breath, hoping that he'll see a more positive side to this than I do. But when the door swings open and my eyes land on the people in the room, all rational thought flies out of my head.

"What the hell is this?" I say calmly. The kind of calm that usually precedes a very big, very violent storm.

"Well?" I stare at my brother, hardly able to believe my eyes.

The four of them—Rhett, Diesel, Zach, and Jax—sitting in Zach's small bedroom, shooting the shit and—

My body locks up the second I spot their bloody knuckles. The dark splotches on their hoodies. My breath hitches as my eyes narrow at the four of them. "What did you do?"

"River, shit." Rhett scrambles to his feet, approaching me with outstretched hands. "It isn't... it's not—"

I lift my hand, stopping him. "You went to Colton, didn't you?"

"Shit, yeah. Yeah, okay." He drags a hand down his face. "Couldn't let that fucker get away with it, Riv. You're my sister. Nobody ever fucking hurts you."

My body trembles with anger, hurt and betrayal. "I begged you. I begged you not to go and you promised me. You promised me, Rhett."

He inhales a sharp breath. "I'm sor—"

"Don't you dare," I fume. "Is he... dead?"

Oh God.

If they killed him...

"No." Diesel stands. "But he'll wish he was for a while."

"You know?" My heart free falls into my stomach.

As if it isn't bad enough walking in on them sitting here, together, and having a beer to... *celebrate*.

Rhett told them.

"You had no right." I pin my big brother with a fierce look.

"River, I— They deserved to know."

"Deserved to know?" I scoff as I feel myself closing down. How foolish I was to believe Rhett when he said he wouldn't go after Henry. And Diesel... I don't even know what to think about his bare-faced lie. "And what about what I deserve, huh? What about what I want? And you..." I pin him with a hard look. "You sat there this morning and lied to my face. How could you?"

I'm pretty sure I'm crying, but they're nothing but tears of rage.

Kat was right. She was right about everything.

And I hate it.

I hate that my life still isn't my own. People will always make decisions for me based on what they think is right, not on what I want.

I didn't want this.

I didn't want any of it.

"River, I—"

"I'm such an idiot." I shake my head, annoyed that I ever believed him. Or Rhett, for that matter. "I trusted you... and this... this is what I get. And what about you two, huh? What have you got to say for yourselves?"

But Jax and Zach say nothing. They just continue staring at me. At least Jax looks guilty. Zach, on the other hand, barely flinches at my tirade.

"You know, it's funny..." My voice is a broken whisper. "Kat gave me this big speech about Sinners protecting their own. About how you guys wouldn't be able to let this lie, but I didn't think... You talk about family, but family doesn't lie to each other's faces. They don't."

"River, come on, you're over—"

"Overreacting?" I scoff. "Nice, Rhett. Real nice. You're all sitting here, covered in blood, and you're going to try to make me feel like I'm in the wrong? Well, fuck you."

His eyes flare with surprise.

"I'm done."

"Done? What the fuck is that supposed to mean?"

"It means, big brother, I. Am. Done. I'm no longer putting up with having my life controlled by you."

Someone breathes, "Fuck," but I don't look around to see who. I storm out of there and take off through the clubhouse.

The few guys sitting around the bar all look up when I enter, frowning.

"Can someone give me a ride home?" My eyes home in on Crank. He knows me. He knows some of the history.

He stands up, running an assessing eye over me. "I'm guessing you saw your brother?"

"Something like that."

Rhett's heavy footsteps sound down the halls.

"Please," I rush out. "I want to go home."

"Sure, come on."

Relief flows through me. But as we get to the door, Rhett's voice cuts through the air. "River—"

"I don't know what you idiots have been up to," Crank says, "but I'm taking her home."

"Crank, man, come—"

"You should think about getting yourself cleaned up, Savage."

Rhett cradles his busted hand, hiding it from view.

"Come on." Crank holds the door open for me. "Truck's this way."

"**W**ant to talk about it?" Crank asks as we head for Savage Falls.

"Not really," I sigh, pressing my head to the window, watching the scenery roll by.

"I'm guessing they did something stupid tonight?"

"You mean, you don't know?"

"I know I saw them sneak back into the clubhouse with split knuckles and blood splattered everywhere. And the fact that I'm driving you back to Savage Falls suggests you know whose blood it might have been..."

"It's a long story, one I'd rather not get into."

"You know, your brother is a good guy, River. One of the best. If he's been up to no good, I'm thinking he probably had a good reason."

I glance over at him. "They lied to me, Crank. My brother. Diesel."

"About that... is there something going on between you and my cousin that I need to know about?" His brow lifts, and I see the humor there. But it's lost on me.

I'm too angry.

Too hurt.

"Look, want my advice?" he asks, but I know he's about to tell me even if I say no. "Sleep on it. Everything will seem better in the morning. I know we Sinners can be a little intense, but it's only because we care, River. Because family means fucking everything to us. Damn, if I found out someone wronged you, I'd want to see them pay as much as your brother or D."

When he puts it like that... But no, I can't soften over this. Going to Colton was dangerous. Not only for Rhett. But for Zach and the club.

It was a risk they didn't need to take.

One I made Rhett promise he wouldn't.

Thankfully, Crank doesn't have any more advice to impart, and we ride the rest of the way in silence.

By the time my house comes into view, I don't feel any better about things. If anything, I feel worse.

Because I realized something.

My brother and Diesel aren't the only ones who lied to me today.

Kat did too.

8

JAX

We agreed to leave River to calm down for the rest of the week.

A fucking week.

Silently, I think we were all hoping she'd cave to her need before then to come back and rip us all new ones.

But as I lie here with my covers resting over my waist on Thursday morning with the hustle and bustle of the compound filtering through my door, none of us have seen or heard anything of her.

Well, that's not entirely true.

Zach's seen her. I caught him sneaking back into his room the other night dressed head to toe in black, looking like he'd been out causing trouble. The thought that he'd gone to her, that she'd let him get close to her when she's avoiding the rest of us twisted me up inside, but that doesn't seem to be the case.

He had seen her, but only from a distance.

There's a lot I don't know about Zach. He's an enigma who turned up here and flipped all our lives upside down, most of all River's. Hearing more about his past in Colton and his involvement with the infamous Night Crawlers makes a lot of sense. But hearing him explain how he's basically been stalking River was a shock.

I understood it, though, More than I really fucking should.

After the horrific night he rescued her from, he's developed an intrinsic need to protect her. Even if he thinks he hates her, which I've still not got to the bottom of.

He's more than happy to call her a whore and treat her as such. Yet her saved her from *that*. Why?

I shake the confusing thoughts about Zach from my head. Something tells me that there's not a living soul who understands that twisted motherfucker, himself included, so instead, I think about her.

The light in all my darkness.

My angel.

The girl who makes my past go quiet, who makes me feel like everything I've heard my entire life isn't actually true. She makes me feel worthy despite all my fucking issues. She makes me feel wanted. And that's a fucking heady thing, after the life I've lived.

My heart fractures as I think about her standing in Zach's doorway with tears cascading down her cheeks as the realization of what we'd done hit her.

I've seen her mad. I've seen her upset. But I've never seen her look like that.

Totally and utterly betrayed by the people she trusted the most in the world.

It fucking wrecked me to watch her suffering. The need to get up and hold her burned through me. But I couldn't, and I knew she wouldn't accept it even if I tried.

I blow out a long breath and just stare at the ceiling, trying to talk myself out from getting on my bike and going over there. Zach's been doing it. In the dead of night, maybe, but why shouldn't I? Why can't I see her? See with my own eyes that she's doing okay, even if she does hate us all.

"Fuck," I hiss, throwing the sheets back and pulling on some clean clothes.

Shrugging on a Sinners hoodie, I shove my feet into my boots and head out, hoping like hell I can escape without being dragged into the clubhouse for breakfast or a friendly chat with one of the old ladies.

The second I pull my door open, I look down the hall at Zach and Diesel's doors. Both are closed, and I can only hope they're hiding behind them. I have no doubt they'll be pissed if they catch me sneaking out, but fuck it.

Only a couple of minutes later, my bike rumbles beneath me, and I'm waiting for Dagger to open the compound gates for me.

The drive back to Savage Falls isn't all that long, especially by bike. But if I thought the journey time would be enough to talk myself out of this, then I was very wrong because as I pass the 'Welcome to Savage Falls' sign, my need to see her is stronger than ever. Even if it is just her slamming the door in my face.

The sight of the Dalton house up ahead brings back a flood of happy memories from when River first arrived. I remember sitting in front of Ray as he laid out all the rules for me keeping an eye on her. No touching. No kissing. No getting any ideas. No letting her get drunk. No putting her at risk. And the list went on and on.

Part of me wondered that day if Prez knew more

about me than I'd ever let on, because the first few rules were things I wouldn't be doing anyway. Shame I couldn't stick to the 'no getting any ideas' rule, though. That sure would have made my life fucking easier.

To be fair, I failed the others, too.

I remember those couple of nights I flung myself straight out of my comfort zone and tried to be normal. A normal fucking horny teenager who needed the girl before me more than I needed my next breath.

I kept her wrists locked in mine, hoping she'd think it was kinky, as I ran my fingers gently over her soft skin. It was fucking mind-blowing, watching her eyes dilate at my touch. Studying her as her breathing increased and a low rumble of need passed her lips.

I'd have given anything to be able to throw caution to the wind and take it further, to go all the way with her. But I knew it was a fantasy I'd never be able to live out.

It's destined to always be that. A fantasy.

I ignore the pain in my chest as I come to a stop in front of Ray's house. Neither his bike nor Victoria's car is here, and I can only hope it means she's home alone. At least I won't have any witnesses when she chews me out.

Killing the engine, I climb off and leave my helmet on the seat before marching toward the front door. My knock goes unanswered, but, not willing to give up that easy, I twist the knob, finding it unlocked, and walk inside.

"River?" I call, but again, nothing.

A lap of the ground floor of the house doesn't help, so I head up to her room with my heart in my throat.

But I quickly find she's not there either.

Assuming she's gone out, I walk back to the stairs, ready to leave and give up, but the sight of smoke from the backyard catches my eye. Rushing down the stairs, I storm through the kitchen toward the floor-to-ceiling folding doors that showcase the view of the lake in the distance, and it's then that I see her.

She's curled up under a blanket on the outside couch with the fire pit roaring in front. She's reading, and as I slide the door open and get a better look at her, I realize she's got headphones in.

I hesitate for a few seconds, just taking her in. Her dark hair is piled on top of her head in a messy bun. Her face is clear of makeup, and she has a slight frown between her brows where she's concentrating on what she's reading. She looks beautiful. So fucking beautiful.

Closing the space between us, I study every inch of her, committing it to memory, because I know everything is about to change when she discovers my presence.

It's not until my shadow falls over her that she startles and screams bloody murder, throwing her book down on the couch and jumping to her feet, allowing me to see the tiny pair of shorts she was hiding beneath the blanket.

Fuck. This girl completely fucking owns me. If only she had any idea of her power.

"Jax, what the hell?" she snaps, her previously soft eyes hardening before me, exactly like I was expecting.

"Sorry, I didn't mean to scare you." I hold her eyes for a beat, but the lure of her bare legs is too much, and they drop after a few seconds to check her out again.

"If that were true, then you wouldn't have," she seethes, dropping back down to the couch and covering her legs once more.

"I called out. I searched through the house."

"Well, you shouldn't have bothered. In case you didn't get the memo, I don't want to see you. Any of you."

Dragging her eyes from me, she stares right at the fire, lifting her chin in defiance.

If she thinks that's going to be enough to get rid of me, then she really needs to reconsider.

"I know, Riv," I say quietly, rubbing at the back of my neck as I take a step closer. "Please, just let me ex—"

"Explain?" she spits. "Explain why you went along with those idiots after they promised me they wouldn't. They promised, Jax."

"I didn't know that," I confess, stuffing my hands into my hoodie pocket.

"Doesn't make it any better. You should have known I wouldn't have wanted that. If I felt like I needed any of your help, then I'd have told you about it all myself. Not waited for all this to blow up in my face."

"I'm starting to wonder if I know what you think about anything these days, Riv."

"Really?" she hisses, finally looking back at me. "You're really going to stand there and spout that shit when you're clearly the one I don't know, Jax?"

"No, that's not—"

"You know all my dark and dirty secrets now, it seems. So how about you start spilling some of yours. Explain to me how you could just sit there and watch Zach take whatever he wanted from me without so much as lifting a finger."

"You didn't look like you needed rescuing."

"I'm not talking about rescuing me, Jax. I'm talking about joining in. Why?" she taunts. "Why did you just sit there and watch when I wanted you? Needed you. Why?"

My lips open and close as I try to find some words for her, anything to put an end to her questioning.

But I can't.

"Because—" Her eyes light up like I'm about to spill everything, but I didn't come here to rip myself open and bleed for her, even if it's what it'll take to make this better. I'm not strong enough, and she sure doesn't deserve me to dump that level of toxic on her. "Because I'm fucked up, River."

Disappointment washes through her as she stares at me.

"Look, I just came to say that I'm sorry. I never meant to hurt you, River. But hearing what that asshole did. Listening to Zach explain how he..." I trail off when her lips purse as if it's physically painful to hear. I understand that pain, more than she could ever know.

"I never wanted you to know."

"I understand that, Riv. But I'm glad we got to do something about it. I hate myself for doing something you trusted us not to. But I'm not sorry for doing it. Anyone who hurts you in any way deserves that and then some."

Pushing from the couch, she walks over to me and I pull my hands free, ready to stop her if she tries to do something stupid like touch me.

She doesn't stop until she's standing right in my personal space and is forced to tilt her head up to continue our eye contact. "Just how sorry are you, Jax? Sorry enough to give me some of your secrets, or sorry enough to kiss me?"

My eyes drop to her lips as she says the final two words.

Need surges through me. My fingers twitch at my sides, desperate to grab her and pull her into my body to take what I need. But while my body might be aching for it, I know my brain, my fear, isn't on board.

Her chest heaves as she waits, her brows pulling together as she begins to come to her own conclusion about how this is going to end.

Closing my eyes, I suck in a breath before giving her an answer.

9

RIVER

Jax's hand snaps out, grabbing the back of my neck as he slams his mouth down on mine.

It's so unexpected, I gasp, and his tongue plunges into my mouth. Claiming me. Devouring me.

"Jax," I whimper, reaching for him to steady myself, but he lets go of my neck and grabs my wrists, pinning my hands behind my back as he traces his mouth down my jaw, licking and sucking my neck.

"Fuck, Riv," he rasps, diving back at my mouth as I struggle against his hold.

I want to touch him. To feel his muscles beneath my fingers. But Jax doesn't let up, taking what he wants from me and giving me nothing.

I want his kisses, yes, but not like this... not if I can't touch him.

"Jax... let me—"

"Shh," he drawls, kissing me harder, sliding his tongue along mine. Shivers run through me, a trace of fear snaking down my spine as he continues to restrain me.

Jax won't hurt me, I know that. But there's something almost violent about the way he holds me. As if touching him would be the worst thing I could ever do.

"I want to touch you." I yank hard, my wrist smarting when he doesn't let up.

"River, come on. Give me this."

My body stills, red hot fury rising inside me. "Why did you come here, Jax?"

"W-what?" His brows knit together as he studies me. The rise and fall of his chest is quick, and I realize then, he lost control just now. Gave in to whatever demons haunt him.

"You heard me. I asked why you came here."

"To check on you. I wanted to make sure you were okay."

"Tell me why I can't touch you."

"I... I can't do that." He releases me like my skin is deadly to the touch and takes a step back, dragging a hand down his face.

He barely looks at me, and rejection seeps into every part of me.

"You should go," I whisper, trying to keep it together.

"River, I... I'm sorry, okay? If I could tell you, I would."

"Do you know how it feels to know you'll use me—"

"I'm not using you. I just... fuck." He kicks the ground with his boot. "*Fuck.*"

"You should go," I reiterate. The sooner he leaves, the better.

I hate feeling like this.

I was ready to give this guy everything. My heart. My body. My soul. And instead of just talking to me, he chose to ruin me by sleeping with that club whore.

"Look, Jax," I sigh. "I know you have your secrets, and that's fine. You don't have to tell me anything. But I'm not your toy to pick up and put down whenever you choose. I deserve better than that."

My eyes bore into his, but his expression remains completely closed off.

"I'm sorry, River, I am. But I can't do this." He backs away, a glimmer of regret in his eyes.

It would be so simple for him to fix this, but he won't. Whatever secret he's hiding, he would rather deal with it alone than confide in me.

"Fine." I fold my arms over my chest. "Then I guess we're done here."

We stare at one another, locked in a battle of the wills. He wants to say more. I can see it in his eyes. But what comes out of his mouth is the last thing I expect.

"I didn't sleep with her."

"Excuse me?"

"The club whore. I didn't sleep with—"

"I saw you together..."

"You saw what I wanted you to see. I needed to put some distance between us, and the guys were—"

"Let me get this straight." The words almost get stuck as my body trembles. "You broke my heart with a lie?"

He holds my stare, and I have my answer.

"Get out."

"River, I—"

"I said get out. And tell Zach and Diesel to stay away too. I can't trust you. I can't trust any of you."

Tears burn the backs of my eyes, but I refuse to let them fall. I'm so angry right now that it burns through me like wildfire.

"Yeah, okay." Jax takes off like the coward he is, and I watch him disappear into the shadows.

Taking another piece of my broken heart with him.

By the time Friday rolls around, I'm pissed. After Jax left last night, I crawled into bed and didn't leave it for the rest of the day.

He lied.

I don't know what's worse. That he chose such a callous way to get his message across, or that whatever he's hiding is so bad that he needed to lie in the first place.

I'm trying really hard not to have any sympathy for him, but it's not that simple.

My cell phone vibrates and I lean over to grab it, groaning at the collection of text messages.

Kat: You can't ignore me forever.

Kat: Come on River, it's almost Christmas. You have to forgive me. I was only doing what my brother asked. I didn't know they were... ugh. Doesn't matter. I get it. I broke the cardinal rule. I put bros before hos. I'm sorry!

Kat: I know you're at home sulking. He said you haven't left your house once this week.

Before I realize what I'm doing, I text back.

River: Who said?

Kat: Ha! I knew that would get your attention. Zach, obviously. Did you know the guy is a Grade A stalker?

River: Zach has been keeping tabs on me?

I don't know whether to be flattered or fuming.

Kat: I'm surprised he hasn't put a tracker on your phone. He has definite psycho tendencies.

My lip curves at that. I can totally imagine Zach doing that, the way Rhett did to Sadie Ray. Maybe that's why my brother got so upset. He realized his little sister has a weakness for all the typical biker traits. Hot-headed. Rash. And one-hundred percent alpha.

River: You're right. I don't know why I'm surprised.

Kat: So does that mean I'm forgiven?

River: I haven't decided...

Kat: That's fair. But you know I only did it to protect you. I didn't know you would sneak over to the compound...

I don't text back immediately, and my cell starts ringing.

"Hello," I say.

"You can't stay mad at me forever. You're my best friend."

"I thought I could trust you, Kat."

"You can," she blurts. "Well, with most things. I tried to tell you that they'd do something like this. They're Sinners, babe. These guys don't live by the same rules as the rest of society."

"Yeah, I know... I just... I'm so freaking angry at them."

"You know what you need? A night out... there's a costume party at Envy Friday. We should—"

"Another party?" I ask with disbelief. Because they never end well.

"It'll be fun. You've been moping long enough. Besides, I miss you. And I have the perfect costumes for us."

"Ugh, why do I feel like this is just another disaster waiting to happen?"

"Say you'll think about it."

"Fine, I'll think about it."

She shrieks down the line. "Thank you. And River?"

"Yeah?"

"I am sorry."

And I don't know if it's the fact that I've missed her or that I know she struggles to make girlfriends the same way I do, but I believe her.

I 'm not sure about this," I say as I stare at myself in the mirror.

"Not sure?" Kat chuckles. "Girl, you look hot with a capital H."

I worry my lip, barely meeting Kat's gaze. "You don't think it's too... much?"

"It's a costume party. I'd say you nailed it."

She smirks, but it does little to ease the knot in my stomach.

"You would say that," I scoff. "It was your idea."

"And a good one at that."

Kat thought going to the costume party as a sexy angel and devil was the 'right statement.' But I'm not so sure. Of course, Kat looks killer in the red skintight skirt and halter top with matching horned headband. Whereas the virginal white dress she insisted I wear is... next to indecent. The feathered wings provide a little bit of coverage, and the halo and fur-trimmed white ankle boots soften the look, but still. I feel half naked.

"Styx is going to freak when he sees you," I murmur, fiddling with my wings for the umpteenth time.

"Seriously, Riv, there's nothing going on with me and Styx."

Her answer is too dismissive to be true. Besides, I know a lie when I hear one.

She wants him. And I'm pretty sure he wants her too.

"You know, I'm surprised D is letting you come tonight." She swipes some gloss over her lips, and I let out a soft sigh. "He's not my keeper, Kat."

Now that we've cleared the air between us, I was wondering when the questions would start again.

"Could have fooled me." She lifts a brow.

"What's that supposed to mean?"

"I've seen the two of you together... well, the four of you."

"I don't want to talk about it."

I really, really don't. Tonight is about the two of us having fun, patching up our friendship.

"So there is something going on?" she adds.

"It's... complicated."

Kat snorts. "When isn't it? Just," she hesitates, "promise me you'll be careful. Diesel is... intense. And Zach is—"

"Kat," I snap, "I said I don't want to talk about it."

"Geez, sorry. I'm only trying to look out for you."

"Don't give me that look," I whisper.

"I'm not... sorry. No judgment, I promise." She holds up her hands. "I just don't want to see you get hurt. Zach doesn't exactly seem the type to share, and D is... do you know what? Forget it. You're a big girl, I'm sure you know what you're doing."

God, I wish I did.

"I don't know what I'm doing at all," I admit. "But thank you. I appreciate your vote of confidence."

"Well, tonight you don't have to worry about them. It's not a club party. We can enjoy ourselves without having to worry about overprotective big brothers or possessive boyfriends."

"Sounds perfect." I smile, grabbing my purse. But as I reach the door, I glance back at Kat, frowning. "Just promise me one thing."

"Anything." She nods.

"Don't let me drink too much tonight." I need to keep a clear head, to make sure I don't make any more stupid mistakes.

A knowing smile plays on her lips. "You have my word."

"You're right, this is fun," I yell over the music as I roll my hips to the sultry beat.

We've been dancing for at least an hour. Laughing and drinking.

The bartender tried to cut Kat off at three drinks, but Kat being Kat found a poor unsuspecting guy to keep us topped up.

"We've got a problem?" Trevor, Kat's new friend says.

"That we do." She motions to his empty hands. "It would appear you forgot our drinks."

"A guy called Styx told me to tell you to consider yourself cut off."

"That motherfucker." Kat's head whips around, no doubt looking for him.

I spot him over by the bar with the bartender, but he only has eyes for Kat, and from his dark expression, he's pissed. She looks ready to storm over there and give him a piece of her mind when he flicks his head to the door.

"Tell me you didn't text them," Kat snaps at me.

"Text whom?" I frown, glancing over to where she's looking. "Oh... *oh*." My stomach drops at the sight of Diesel, Zach, and some of the other members walking into the club. "Of course I didn't text them. Dammit."

"Well, somebody told them," Kat huffs.

"Styx, maybe?"

"Who is that guy, anyway?" Trevor asks.

"Listen, Trev." Kat taps him on the shoulder. "It's been a blast, but me and my girl need to go."

"You're leaving? But I thought—"

"You thought wrong, buddy."

"But I—"

"See those guys over there?" She points toward where Diesel is cutting through the crowd, making a beeline for the bar.

Why are they here?

Ugh. I knew this was a bad idea.

"Yeah, what about them?" He puffs out his chest, getting ready to fight for Kat's honor, no doubt.

"Ever heard of the Red Ridge Sinners, Trev?"

The blood drains from his face as realization dawns on him. "Well the dark-haired one at the front? That's my big brother. And when he realizes I'm here, he's going to be pretty damn pissed."

"Shit, that's..." He swallows nervously, raking a hand through his hair. "I should probably go."

"Yeah, run along," Kat calls after his retreating form. "Pussy."

"Kat," I sigh. "That was mean."

"Seriously? The guy was only buying us drinks because he wanted to bang one of us. Maybe both. Shit. They're looking over here."

"Who?" I play dumb.

"Cute, Riv. Real cute. My brother, Zach... and Jax. Wow, three for three."

My heart falters in my chest.

Crap.

"What? They're all here?"

They all came.

I can't even process what that means.

"Yep." Kat purses her lips, clearly annoyed by the turn of events. "Question is, what are you going to do about it?"

"Nothing." I shrug. "I'm here with you. They can all go fuck themselves."

"Feisty, I like it. But I give it an hour." Kat smirks.

"I'm serious, Kat. I'm not going anywhere."

She pins me with a knowing look and shrugs. "We'll see."

And although it feels like a betrayal, to her and myself, I can't help the little thrill that goes through me.

10

ZACH

I fly through the compound gates and pull to a stop right outside the main entrance to the clubhouse.

Peeling my fingers from the handlebars, I kill the engine and jump off, running inside. "Get dressed. We're going out," I bark at D once I've stormed up to the table he's sitting at with Crank, Ryder, and Bones.

"Uh... are we?" he asks, his brows lifting in shock, although the second he turns his head to look at me, his shock is soon replaced with concern. "What's happened?"

"I need to change. So do you," I say, looking down at his grease-covered wifebeater.

He looks back at the guys who are also staring at me, wondering why the fuck I'm standing here, ordering around their Sergeant-at-Arms.

Diesel throws back his whiskey and stands, pushing his chair out loudly behind him, causing a few others to look our way. "Lead the way then," he says, gesturing toward the door that leads to our rooms.

"Wait," Crank says. "Is everythi—"

"It's fine. Nothing we can't handle," I say, cutting off his concern.

We're halfway across the clubhouse when I spot Jax. "You too, Pitbull. Let's go. You're gonna need to put on your prettiest dress," I quip, and he jumps up like his ass is on fire.

"What's going on?" he demands.

"I think it's time to finally make River forgive us," I explain.

Each of us might have tried to make peace with her after she caught us doing the exact opposite of what Rhett promised her. But we all stand by our decision. We just need her to see it our way. We were protecting her. Protecting the girls of the future. Or at least, I hope we were.

"Oh, and how exactly do you intend on doing that? She's barely talking to us," D asks.

"I know exactly where she is. And something tells me we can get her to see things our way."

Diesel doesn't look convinced, but Jax seems to be immediately on board.

I'm hardly surprised, seeing as he's managed to dig himself an even bigger hole with River after his lame-ass attempt at an apology the other day.

He didn't want to tell me about it, understandably, but after plying him with enough liquor, I finally got him to confess. I want to say I was happy that he'd managed to put whatever bullshit stopped him at the motel aside, but seeing the pain on his face as he explained River's reaction, I mostly just felt sorry for him.

He cares about her. A lot. That is more than obvious. But he's built up his walls so high that even River can't seem to scale them.

I'm worried that if she can't do it, how is anyone else ever going to?

"Where is she?" Diesel demands.

"Envy."

"Again?" he spits, his eyes blazing as if that one word ignited something inside him.

"Again," I confirm. "They're throwing a costume party."

"I'm not fucking dressing up."

"You think I am?" I hiss, coming to a stop at my room door. "Ten minutes and we're leaving. I don't know about you two, but there's no fucking way any other cunt is getting their hands on her."

I look between Diesel and Jax. D might be angry, but I can still see hesitation when it comes to River. He doesn't want to want her. But he also can't stop himself craving her, despite all his reservations with the age difference. Not that it's even that big a difference. He's just being a pussy.

Leaving the two of them out in the hallway, I blow through my room, having the fastest shower of my life before pulling on a pair of dark jeans and a black button-down. I'd much rather be wearing a hoodie, but there's no way I'm risking not being allowed in that place when I know she's inside.

Something akin to excitement twists up my stomach at the thought of walking up behind her, taking her hips in my hands and moving along with her.

My cock swells.

It's been far too long since I had her. I'm still longing for our lost opportunity on the rooftop a week ago. Barely getting the tip in really didn't cut it.

I run some wax through my hair, shove my feet into

my boots, and rip my door open, more than ready to go and find her. I'm hardly surprised to find Jax already waiting and for D to emerge only thirty seconds later.

"If she and my sister are wasted again, I'm gonna—"

"Finally make the most of the situation?" I suggest, interrupting his rant.

"She's too young for me," he argues, grumbling, "My sister's best friend."

"You sound like a broken fucking record, Walker. Man the fuck up and admit that you want her."

"It doesn't matter," he spits. "I can't have her."

"But you have, haven't you?" I growl.

I'm not paying enough attention to where I'm going and collide with Jax when he stops dead in front of me.

"What the—" He spins on Diesel. "You've had her too?" he asks, a wrecked expression on his face.

"U-uh..." he hesitates, looking over to me as if I'm going to help him out.

Fuck that. He really should know me better by now.

"Truth time, D. Are you man enough?" I taunt.

"I... uh..." He lifts his hand to push his hair back from his brow. "I haven't fucked her, if that's what you're getting at."

Jax's hard expression doesn't falter.

"Fine," D sighs in frustration. "She spent the night in my bed a few weeks ago when I'd had a bad time of it with Mom." Jax's brow lifts, wanting to hear more. Although for the life of me, I have no idea why he wants to torture himself more than he already is by having this information. "I ate her until she screamed my name. Is that what you want to hear?" Diesel asks, his patience running thin.

Jax's jaw tics, his fists curling at his sides as his chest heaves with anger.

Silence crackles between them as the tension becomes oppressive. Jax takes a step forward, and I'm just about to jump between the two of them, thinking he's about to throw one of his improved punches in Diesel's face when he suddenly turns and storms out of the building.

The door slams back against the wall as he crashes through it, and thankfully, the air thins out enough to take a decent breath.

"I think he's pissed," Diesel mutters.

"Nah, he's just so fucking horny he can hardly think straight."

"Come on." D shakes his head as if he can't actually believe we're doing this. "Let's go, before they get themselves in too much trouble."

Following him out, we both climb into the truck Jax already has running, and without a word said between us, he pulls out of the space and heads toward Envy.

The second we walk up to the entrance, Diesel sparks up a conversation with the doorman which results in us getting to skip the line and head straight inside.

My eyes widen the second the room opens out and we get a look at the variety of costumes on display. There are school girls, nurses, army women... everything a guy's imagination could conjure up.

"Holy shit," Jax gasps behind me as two guys dressed as nuns wearing only a pair of boxers walk past us.

"Feeling like you're missing out, Jaxy boy?" I ask, throwing my arm around his shoulders, my eyes continuing to scan the crowd, but I ignore all the skin and tits on display in favor of searching for River.

The second I find her, a laugh falls from my lips. "Angel my fucking ass," I scoff, slapping D on the arm and nodding toward where River and Kat are dancing.

Despite the booming music that's making the floor beneath our feet vibrate, I hear the growl that rumbles in his chest. With one look, we take off, our legs eating up the vast space between us.

The second Kat notices, she bolts for freedom, leaving River alone. Diesel takes off after his sister, and Jax and I descend on our angel sent from fucking heaven.

Her eyes widen in horror the moment she spots us prowling toward her. She backs up, as if she actually thinks she's going to be able to outrun us now that we've found her.

"If you were going for virginal, then I'm pretty sure you failed, Blondie," I growl, taking her chin between my fingers and forcing her to hold my eyes.

"W-what are you doing here?" she asks, her voice raspy from the alcohol she's consumed.

"Wanted a night out. What are *you* doing here?"

Defying me, her eyes shoot to my side where Jax is standing. "Trying to forget about you all," she hisses.

"It's cute that you think that's possible, Blondie."

"You're not dressed up. Why are you really here? How did you know where I was?"

A smirk pulls at my lips before I close the space between us and brush my lips over the shell of her ear. "A little bird told me that we might find you here. Hoped the alcohol might loosen your inhibitions a little. Give us a better chance at forgiveness."

She shudders as my breath skates down her neck. "No chance. I don't want any of you here. I don't want you anywhere near me."

She tries to pull her face from my grip, but I'm having none of it, reaching out to clamp my other hand around her hip and tugging her into my body instead. "You're a filthy liar, Blondie. What you really want is to dance with me." I lower my voice, ensuring it rumbles through her. "To dance with us."

She gasps, giving her desire away, and the second I slide my hand around her back and press her body into mine, she's powerless but to sag against me, her hips moving in time with mine as I roll them in time with the music.

It takes her a few seconds before she comes back to herself, and I smile, knowing that I was able to make her lose sense of everything with just one touch and a roll of my hips.

"No," she snaps, slamming her palms against my chest in an attempt to make me back up.

"Aw, Blondie, you know it only makes me hotter when you fight me."

"I hate you," she hisses, but the second I press my quickly growing cock against her stomach, her fingers twist in my shirt, holding me against her.

"Yeah. It's fucking sweet, right?"

She continues moving with me, spurred on by the alcohol running through her veins, and the beat of the music flows through her muscles.

"Gonna join us, Jaxy boy?"

His eyes are glued to us, watching as we move

together. They're almost as dark as they were the night he watched me make her come in front of him in that motel.

His entire body is pulled tight with tension. It's obvious how much he'd love to step up behind her and pin her hot little body between ours as we set about driving her crazy. His lips part to refuse, because despite the desire and need swirling in his eyes, I know he's not about to step up. But before he manages to say anything, Diesel appears.

His eyes find mine over River's head before they drop down her body, taking in her almost indecent outfit. His jaw tics as he closes the space between us, but to my surprise, he doesn't stop at a distance. Instead, he takes up the position I just offered Jax.

His hands brush mine, which are resting on her waist as he grips her hips.

"Oh God," she moans before he dips his head and whispers something in her ear.

I have no idea what it is, but his words make her eyes widen and her lips part. And I know for a fact that if I were to dip my hand under her skirt, I'd find her dripping for the pair of us—the *three* of us.

"What do you think, D? What should we do with our girl to show her just how sorry we are?"

A smirk pulls at his lips.

I have no idea what's changed since his argument at the compound. But something quite clearly has.

And I'm here for it.

11

RIVER

"Do you trust me?" Diesel whispers as he and Zach slide their hands over my waist.

Their touch, although innocent, feels possessive and full of promise.

"River," he hisses. "Do. You. Trust. Me?"

My lips part and I nod. Their touch is electric, lighting me up inside.

I should tell them to go away, scold them for turning up here like they have every right to ruin our girls' night out.

Speaking of... my eyes flicker over to Kat, but I don't see her anywhere. Huh. The rumble of Zach's voice sends shivers through me, and all thoughts of Kat flutter away.

She won't care. She's probably already found some unsuspecting guy to dance with.

"What do you think, D?" Zach drawls, running his thumb over his jaw as he watches me, devours me with his dark gaze. "What should we do with our girl to show her just how sorry we are?"

Zach's words reverberate in my chest.

Our girl.

I can barely think straight as Diesel takes my hand and guides me out of the club. Nobody pays us any attention, everyone too drunk and high on the party to care that I'm leaving with three guys.

Three Sinners.

My head swims with lust and liquor and so many things that I wrap my arm around Diesel and stick close to his side as we leave the club and head for...

The truck?

I frown.

It's just waiting out here, as if they planned this.

I should be pissed at them, and part of me is, but I can't deny the trickle of anticipation zipping up and down my spine.

"Where are we going?" I ask as we reach the truck. Jax grabs the door and Diesel lifts my hips. "Up you go."

I climb inside and slide over the bench so the guys can get in. Zach first, then Jax. He stares down at me, his eyes blown with lust.

"You're not fooling anyone with this costume, Blondie." He smirks, running his finger along the inside of my knee.

A shudder goes through me and my breath catches when his hand disappears under my skirt and grazes my thigh.

He's right, I don't feel very angelic right now. I feel... I feel wound so tight I want to beg him to touch me. For them all to touch me.

But I won't. Not yet.

Not until I find out what they've got planned as way of an apology.

The driver's door clicks open, startling me, and I slap

Zach's hand away. "You don't get to touch me, I'm still mad at you."

His mouth brushes my ear and he whispers, "We'll see."

"You good?" Diesel asks the second he climbs in.

I nod, swallowing over the lump in my throat.

Now that we're out here, together, with no one else around, I don't really know what I feel.

"We need to talk, all of us," he adds, gripping the steering wheel in both hands. "I have a place, but it isn't exactly—"

"It's fine," I say, trying to disguise the slight quiver in my voice.

"Don't chicken out now, man," Zach taunts. "The fun is only just getting started.'"

Diesel lets out a little grunt and fires up the engine. The truck rumbles to life, and I'm grateful for the sound...

Because it drowns out the wild beat of my heart.

***

By the time we pull up outside the rickety old cabin, my skin is too tight and my heart is like a runaway train in my chest.

"W-what is this place?" I gulp, staring up at Diesel. His eyes swirl like a storm, the air crackling around us.

Zach's fingers toy with the hem of my skirt, the way they have the entire ride here.

We didn't talk, not really, which only made the anticipation in the air thicker. The knot in my stomach tighter.

It's the first time we've all been in the same vicinity, acknowledging this... whatever this is.

Diesel's gaze drops to where Zach is touching me, and his nostrils flare. "Zach," he warns.

"Too late to back out, bro." Zach inches his hand higher and a whimper spills out of me as I fist the edge of the seat.

I shouldn't be letting him touch me like this. But all rational thought went out of my head the second I found myself sandwiched between them in the club.

For a second, it was like all my fantasies have come true. The three of them watching my every move, stalking me, undressing me with their eyes.

God, I want this.

I want it so much, and I don't really understand what *it* is. All I know is that if somebody doesn't touch me properly soon, I'll combust.

"Look at her, man." Zach lowers his mouth to my neck and ghosts his lips over my skin. "She's gagging for it."

Diesel blinks, jolting himself out of it, and grumbles, "Come on, let's go." He climbs out and Jax follows out of the passenger door, leaving me alone with Zach.

"Scared, Blondie?" he asks.

"Of you?" I quirk a brow. "Never."

"Such brave words for an angel." He toys with a loose curl, wrapping it around his finger.

A loud bang on the door startles me and Zach chuckles. "Looks like D is getting impatient. Out you go." He nudges me toward the door and Diesel helps me down, his eyes sweeping over my body.

"Never stood a fucking chance," he murmurs under his breath before stalking off toward the cabin.

"What is this place?" I ask, hurrying after him. I wrap

my hand around his arm again so he can't leave me behind.

"It's a project, but I don't get to come out here much."

"It's yours?"

"Yeah, always wanted my own space. Crank's place is just around the lake. It's quiet out here, peaceful. Figured it would be a good place to raise a family one day."

My chest squeezes at his words.

"You want—"

"Didn't bring you here to talk about me, pretty girl." He runs his knuckles down my cheek.

"Sweet place." Zach catches up to us. "You're renovating it?"

"It's a work in progress," Diesel replies, isolating a key on his key chain.

"Nice."

"You haven't seen the inside yet."

"I'm sure it— Oh." My eyes widen at what can only be described as a demolition site. The living space has been stripped back to bare wood, a dust sheet covering a few pieces of old furniture. There's an unfinished open fireplace and the bones of a new kitchen, but it needs work.

A lot of it.

"It's fucking freezing in here." Zach rubs his hands together.

"I have a couple of heaters. Give me a second." Diesel disappears down a hall and we hear the bang of a door.

"Hey, Jaxy boy," Zach calls over to him.

Jax has barely looked at me, and his obvious discomfort at being near me makes my stomach twist.

"Come here."

"Come on, Zach, don't be such a—"

"Relax, I'm not going to do anything you can't handle. Just get over here. River looks cold. You don't want her to be cold, do you?"

Zach steps up behind me and takes my hands in his, yanking them behind my back.

"Zach," I cry.

"Don't worry, Blondie," he whispers, his warm breath tickling my neck. "I got you. Jaxy boy is going to get you nice and warm. Isn't that right?"

He takes a step toward us, his eyes darting wildly over every inch of me, burning with lust.

"Fuck, you're beautiful," he rasps, dragging his lip between his teeth and biting down hard, as if he's trying to temper whatever storm is raging inside him.

"Come on, bro," Zach drawls. "She won't bite. But I will." He latches his mouth onto my neck and bites down —hard—making me cry out. "She wants it. She wants your hands all over her tight little body. And you want to make it up to her, don't you? You want to apologize."

"River, I—" Jax stops himself, almost close enough that I could touch him, if Zach wasn't restraining me.

"Do it, man. Just fucking touch her. You know you want to."

My body trembles with anticipation, heat curling in my stomach. This... this is what I need. Zach's rough touch, his dirty words. The way Jax is looking at me like I'm the single most important thing in his world. It's addictive, and I want more.

So much more.

And when Diesel steps back into the room, I get it.

His hungry gaze is like a brand over my skin, burning me up and making me shudder.

"What's going on?" he asks in a low voice.

"Worried we started the party without you?" Zach chuckles. "Don't worry, Walker, Jax is just getting started. Isn't that right, Jaxy boy?"

"I-I... fuck, I can't." He glances down, and rejection weighs heavy in my chest.

"Jax, look at me," I say softly.

Slowly, he lifts his head, meeting my gaze with a pained expression.

"It's okay," I whisper. "I want this. I want all of you."

"Fuck," Diesel hisses, moving closer to Jax but remaining on the periphery.

"I want to, Riv. So fucking bad. But I'm... I... can't."

Diesel leans in, whispering something to him. Jax's eyes spark with hunger as he zeros in on me.

"There he is," Zach says.

"You can touch her," Diesel adds. "She wants it. Look at her. Her skin is flushed, her eyes are glazed over... Zach won't let her touch you. It's safe."

Safe?

What the hell does that mean?

But there's no time to consider his words as Jax reaches out as he gently collars my throat. My eyes flare, my lips parting on a gasp.

"Go easy," Diesel warns.

"Or hard," Zach teases. "She likes it rough."

My pussy clenches at his words, and Zach must sense my reaction because he chuckles again. "She's fucking dripping for you, man. Feel her. Tell us..."

Jax brushes his thumb along my pulse point, making my eyes flutter. "Kiss me," I whimper. "Please."

I'm a riot of sensation, restless and needy. I can barely stand the way they're looking at me, eating me up with their eyes.

Jax dips his head and closes his mouth over my lace-covered breast, biting down hard.

"Oh God," I cry, my legs threatening to buckle.

"I got you." Zach moves both of my wrists to one of his hands and slides his other arm around my waist, anchoring me to his hard chest.

"Jax... please..."

His hand grips my leg as he tentatively slides it up my thigh in jerky, uncertain movements. His breaths come in short, sharp bursts as if it's taking everything he has not to break.

I realize then that something is happening—something is changing—between the four of us.

He's never touched me like this before, never allowed himself to. But with Zach and Diesel's guidance, their encouragement, he's finally giving himself permission.

His fingers finally reach the apex of my thighs, brushing the damp material.

"Fuck... fuck," he chants. "She's soaked."

"Told you, man." Zach smiles against my shoulder, his tongue licking my skin.

I'm on fire. Burning from the inside out. Diesel shifts closer, his arms folded over his chest as he watches Jax explore my body.

Then he says five little words that make me melt.

"Put a finger inside her."

12

DIESEL

Jax looks up at me, his eyes wide with fear.

I might not understand, or even have the slightest fucking clue what his issue is, but I can see just how badly he wants to break through it.

I understand that kind of determination. To force yourself to do something you never thought possible, despite all your demons telling you it's not.

Hell, I'm standing here despite my own with my heart damn near beating out of my chest and my cock trying to burst out of my pants.

"It's okay," I breathe.

"See, Daddy D says it's okay," Zach quips, making my teeth grind, but the second River's eyes find mine and I discover the depth of the blue staring back at me, I decide that he could have called me worse.

River's gasp rips through the dusty air of my cabin, but she holds my eyes as Jax must force himself to do as I said.

"Oh God," she whimpers.

"Watch him, pretty girl. Let him know how good it feels."

I hate to do it, because I know I'm about to lose my contact with her, but he needs this more than I do right now.

"Jax," she whimpers when she looks down to find him staring back up at her with an awed expression on his face.

"Two fingers," Zach instructs—I guess assuming, like I have, that he's not very experienced with this.

River's moan tells us that he's complied.

"Now, bend them a little and rub. You'll know when you hit the right—"

"Jax," River cries, making both Zach and me laugh.

"Someone's a quick learner," Zach mutters with a strange tinge of pride. "You want to make our girl come, Jaxy boy?"

"S-say that again," he stutters, his voice rough with desire.

"Tell me why and I might," Zach demands.

"She got so fucking wet."

Zach dips his head once more and brushes his lips against the shell of River's ear. "Our girl," he whispers.

"Holy shit," Jax breathes as I assume she gushes for him.

"That's right, isn't it, Blondie? You're ours." His free hand slides up her body until his fingers tangle in her hair, giving him control of her head.

He tugs until she has no choice but to look right at me.

"Diesel wants you. You know that, don't you, Blondie?" She sucks her bottom lip into her mouth before nodding slightly. "Look how hard he is for you." He

96

pushes her head down, making her eyes drop to the more-than-obvious tent in my pants.

"And Jax," he says, turning her to look back down at him. "Look what he's doing for you, Blondie. Just. For. You."

"Jax," she whimpers, the blush on her cheeks spreading down her chest as her release begins to crest.

"Keep going, man. Press your thumb to her clit too. Circle it, make her fucking shatter," he demands before dragging her head back so she has no choice but to look at him. "And me. You know exactly what you're doing to me, rubbing my dick through my pants while Jax finger fucks your pussy. We own you, don't we, Riv? You're our dirty little whore."

She stares at him, her chest heaving, her skin burning up as she begins to come apart.

"Answer me, or I'll make Jax stop," he warns. "And we don't want that, do we? We want him to know what it's like to feel you fall. After all, both D and I have already experienced it."

"Asshole," she hisses, making his eyes flash with wicked intent.

"Who owns you, Blondie?" he grits out.

"Y-you do."

"Fuck, yeah," he grunts before claiming her lips as Jax continues driving into her.

Zach's eyes find mine as pushes his tongue past River's lips.

"Jealous, bro?" he mutters into their kiss. "I'm sure River would be on board for you joining the party."

My heart rate spikes at the thought, but I don't move. I just stand there and watch them with her.

"This is Jax's moment. Let him have it."

"Yeah," he mutters, kissing across her jawline. "And she's so fucking close, aren't you, Blondie?"

She whimpers in response.

"Now watch," he demands, forcing her to look down at Jax once more. "Watch as he makes you come."

"River," Jax grunts when their eyes collide.

"Please," she begs.

His movements don't falter, and in only a few more torturous seconds, she falls.

Her eyelids lower, her chin falls slack and her entire body convulses in Zach's hold as she rides out the waves of pleasure Jax provided her with.

He sits back on his heels, looking equally as pleased with himself as he does in fucking agony from being a part of that while she sags back against Zach.

"We forgiven yet, Blondie?" Zach asks, clearly hoping a good orgasm might help soften her anger at the three of us.

She doesn't respond right away. She just stares down at Jax while he silently shatters before us.

"Let go," she snaps, tugging her arms out of Zach's grip before dropping to her knees in front of Jax.

He startles but doesn't move, and she wisely keeps her hands in her lap.

Zach shoots me a confused look, but I just shake my head at him. "There's beer in the fridge and vodka in the freezer. Go get them," I tell him, not willing to leave these two alone.

I know Jax won't hurt her, but equally, I don't want him to freak out and run.

He might be in all kinds of agony right now, but he needs this.

"I wanted it," River says softly. "You were amazing."

His eyes flash with something—confusion, I think.

Has no one ever said something like that to him before?

"Tell him how good it felt," I tell her.

"So good, Jax. You were perfect."

Pride and shock wash through his features once more.

Zach marches back in with drinks, his presence ruining the moment between River and Jax. Although it doesn't stop her.

"I know you'd never hurt me, Jax. I trust you. And I want you to trust me too."

He nods once, and when she reaches for his hand, he doesn't flinch. Much.

"Jaxy boy, get over here. You deserve the first shot for getting our girl off."

Just like before, River's expression completely changes the second Zach says those words.

Standing, Jax takes the bottle of vodka Zach offers him, and he swallows down a couple of shots before River steals it, drinking more than I thought she'd be able to in one go before looking each of us dead in the eyes.

"I don't forgive you for that stunt you pulled. I trusted you to let it go and not go storming in there like some violent fucking thugs," she spits. "And you should know, I'm not just angry. I'm really freaking disappointed. Zach," she says, turning to him. "I kinda get it. Although, what I don't get is why the hell you're here instead of Colton."

Guilt flickers through Zach's eyes. Due to her giving us the cold shoulder, he hasn't had a chance to properly explain yet, although I know he wants to.

"Riv, I—"

"No," she spits, the alcohol running through her system giving her the confidence to say exactly what she thinks. It's refreshing, and I can't deny that I'm not enjoying this fired-up side of her. "I'm talking." She holds his eyes, daring him to say more, but he wisely shuts his mouth.

"Jax," she sighs. "I understand why you want to fight for me. And I appreciate your need to do that, but it really pisses me off that you won't let me help you in your battles in return."

He doesn't respond, but the defeat in his shoulders kinda says it all.

"And you," she says, stepping up to me confidently. So fucking confidently, it makes my cock ache for her.

My fingers twitch with my need to reach down and rearrange myself, but I hold still, waiting for her to finish.

"I'm really fucking disappointed in you. I thought you were the sensible one. The one who would stand up for what I wanted and not just run off and do the opposite."

"It's you, Riv. I told you. I'd do anything for—"

She holds her hand up, cutting me off from explaining myself. "So I might not forgive any of you, but that doesn't mean I'm not willing to let you try to convince me otherwise."

My heart skips a beat at her words.

"I'm fed up with everyone thinking they know me. Of thinking I'm this precious petal that might break any second. Well, I'm not. There are things I want. Things I can't stop thinking about."

Her eyes leave mine as she quickly looks at the others. "And you're going to give them to me. You owe it to me, after all."

"Riv, are you sure you— shit," I gasp when her fingers

grab my waistband, pulling my belt free and tugging at the buttons of my pants.

"All bets are off tonight. To hell with the rules. The right thing to do. Your questionable morals. I want you. All of you. In any way I can get you." She locks eyes with Jax as she says the final part of that statement, and he swallows nervously. "But then we walk out of here after, and I call the shots. You got that?" she asks, dropping to her knees and dragging my pants down with her.

"Whatever the fuck you want, Blondie. You just make sure I get some of that special treatment in the near future," Zack barks, dragging a dust sheet off the old couch in the middle of the room and falling down onto it, sending a plume of dirt and debris billowing around him.

He rips his own fly open and shoves his hand shamelessly into his pants.

"Riv, you don't have to—"

"Either forget the big brother act, *Daddy*," she taunts. "Or walk out right now."

Her ultimatum ripples through the air as she waits for me to make a decision.

But there isn't one to make. Not really.

Since that very first kiss we shared after Jax broke her heart, there's only been one thing I've truly wanted.

Tucking my thumbs into my boxers, I shove them down my hips, letting my cock bob in front of her. "You owe me one, after all," I tease.

"Me too, Blondie," Zach chips in. "You take the edge off and we'll make sure you're screaming our names all fucking night."

Jesus. What the fuck am I doing?

My eyes move between Zach, who's laid out like this

is just another Friday night lazing on the couch with his hand on his junk, to Jax's shocked but intrigued eyes.

But then, I look down and find her on her knees for me, and every single hesitation I had about this happening, about giving in to what I so badly fucking need, sharing her with these two assholes vanishes as she licks her top lip and then bites down on the bottom one.

"Maybe Zach was on to something all this time," I murmur, making her brow shoot up. "You are a whore." Her eyes widen in shock. "*Our* whore."

"Fuck yeah," Zach barks. "Get the fuck over here, Jaxy boy. Come and watch our girl at work. It can all be yours one day. Remember that." Zach slaps him on the ass as he passes before dropping down, his eyes locked on River as she reaches out and wraps her delicate fingers around my aching shaft.

"Fuck. It's been a while," I warn her. "And I've been dreaming about this for... a fucking long time."

"What about Lucy?" she asks, a frown between her brows.

"Riv, the only girl I've wanted since you kissed me has been you."

A smile twitches at her lips before they part and she sinks down on my cock.

"Fuck," I bark as the heat of her mouth damn near burns me. Eyes on me make my skin tingle, but I couldn't give one single fuck that they're watching us right now.

If anything, it just makes it that much hotter.

13

RIVER

What am I doing?

The words replay over and over in my head, but that little voice of reason isn't loud enough to make me stop sucking Diesel's hard length into my mouth.

"Fuck," he barks, fisting his hand around my hair and guiding himself deeper past my lips.

His salty taste floods my mouth, but I love it. I love how he's grunting and groaning, gently thrusting into my mouth as if he's barely in control.

I don't know what came over me earlier, but the words that spilled out were true.

I'm fed up with everyone thinking I'm some precious flower. That I need shielding from the world and wrapping up in cotton.

I have wants and needs and desires, just like anyone else. It might be scary and overwhelming at times, and I might not have an idea of what I'm doing, but I'm not afraid.

When they look at me, I feel... alive. I feel like—finally—I belong.

"Look at her, Jaxy boy. Imagine how good her pouty mouth feels."

"So fucking good," Diesel hisses, letting his hand drop to my cheek so he can rub his thumb along my skin. I look up at him, flushed and breathless. "Do you have any idea how good you look like this?" He pushes his thumb past my lips and I make a show of sucking on it, swirling my tongue around the tip.

"So fucking dirty," Zach drawls, and I glance over at him and Jax, putting on a show for them too.

"Don't forget, Blondie. You owe me too." A wicked smirk tugs at his mouth, full of intention and promise, making my stomach tighten.

"Suck me, River. Show me how much you want this." Diesel feeds me his cock inch by inch, and I hollow my cheeks, breathing through my nose. "Good girl. Such a good, pretty girl." He pets my hair.

I slide my hands around the back of his thighs and drag him closer, needing more of him. Needing everything he'll give me.

"Jesus, fuck, Riv." He begins to fuck my mouth. "Feels like heaven. I'm so fucking close..."

"Holy shit," Jax breathes, leaning forward on his fists, trying to get a closer look.

Diesel groans, his body going still, and then he's jerking in my mouth, spilling his hot cum all down my throat.

Yanking me to his feet, he crushes his mouth to mine, kissing me hard and deep, tasting himself on my tongue. It only makes him groan more.

"Amazing," he whispers against my lips. "So fucking amazing."

Diesel kisses me into submission, until I'm trying to climb his body just to feel some friction where I need it most.

"Such a greedy little bitch." Zach chuckles darkly. "Now get over here and put your mouth on me."

Diesel tenses, and for a second, I think he might put an end to this. But when he searches my face, he must not find whatever he was expecting, because he says, "Go... go to him."

I stumble over to the couch and sink to my knees. I'm mindless with anticipation, my body on fire from watching Diesel fall apart because of my touch, my lips wrapped around his impressive cock.

Before I can slide my hands to Zach's jeans, he leans down and grabs the back of my neck, slamming his mouth down on mine.

He isn't sweet or tender. He takes what he wants without apology. His tongue plunges into my mouth, so deep I can barely breathe. His hand slips to my throat, collaring me, and for a second there's only him and me and a kiss that sets me on fire.

But then I feel them—Jax's inquisitive, awed stare, and Diesel's reluctant but hungry gaze.

"I don't think I can wait," Zach says. "I need to fuck her."

"We didn't agree—" Diesel starts, but I cut him off with a whimper.

"Yes, yes. Fuck me, please." My head swims with desire. It's like the liquor in my veins. Hot and fiery and all-consuming.

"Look at me," Zach demands, pulling away slightly.

I blink up at him, lips parted and heart crashing violently against my chest.

"You want this?"

I nod, breathless.

Zach pulls me onto his lap, forcing my legs either side of his waist. "You looked good on your knees, sucking D." His fist tightens in the back of my hair, keeping my face right where he wants it. "You really want this, don't you? The three of us. Together."

"Zach..." Diesel warns, and I sense him move closer.

"We could both fuck her and she'd let us. Wouldn't you, Blondie? I could get nice and deep in your pussy and D could have your ass. Poor Jaxy boy will have to settle for watching... for now."

My blood turns molten as I grind down on him, desperate for him to touch me.

"Look how responsive she is, man." His eyes go over my head to where Diesel is standing. "Think of the shit we could do to her. She'd love every damn minute."

"Zach," I moan. "Please..."

"Please, what? What do you want?" His eyes are hooded. Dark and dangerous. But I only feel the delicious lick of anticipation up my spine.

"You," I say, "I want you to..."

"Say it."

"Fuck me. I want you to fuck me."

He stands up with me, and I wrap my legs around his waist. "A little help, D."

"Shit, yeah."

The next thing I know, Zach lays me down on a table and Diesel grabs my arms, pulling them above my head.

"Relax," he says, looming over me. "I've got you."

Zach grasps his cock and wedges himself between my thighs. "Remember to scream for us."

He slams inside of me and pleasure flashes through me. It feels so good, I can hardly breathe.

"Fuck, D. Wait until you get inside her."

Diesel murmurs something under his breath, but I'm too lost to the sensations Zach is wreaking on my body. One hand grips my hip as he rides my body hard and fast while the other plays with my clit, circling and rubbing it in a way that has me crying out his name.

"She's so fucking tight, fuck... *fuck.*" He slides both hands under my ass, lifting me onto him, driving deeper... harder.

"Oh God," I moan.

"Look at you taking him, pretty girl."

My eyes look up to find Diesel watching Zach, watching where his cock disappears into my body.

"I thought I'd hate it... I thought... fuck, you look so fucking hot, River." He strokes my cheek.

My cries fill the room as intense waves of pleasure crash over me, again and again, wrecking me. Ruining me.

"Fuck... you should feel her, man. She's gripping me like a vise. I'm not gonna last much longer."

I tug one of my arms a little, and Diesel releases me so I can wind it around the back of his neck and yank him down to kiss me.

Our tongues slide together, his free hand gliding down my chest to my breast. He squeezes hard enough to make me gasp.

He chuckles. "You like a little pain, don't you, pretty girl?"

"Yes... yes." My voice is choppy as pressure builds inside me.

"She's close..." Zach confirms.

"One day, we're both gonna fill you up, River. Would you like that?" Diesel teases the words against my lips.

I whimper, unable to stop the needy, wanton sounds falling from my lips. My body trembles, the coil inside me snapping.

"Oh God... yes... yes, yes, yes..."

Zach cusses, slamming into me a couple more times before pulling out and coming all over my pussy and thighs.

"Fuck," he grunts, jerking himself until he's spent. Using his fingers, he spreads his cum through my folds, pushing it back inside me.

A loud groan fills the air, and I look over just in time to see Jax come all over his hand.

"Fucking hell, Jaxy boy, didn't know you had it in you." Zach tucks himself back into his jeans. "Got anything to clean her up with?" He sucks our combined juices off his fingers.

"Asshole," Diesel murmurs, but he stalks off, leaving me splayed over the table. I'm too weak to move, my legs like jelly and my heart a runaway train in my chest.

"Z-Zach..."

"Yeah, Blondie." He peers over me, something flashing in his eyes.

"Thank you."

"Fuck," he hisses, running a hand down his face. "What the fuck are you doing to me?"

I don't have time to ask what he means, because Diesel returns with a warm washcloth and cleans me up. When he's done, he tosses it on the counter and scoops me up in his arms, moving over to the now empty couch.

"Where's Jax?" I ask, curling against him as he sits down.

"Don't worry about him. Zach will go check on him. Right, Zach?"

"Oh, it's like that, huh?"

Something passes between them, but I'm too exhausted, crashing too fast to give it much thought.

"Just go..." Diesel says, running his hand down my hair.

Heavy footsteps sound in the air, then a door slams.

"He left?" I whisper.

"Yeah. How do you feel?"

"Like I could sleep for a week." I nuzzle against his chest, breathing in his manly scent. Leather and cologne.

"What happened..."

"Shh." I manage to press a finger to his lips, opening my eyes to meet his concerned gaze. "I wanted it, D. I wanted all of it."

"It's messed up, Riv. The way Zach—"

"Don't. Don't do that. I like how he makes me feel. I like how you make me feel. Please don't ruin it by making it out to be wrong or dirty. I've never felt more... more alive than I do when I'm with you all."

"You really want this. Me? Him? Us?"

"I do. I really, really do." A soft sigh escapes me. "But Jax... he worries me. The way he holds himself back. Something happened to him, D. Something bad."

"Yeah." His jaw tics. "You know, I didn't plan on it going this far when we came looking for you tonight."

"Do you regret it?"

Indecision flickers in his eyes. "I wish I did... I wish I could be a normal guy. A good guy. The kind of guy that could give you a better life than... than this." He glances away from me, but I grip his jaw gently and drag his face back down to mine.

"I want this." I press a kiss to his lips. "I want you. All of you. I won't apologize for that. Not now, not ever. The question isn't what I want, though... it's what the three of you want..."

I snuggle closer, letting my words hang in the air around us.

He's quiet for the longest time as I slowly slip into oblivion. And as darkness washes over me, I'm sure I hear him say, "I want you too, River. However I can get you."

14

JAX

"ARGH," I scream as I step out into the silent night.

I startle a few birds that are nesting above me, and they quickly take flight to get away from me.

Smart. Really fucking smart.

Shame everyone inside that cabin didn't think to do the fucking same.

Instead, they dragged me out here with them, inviting my many shades of fucked up and the poison that lives inside my veins with me.

"FUCK," I bark, surging forward, my fist colliding with the first tree trunk I find.

I hit it over and over, feeling my knuckles splitting open. Pain sears up my arm, but I don't stop. I can't.

I fucking deserve it.

I deserve it for being such a fucking screw-up. For letting everything *he* ever said and did to me rule my life, hold me back from the things I want the most in the world.

Her.

A sob rips up my throat as I think of her. Of her giant blue eyes staring down at me as I pushed her over the edge.

The awe that covered her face, the pride that swelled within me knowing that I did that to her. I brought her that pleasure, it was so fucking overwhelming, I could barely stand it.

I was fucking flying as her juices dripped down my face and her muscles rippled around my fingers.

I'd done it. I'd done one of the things I've fantasized about for fucking months.

But I knew that was all I was going to be able to do. Even with D and Zach's encouragement, I knew I'd already pushed myself too far, opened myself up to all kinds of fucking nightmares when I finally allow myself to close my eyes at some point in the near future.

My chest heaves as I wrap my arms around the tree trunk, the image of River on her knees for D filling my mind.

Fuck. I want that.

I want it so fucking badly.

My entire fucking body aches for it. But I know the second she touches me that I'm going to freak out, and I can't do that to her.

I can't let her put herself in that position for me to rip apart her confidence like that.

But fuck... Watching D's expression as she sucked him... I bet it feels fucking insane.

Why can't I have that? Why can't I allow myself to get lost in the girl I handed my heart to the second her kind, soft eyes landed on me the day she moved to town.

What have I ever done in my fucking like to deserve this kind of torture?

A pained sob rips from my lungs a second before the sound of a door slamming hits my ears. My skin tingles with awareness as I continue to drown in my own darkness, my own nightmares.

Footsteps get closer, and my arms fall from the tree, although I don't move my head from it. I don't have the strength to face whoever it is.

They all witnessed too much tonight. My weakness, my innocence, my constant battle with my own body.

Movement stops and something creaks. I want to look back, to at least find out who it is.

If I wasn't convinced it was one of three people, I would never keep my back to them. But other than discovering the truth and the agony that would be, I know the three of them would never hurt me. That's what makes it so much harder.

For some fucking reason, I trust them. Just not enough to tell the truth. To reveal just how fucking ruined and irreparable I am.

"Come sit." Zach's deep voice rips through the air, and I release the breath I didn't know I was holding.

I have no idea if I'm grateful or disappointed that it's not River.

At least I know Zach's not going to try to touch me or make me want to touch him.

With my shoulders lowered in defeat, I push away from the tree and walk over to where he's dropped down on the old deck's stairs.

"It's okay, Jax," he says quietly, almost softly, like he could actually understand.

I sigh, resting my forearms on my knees once I've

lowered my ass beside him. "It's not. She deserves more than this. Than me."

"That's bullshit and you know it. River cares about you so fucking much."

"She shouldn't. I'm not good enough for her."

"And you think we are?"

"Fuck no," I spit, thinking of the way he treats her but equally aware of just how much she responds to his dirty words and vicious touch. "But at least you can give her what she needs."

"So can you. You did. She fucking shattered for you, man. It was beautiful."

A smile twitches at my lips as I replay that moment over and over in my head. "She's so fucking beautiful."

"Now imagine her lying beneath you, naked. Her tits right there, her nipples hard for you, her hair splayed out over your pillow and your cock buried so fucking deep inside her that you swear you'll never be the fucking same again."

"That good, huh?" I mutter sadly, knowing that I'm never going to experience it.

"Yeah. That fucking good."

"I can't," I whisper, hoping that the cold wind whipping around us is enough to carry the words away before they reach his ears.

It's fucking wishful thinking, though.

"You wanna talk about why? If you—"

"No," I snap, immediately trying to shut that topic of conversation down. "I'm fucked up. Fucking hardwired this way. I'm never gonna—"

"If you explain, we could help. Fuck knows how. D and I are just two biker fuck-ups. But, fuck, man. You need to work through this shit. You need to be able to take your girl."

"She's not mine," I mutter, pain ripping through me at the admission.

"Seems to me that you own a serious chunk of that girl's heart. But hell, I'm just a Colton gangster. What the fuck do I know about love?"

My lips part to respond, but I think better of it.

Silence follows his words, but they never stop ringing in my ear. I can't deny that hearing him say that River cares makes my heart soar, but at the same time, it slices right through me, damn near carving the thing right out of my chest because I know I can never be what she wants, what she needs, what she deserves.

She deserves to have guys like D and Zach, who can give her everything.

Unlike me, who's only able to offer her the slightly less broken parts of myself.

I have no idea how much time passes as we sit there in silence with only an owl hooting in the distance and the rustling of the trees filling the air around us. But when Zach finally speaks, my entire body jolts in shock.

He notices too, the heat of his curious stare burning into me. "What happened to you, Jax? *Who* did this to you?"

My insides knot up painfully as his guess hits way too close to home.

"You don't have to give me details. Just... I'm right, aren't I? Someone hurt you."

"Y-yeah." I force the word out through the messy lump of emotion that clogs my throat. I've never confessed to anyone what happened to me, and I have zero intention of doing it now.

I drop my head into my hands, feeling the weight of his unasked questions pressing down on my shoulders. I know they're coming, and I know there's not a damn thing I can do to stop them.

Thankfully, fate gets involved and the door behind us slams closed again.

"Is everything okay?" D asks hesitantly.

Zach stands, but I don't move a muscle. I can't. I'm too busy drowning in my own misery.

"Where's River?" he asks D in concern.

"She's passed out on the couch. Caring looks good on you though, man."

"Fuck off," Zach scoffs.

"We should probably get her back to the compound. We can hardly crash here."

"Slept in worse places," I mutter, the words falling from my lips before my brain catches up with my mouth.

"Uh..." D starts.

"Let's just get her back. I need a fucking drink anyway."

I take off around the front of the cabin, leaving them both watching me with what I know is concern. I don't need to turn around to see it. I feel it. And I fucking hate it.

I don't need their pity.

I just need... Fuck knows what I need.

A goddamn miracle would be a good start.

When we got back to the compound after a painfully silent journey with River laid out in the back with her head in Zach's lap, they reluctantly agreed to let her sleep in my bed.

I already knew there was no way I was going to be getting any rest anytime soon, and fuck if I wanted to be awake, knowing she was sleeping soundly wrapped in their arms.

I expected them to argue, to fight over her like she's some kind of possession they think they own, but they never did. After sharing a knowing look, they nodded, and when we finally pulled up, D carried her straight down to my room.

I set my ass down on the couch with a fresh bottle of vodka in my hand and I drank it, watching her peaceful face pressed against my pillow, until I passed the fuck out.

Getting wasted is the only way I can make the memories subside enough to get some rest. Although, after the events of the night, my sleep was anything but peaceful as my mind took me right back to D's cabin, letting me imagine how things could have gone if I wasn't such a fuck-up. And when I finally woke, it was with a raging boner and an unforgettable need for her to do all the things I'd been dreaming of.

Cracking an eye open, I find myself at an awkward angle on my couch, but I've got a blanket thrown over me that I'm fucking sure I didn't put over myself before I passed out. It's not until I glance at my bed that everything comes crashing down around me.

The sheets are neat, making it look like no one even spent the night there.

She left.

The thought hits me like a fucking truck.

She's probably embarrassed, ashamed, mortified about what I showed her last night. It doesn't matter that I made her come. She saw more in me last night than she ever has, and she has every right to be disgusted.

It's how I feel about myself most days, so it's only right that the person I care about the most in the world understands who I really am.

I'm still in the exact same position sometime later when a soft knock sounds on my door.

"Yeah," I call, although the last thing I want right now is a fucking visitor. But then I guess misery loves company.

"Hey," D says, poking his head into the room. "Where's Riv—"

"Gone," I spit.

"Uh... gone where?"

"No idea. I woke up and the bed looked like that." I point out, not that it's really necessary.

"She wouldn't have just left," he says confidently, but I see the truth in the creasing of his brow.

"Maybe we don't know River like we thought we did."

D rubs the back of his neck. "Last night was something else, huh?"

"Yeah, you could say that."

Closing my door, he invites himself in and lowers his ass to the bed. "I don't need your secrets, Jax. You don't have to tell me fuck all about any of it. But, please, tell me how to help. How can we push through whatever walls you've built around yourself?"

I blow out a pained breath and admit a little bit of the truth. "I hate being touched."

"I figured as much. But we can totally work with that. It doesn't have to stop you enjoying yourself, River enjoying herself."

I narrow my eyes at him and he smiles, knowing he just hit my weakest spot. Because hell knows I'd do anything for that girl.

Even reveal my dark, ugly truths to my brothers.

Maybe even River.

15

RIVER

"I swear to God, River Savage, if you don't open this door right—"

"Hey," I say as the door swings open.

"About fucking time." Kat barges past me and stomps down the hall toward the kitchen.

"Come in, make yourself at home," I murmur, trailing after her.

"Well," she seethes. "Are you going to explain to me what the fuck happened to you last night, since you haven't returned a single one of my text messages?"

"I texted to say I was okay."

"At eight-thirty this morning. Do you have any idea—"

"Do you have to shout?" I groan, dropping into one of the chairs.

"You're hungover." She studies me.

"You could say that."

But it isn't just last night's liquor causing me a headache this afternoon. It's... everything.

When I woke up in Jax's bed this morning and found

him asleep on the couch, brows drawn together, his hands fisted in his lap, I panicked.

I was drunk last night, but not drunk enough to forget. I remembered everything. Every single little detail. The way Jax had made me come apart under Zach and Diesel's instruction. I could still taste Diesel on my tongue, feel Zach buried deep inside me.

The only thing I couldn't remember was getting back to the Red Ridge compound. I guess I must have passed out after Zach gave me what I wanted—what I begged for.

Oh God.

Who had that girl been last night?

I drop my head onto my arms and smother another groan.

"Riv? What's wrong?" Kat asks, and I slowly lift my eyes to her concerned ones.

"Everything... every damn thing."

"I'm guessing something did happen last night then."

There's no judgment in her eyes, only mild curiosity. But it doesn't stop a sticky trail of guilt slithering through me.

"I'm sorry I left you."

"Don't worry about it. I made my own fun." A sly smile tugs at her mouth, and I sit up straighter.

"Did something happen... with Styx?"

"We're not talking about me right now. We're talking about you and my brother... and Zach... and Jax. It's like Sadie Ray all over again." She rolls her eyes.

"Not funny."

"Wasn't supposed to be." She shrugs. "But I won't deny I'm a little worried. Zach on his own is a lot to handle. But the three of them together? I hope you know what you're doing."

"I wish I did." A soft sigh escapes my lips, a heavy ache settling in my chest. "Everything got a little wild."

"They didn't make you—"

"God, no. No, nothing like that. I wanted it. I mean, I want them. All of them. But it's like, when we're in the moment, I get swept up in it. But then afterwards, I feel..."

"Overwhelmed?" Kat answers.

"Yeah." Overwhelmed. Ashamed. Embarrassed. There are a ton of emotions going through me. "It can't work, can it? All of us? I mean, I'm not even sure Zach likes me—"

"He likes you." She scoffs. "He's just got that doesn't-give-a-shit attitude working for him."

"But I can't imagine him wanting a relationship."

"Is that what you want?" Her brow cocks. "A relationship with all of them?"

Yes. Yes it is, I want to say, but I swallow the words. Because it's not that simple.

"In a perfect world?"

A wry smile plays on her lips. "We don't live in a perfect world, Riv. And what Sadie Ray has with your brother, Dane, and Wes is—"

"Special, yeah. I know."

Rhett and Dane have been best friends for as long as I can remember. It isn't hard to believe they would share a girlfriend when they've shared so much of everything else in their lives. And Wes slotted into their dynamic like he always belonged there.

But Diesel, Zach, and Jax aren't exactly friends. I'm not even sure they like each other half the time.

"Look, I can't speak for Zach or Jax, but my brother can be intense... about sex, I mean." She sucks in a sharp breath and chuckles. "That's something I never thought I'd say. Have the two of you..."

"Kat!" My cheeks flame. "You really want to talk about this stuff?"

"Hell no, I don't. But you're my best friend, and I'm guessing you probably don't want to have this conversation with Sadie Ray or Quinn. So I'm here, whatever you need. Except sex tips. I draw the line at helping you learn how to get my brother off."

"Oh my God," I breathe, barely able to look her in the eye.

She chuckles again. "You know, if you're going to be with all of them, you're probably going to have to get less embarrassed by this stuff. Just promise me you won't let them push you into anything you're not ready for."

I nod, because I can't formulate a reply that will make sense right now. And I definitely can't tell her that I like how they dominate me. How they bend me to their will and make me shatter.

"Do you think I'm crazy? For wanting this, I mean?"

A knowing smile plays on her lips. "Less crazy than you might think."

"What the hell is that supposed to mean?"

"Nothing." She smirks again.

"Something you want to tell me?" I level her with a knowing look.

"Nope. But I'm starving. Want to order pizza and watch a movie?"

"You're hiding something."

"No, I'm not." Kat pulls out her cell phone and pulls up the food delivery app. "Pepperoni good?"

"Yeah, whatever," I murmur, not really paying attention. Because she's lying to me. Again.

Which means I'm not the only one keeping secrets.

―――――

"Hey, sweetheart." Victoria breezes into the kitchen. "I got takeout. You want some?"

"No, thanks. Kat and I got pizza earlier."

"Oh, Kat's here?"

"No, she already left."

"That's a shame. We could have hung out. How was the party?"

"Fine. It was fine."

"Did you meet any nice boys?"

I almost choke on my soda.

"I... uh, no one special."

She looks up from the containers of Chinese food and smiles. "You're a beautiful girl, River. You must have a ton of guys lined up to date you. Is there someone at school perhaps?"

My heart hammers against my chest. This is the last conversation I want to have with her.

It was hard enough deflecting Kat's questions earlier. It's nice having her to talk to, knowing that she doesn't judge me or the situation. But I'm still not ready to discuss everything with her. Especially not where her brother is concerned.

It's weird.

"And what about Jax..."

"What about him?" I snap a little too harshly.

Victoria stops what she's doing and smiles up at me with her pity in her eyes. "Well, he left Savage Falls, and we haven't really talked about it."

"There's nothing to talk about." The lie sours on my tongue. "Has someone said something to you?" I ask.

"What? No, sweetheart. That's..." She lets out an exasperated breath. "I'm just aware that Ray and I have been a little preoccupied, and with Sadie gone, I didn't want you to feel like we've all abandoned you."

"I'm fine." I offer her a tight smile.

"Okay, sweetheart. I just want you to know that I'm always here for you. No matter what."

"Thanks."

"I was actually thinking, maybe we could—"

The doorbell chimes down the hall, saving me from the awkward tension swirling around us.

"I'll get that," I say, rushing out of the kitchen.

But when I yank the door open and find Jax standing there, I wish I had stayed in the kitchen.

"Hey," he says, a sheepish smile tugging at his mouth. "Can we talk?"

"I... uh, Victoria is home." His smile falls and I quickly add, "But we could sit out back and start a fire?"

"Sounds good. I'll meet you round there?"

"Okay. Give me five while I get some blankets and supplies."

Jax nods, his gaze lingering on mine as if he wants to say something else, but he doesn't. Unable to stand the tension simmering between us, I blurt out, "I'll see you soon," and shut the door in his face.

Because Jax Pitman standing at my front door was the last thing I expected tonight.

"Hey." I find Jax outside. He's already got the fire started and has pulled the couch a little closer to the pit.

"Hey." He offers me an uncertain smile.

"I got you a beer and some chips. Victoria said if you want some Chinese food there's plenty, but if you go in there it's likely we'll never get rid of her."

"I'm not hungry," he mumbles, running a hand down his face. But when his eyes find mine again, I see nothing but hunger in his gaze.

My stomach curls as I wrap a blanket around my shoulders and sit down.

The silence stretches out before us, but I don't speak, letting him find the courage to say whatever it is he came here to say.

After a minute or two, he releases a steady breath and says, "You were gone. This morning when I woke up, you were gone."

"Jax, I..."

"It's okay, I get it. You hate me. And I don't blame you. I don't—"

"You think I hate you?"

His eyes dart to the ground, away from me. I want to reach over and touch him, but I don't want to scare him. So I wait.

And wait.

I wait until blood roars in my ears and my heart crashes against my chest.

Whatever haunts Jax, it skews every good thing in his life.

"Jax, look at me," I whisper softly.

He relents, his tortured gaze meeting mine. "I don't

hate you. I couldn't if I tried—which I have." His brows draw tight. "But you left".

"I panicked. But it wasn't about you or what happened... well, maybe a little about what happened. I just needed some space. I'm sorry."

"You don't hate me." Awe glitters in his eyes as he stares at me with wonder.

"Of course I don't hate you. What happened between us last night was... it was everything."

"Fuck," he rasps, scrubbing his jaw. "I didn't think... I didn't know... I don't know what to say."

"You don't have to say anything. I'm sorry I didn't stay this morning, but I was overwhelmed. I'm still a little overwhelmed."

"But you're really okay with what happened? Fuck, River, it was the hottest thing I've ever seen."

"Jax." I worry my lip, not wanting to push him but needing to at the same time. "Why can't I touch you?"

"Shit, I... yeah, okay. Okay," he murmurs to himself more than me.

"Whatever it is, you can tell me. You know that, right?"

He nods, but I see the fear in his eyes. "Zach said I should talk to you. Diesel too. They kinda encouraged me to come over here."

"They did?" My heart swells at his words.

At what it possibly means.

"Yeah, but it's hard for me. I don't... I don't talk about it with anyone."

I look him dead in the eye and whisper, "Try, Jax. Try for me."

16

JAX

My eyes hold River's as she silently begs me, pleads with me to give her something. Anything.

My heart pounds and my hands tremble. Curling my fingers into fists, I try to force my fear down as I attempt to come up with some words.

Before Zach and D, I've never spoken about my past to anyone. Ever.

The thought of doing so now, to the one person I so desperately want in my life but who will ultimately be repulsed by me once she finds out the truth, is terrifying.

Worse than anything I've ever suffered.

My stomach churns as bile burns in the back of my throat.

"It's okay, Jax. I'm here, right fucking here, and I'm not going anywhere. No matter what you tell me."

Her hand twitches on the couch between us, and my body turns for her touch, her comfort. But that only makes all of this worse, because I know I can't handle it, despite how much I crave it.

"M-my childhood..." I whisper, the words barely audible. River's brows pinch in concern at whatever she must hear in my tone, but a soft, encouraging smile plays on her face. "Fuck, Riv," I sigh, ripping my eyes from hers. I slump down on the couch and rest my head back. I close my eyes but quickly discover what a fucking mistake that is, because all I see is a hungry and scared little boy shivering in the corner of a dark and dank room.

I gasp, my eyes flying open. My chest heaves as I try to force the image out of my head.

The cushion beneath me moves as River slides a little closer, but she never touches me, or even tries. Her warmth is comforting though, and I wish I could explain how much it means to me that she's still here.

"It was awful," I continue, my eyes locked on the clouds that are floating above us. "I never knew my dad. My mom, from what I remember, was a mess. She left when I was five. Someone promised her a better life elsewhere, and she didn't deem me important enough to take with her."

"Jax," River breathes.

She gets this shit, I know she does. She's lost both her parents. I recognize the darkness in her eyes from that loss. I think it's probably one of the things that first drew me to her. She'd seen some of the same darkness I have with her mom's addiction. Although, I've prayed every day since I first laid eyes on her that she hasn't experienced anything half as bad as I have. I wouldn't wish that shit on my worst enemy.

"I was left behind with my uncle. He was a fucking deadbeat. I'd always hated him, but I never really understood why I was so wary of him until I was given no choice but to live with him."

Blood whooshes past my ears as I think back to walking into that place with my few belongings under my arm. The smell... My stomach turns over all these years later at the memory. The place was a dump. Something he expected me to fix.

"If I wasn't at school, then I was expected to work. Either cleaning his shitty trailer, which really needed to be burned to the ground, or in his auto shop. Although it was less of a shop, nothing like we have at the compounds.

"If I did my jobs well, I might get fed, be able to go to bed. If I didn't, which was more often than not, then..." I trail off.

"He hurt you?" River whispers eventually when it becomes clear I'm not going to say any more.

"He was brutal." I think about the scars that still litter my body because of him.

"Wasn't there anyone to help? To get you out of there?"

I can't help the listless laugh that falls from my lips. "He controlled everything, Riv. Overtook my thoughts, my feelings. Everything. I thought it was normal. Right." I shake my head, ashamed of the little boy I was.

I knew better, I did.

But I'd been abandoned by the one person who gave a shit, and she wasn't exactly winning mother of the year any time soon. I desperately wanted a family. My uncle was it. And I naïvely believed every word he said to me for years.

"The school I went to was full of dirty, tired kids. The town we lived in was depraved, forgotten. Everyone was too busy trying to survive their own nightmares to dig too much into anyone else's."

"I can't even begin to imag—"

"Good," I snap. "I don't ever want you tainted with this shit. I don't want anyone to be. It's toxic. I'm toxic because of it."

"No, Jax. No," she pleads. "It's your past. You're not that little boy anymore."

I scoff, unable to believe her.

"You're such a good person, Jax. Look at all the people you've helped at the club. You looked after me. Went with the guys to protect Sadie, Dane."

I swallow thickly, emotion welling inside me.

"You're my best friend." I squeeze my eyes closed as the pain in her voice flows through me. "You were there for me when I needed you most when I first moved to town. No one else saw my pain the way you did. No one understood me like you did."

"He poisoned me, Riv. That person I let you see was a lie. I'm fucking broken. Irreparable." The final word rips from my lips like a curse.

Sitting forward, I rest my elbows on my knees and hang my head.

I know it's not intentional. I know she's a good person and she's hurting for me, with me. But it doesn't stop me jumping a fucking mile the second her tiny hand lands on my back in support.

"Oh my God," she gasps the second I'm on my feet. "I'm so sorry. I'm sorry. I didn't think. I—"

"Stop," I demand, my voice cold and hard, forcing her to follow orders instantly. "You shouldn't have to be sorry for trying to comfort me. This is so fucked up," I bark, kicking the fire pit before me, sending pain shooting up my leg. "I'm so fucked up."

"You're not, Jax. You're just you and I think you're—"

"I've only touched on the least painful parts, Riv. The rest of it, the things he—" A sob rips from my throat at the thought of having to confess the things I can't even think about without throwing up.

"Kiss me," River demands, hopping up and coming to stand right in my space, although not touching me.

She puts her hands behind her back, forcing her back to arch and her tits to push forward.

"Riv, you don't want—"

"How about you let me decide what I want?" she snaps more forcefully than I'm used to from her. "I know you can kiss me. You *have* kissed me. I know you want to."

My eyes bounce between her eyes and her lips, my mouth watering at the possibility of getting a taste of her.

"When you kiss me, it makes me forget," she confesses, her teeth sinking into her tempting bottom lip. "It makes me forget about Mom, about Colton, about the pain. Tell me you don't feel the same when you kiss me?" she taunts.

My breaths rush out as she offers me everything I fucking want.

"I'd give you everything, Jax. If it helped take the pain away. Helped you forget."

Tension crackles between us, images of what we've already experienced together flickering through my mind.

"You don't need to be afraid of me. I'll never hurt you. I promise."

"It's not about that, Riv. I know you wouldn't."

She shrugs, looking confused yet determined. "You have two options," she tells me. "Keep talking or kiss me."

My lips part to argue with her once more. But then I hear her ultimatum in my head again and wonder why the fuck I'm hesitating.

I step closer so there's only a hair's breadth between us.

Her gasp rips through the air when I collar her throat with one of my hands while the other goes to her wrists behind her back, holding them in place to squash any lingering fear I might have that she'll lose herself in her need to touch me again.

Staring down into her eyes, I allow myself to drown in the blue depths. I lose myself in her strength, her compassion, her... everything.

"You're all I can think about, Riv." Her pulse thunders beneath my fingertips, telling me that she's just as affected by me as I am her. "Last night... watching you come..." Her cheeks burn bright red at my words, but her eyes darken with desire. "Fuck. You were so fucking beautiful. You have no idea what you gave me."

"Let me give you more," she pleads. "Let me help you through this. Let me show you how it could be."

My eyes close, my brow resting against hers as images of what she's offering fill my mind.

"One day," she continues. "I could be on my knees in front of you."

"Fucking hell," I grunt, my cock straining against my pants.

"Trust me, Jax. Trust me to stand by your side, to do whatever you need. No matter how fucked up you think it is. I can handle it."

I shake my head against hers. "You have no idea what you're asking for."

"I'm offering to be whatever you need. Let me. Please," she begs.

"Fuck. Riv. Fuck," I grunt before slamming my lips down on hers.

She sags in my hold, but she doesn't close the final bit of space between us as her lips part, letting me inside.

A deep growl rumbles in my chest as her tongue slides against mine.

My grip on her tightens as my need for her surges forward. I take everything she's offering me—her support, her comfort, her desire to push me to help me. I take all of it selfishly and allow myself to drown in her.

River.

My angel.

It goes on and on, and fuck if I never want it to stop, never want to pull away from her. But all too soon, she pulls back.

"Jax," she breathes, her eyes full of unshed tears.

"Don't, Riv. Please. Not for me."

She shakes her head. "That's not... It's relief. Keep going," she urges.

"I can't."

"I'm not asking for anything more than your kiss, Jax."

"Shit," I hiss when she tilts her chin up in offering.

"One step at a time for as long as it takes."

Walking her backward, I don't stop until she's lying with her arms pinned beneath her and her back against the cushions of the couch.

Standing, I stare at her. Her chest is heaving, her eyes are blown with desire, and her lips are swollen.

I did that.

I made her want more.

She's not running.

"Jax," she whispers, parting her thighs, her eyes shooting down to the space between them. "I won't move my hands. It's all on you."

"How am I meant to say no to you, Riv?" I ask, reaching down to rearrange my aching cock.

"You're not." She smirks.

Hesitantly, I crawl between her legs and drop my hands on either side of her head.

"Please, continue," she teases.

"Fuck, I don't deserve you."

"Kiss. Me."

17

RIVER

We kiss and kiss.

We kiss until I can't breathe, until I feel like I might combust from the flames licking my insides.

I want to touch him, to reach out and hold his face, run my fingers over his jaw and link my hands around his neck. But I don't.

I won't.

Not until he's ready. Until I have his absolute trust.

When Jax opened up to me about his past, my heart cracked for him. For the man he is today and the little boy he used to be.

"Fuck, River, I don't think I'll ever get enough of this." He breathes the words onto my lips, his grip on my hips almost desperate. But I don't tell him that I think he'll leave bruises because I don't want him to stop, and his confidence is a fragile thing right now.

"Can I touch you?" I whisper, gazing up at him.

"I..." A shudder goes through him. "I-I don't think... fuck, *fuck*."

He goes to pull away and I rush out, "Don't. Please don't. It's okay, Jax. We'll figure it out. Together."

"I can't ever lose control with you, River." His eyes darken, the rise and fall of his chest a jerky staccato.

He leans back down to kiss me, harder this time. His tongue sweeps into my mouth and claims me. I lift my hips involuntarily, and a groan catches in his throat.

"River." The pain in his voice makes my blood turn to ice. "Shit, I'm sorry... I... I can't."

"Hey, hey, Jax, look at me," I beg, hating that he can't. "It's okay, we can stop."

His eyes lift back to mine, blown with lust but swirling with torment. He wants this—wants me. He just can't see past his demons.

"Maybe we should stop for tonight." My wrists smart as I slowly bring my arms up over my head, but Jax snags them in his hand and pins them back in place.

"Wait," he says. "Let me try something. Don't move, okay?"

I nod, pressing my lips together. Anticipation sings in my blood, making my heart race as he hovers over me.

Slowly, he rocks forward, pushing his hips into mine. A whimper catches in my throat and I strain against him.

"Don't. Move." He grits out, rocking slowly against me, circling his hips until his dick nudges up against my clit every time.

"Can you feel me?" he asks, and I nod, my body bowing into his of its own volition.

Jax clamps his hand around my hip as he rides my body, clothed and cautious. Handling me like a new toy he wants to play with but isn't sure about.

"Fuck," he hisses, and I suppress the tiny moans of pleasure building in my throat.

It feels so good.

Even though there are layers of material separating us and I want more, so much more, I'll happily take this.

I'll take whatever he can give me.

Slipping his hand under my thigh, he lifts my leg slightly, letting him change the position slightly so that every press of his hips grazes my pussy.

"Jax," I cry, an intense tidal wave building inside me.

"I'm gonna make you come like this, Riv. I want to watch your face as you fall. Imagining that I'm buried deep inside you." His movements become harder, jerkier as he rocks our bodies together, all while restraining my hands above my head.

"Fuck, you feel so good, and I'm not even inside your pussy yet."

"Kiss me," I rasp. Beg. "Kiss me, please."

Jax gives me what I desire, capturing my lips in a bruising kiss, his tongue licking the inside of my mouth in slow, indolent strokes.

He's fucking me now, his brows pinched with concentration as he ruts against my body.

"More," I cry, lifting my hips, desperately searching for more friction.

"Don't move," he grits out, his jaw as tense as his words.

But I'm too lost in him, in the little bursts of pleasure sparking through my body as he takes me higher... and higher...

"Oh God, Jax... God," I cry, the sensation of being restrained only intensifying everything as a wave of pleasure crashes over me.

"Fuck, Riv, you're so fucking beautiful when you

come." He releases my wrists, stroking his finger down my cheek and kissing me softly.

"D-did you?" I ask, flushed and breathless.

"Don't worry about me." He sits up, tugging me with him. But I notice the ocean between us already. He's closing down. Pulling away.

And I hate it.

I hate that what his vile uncle did to him prevents him from enjoying this. Because while Jax might be battling the scars from his past, I'm falling a little bit more and more into him every time we're together.

"Shit," he bolts upright at the sound of a rumble in the distance.

"What's wrong?" I ask with a frown.

"You don't recognize the sounds of that bike?"

"Should I?"

"I would think so," he murmurs. "Ray's home."

———

The next morning, I'm still replaying every little detail over in my head when my cell phone vibrates.

Zach: Heard you and Jaxy boy had fun last night...

. . .

A smile tugs at my mouth. I wondered how long it would take for Zach to text me. Turns out, it didn't take long at all.

It's dangerous to hope it's a sign that he's going to be able to overcome his issues and be okay with all of this. But the thought is already planted in my head—and heart.

M **e: The three of you are worse than little old ladies gossiping. Did he seem okay to you?**

R ay's unexpected arrival had put a damper on things. But Jax had still kissed me good night before disappearing, and I'd managed to sneak into the house and upstairs before Ray was any the wiser.

Z **ach: Don't worry about Jax. We have a plan.**

M **e: We?**

. . .

H is reply doesn't come, so I lock my cell and head downstairs in search of breakfast.

"Morning, sweetheart." Victoria smiles, nodding to the coffee maker.

"Please," I say, sliding onto a stool.

"Mornin'," Ray stalks into the room, going straight to Victoria and dropping a kiss on her head. She nudges him and motions to me, and he grunts, "River."

"Morning," I whisper, suddenly feeling like the odd one out.

"How was Jax, sweetheart? Did you two clear the air?"

Ray frowns. "Jax was here?"

"I... uh, he came by last night."

"I see." There's something in Ray's hard gaze that makes me shudder. "Good kid, but he's been distracted lately. Thought the move to Red Ridge would do him good. But I dunno... What else is new?" Ray asks, and I frown.

"Nothing."

Victoria murmurs something under her breath and my spine stiffens. "Sweetheart, you know you can tell us anything, right?"

"W-what?"

"Ray, perhaps you should..." Victoria flicks her head to me again.

"Hmm, what's going on you guys?"

"River, sweetheart, Ray's been meaning to have a little chat with you. Haven't you, Ray?"

He scrubs his jaw, releasing a heavy sigh. "Vic's right. We should talk."

"We should?"

This can't be good.

Victoria moves over to where Ray is sitting at the table and squeezes his shoulder. "I'll leave you two to it."

Before I can beg her not to go, she disappears, taking the air in the room with her.

"So..." Ray shifts uncomfortably.

"So..." I brace myself for whatever he has to say.

"Firstly, I feel like we owe you an apology."

"Ray, you don't—"

"Yes, I do, sweetheart. Didn't anticipate how hard it'd be on you with Sadie Ray moving out, settling down with Rhett and the guys."

"It's fine, I can take care of myself."

"Damn, River. You think I don't know that?" Pain ripples in his gaze. "The club is my life. Always has been, always will be. But it wasn't the life you were born into. Doesn't make you any less family, but I know the transition hasn't been easy."

"Ray, you don't need to do this. I'm fine. Totally fine." I stand, ready to bolt from the kitchen and this god-awful conversation.

"Sit," he says. And it isn't so much a command as it is a plea.

I drop back down and run a hand through my hair.

"I heard something at the club... something that got me all kinds of twisted up inside. Now I spoke to Rhett, and he said it's nothing to worry about, but I'm going to ask you, and I want you to know you can tell me. If something happened, you can tell me. Okay?"

Crap.

Crap.

My body trembles as he says the words I've been dreading.

"Is there something going on with you and Zach

Stone?"

"I... what?"

Ray inclines his head, studying me. "I know something happened up on the roof at Red Ridge. Rumor has it, Rhett shot him. Now I know Rhett is a hothead, but I also know he doesn't act without good reason. Your name came up, and well, I gotta say, sweetheart, I'm putting two and two together and not likin' the answer I'm getting."

"I... I don't know what to say."

"The truth might be a good place to start."

Not an option.

If I tell Ray the truth, it won't only be Rhett gunning for Zach's blood. And this doesn't only concern me and Zach. Not anymore.

So I do the only thing I can.

I lie.

"I knew... about their altercation. But I don't know what happened."

"You don't?" His eyes narrow, and I'm almost certain he can see straight through me.

But I've committed now, and I'm not ready to admit the truth. Not to Ray or anyone else who wasn't there that night.

"You know how Rhett gets." I shrug. Easy. Casual. Hoping I'm playing this better than it feels.

"Yeah, I do." He doesn't add anything else, silence stretching out between us. "I get it, you know. You're young, caught up in a world full of young guys all looking for their next piece of ass. But you're better than them, sweetheart. You're better than this club. And I want more for you, River. So much more than the likes of Zach Stone or Pitbull. Just... promise me you won't give your heart to any of these dirty bastards, okay?"

"I thought the club was your family?" I lift my chin in silent defiance, my heart aching at his words.

He'll never accept this thing between me, Zach, Diesel, and Jax.

I guess I was a fool to think that one day he might.

That maybe, just maybe, all my dreams would come true like Sadie Ray's.

"It is, and it's your family now too. But that doesn't mean I want to see you shackled to it forever. Not you, River, sweetheart. Not when there's so much more out there for you." A hint of sadness flickers in his eyes, and I wonder if he has regrets about clipping Sadie Ray's wings so much when she was younger. Because now she's tangled up with not one but three bikers, and we all know she's in for life.

I get up and move toward him, stopping just in front of the table. Ray smiles up at me. "We good?"

"Yeah, we're good," I say, despite how the words coil around my heart like barbed wire.

Despite how much they sting.

18

DIESEL

"Yeah," a croaky voice comes over the line as sweat runs down my spine, soaking into the waistband of my sweats.

"Get up, get Zach, and get your lazy asses to my cabin," I bark.

"D-Diesel?" Jax stutters, clearly still half asleep.

"Yeah, who the fuck else would it be? We've got shit to be doing, and I'm fed up doing it alone."

"Uh... y-yeah, sure. We'll be there."

"Good. I'll be waiting." I hang up before I get a response and reach for the can of soda on the counter.

This place needs a hell of a lot more work than we're able to do in a few days, but we can do what we can to make it a little more comfortable for the plan Zach and I came up with.

I drain my drink, throw the can into the trash in the corner of the room and head back toward the bedroom. We figured it was the best place to start, seeing as we're short of time. It's been stripped back to bare walls, but by the end of the day, I want it to resemble something like a functioning room. Paint, baseboards, flooring, furniture, the lot. But there's no way in hell I'm doing it alone.

It's almost an hour later when the rumble of two bikes finally pulls up outside. I'm more than halfway around on my second coat of paint with dark gray splatters covering most of my exposed skin.

"D?" Jax shouts, obviously expecting to find me waiting.

"Through here," Zach tells him, his footsteps getting louder as they get closer.

"Oh shit," Jax gasps, taking in the transformation.

"What did you think we were doing while you were busy rubbing one out over River yesterday?" Zach asks, clapping Jax on the shoulder.

"I wasn't—" he starts to argue, but Zach's knowing smirk makes him stop.

"Tell me more," I urge, not that it's really necessary. Zach gave me a quick rundown last night.

"We... uh... we just kissed a bit." I can't help but smile at the heat that creeps onto his cheeks at his admission.

"Yeah, bro," I say with a beaming smile which I really fucking hope covers the jealousy that's twisting up my stomach so hard it hurts.

"Made her come too," Zach adds, making that knot inside me ten times worse.

I know just how beautiful it is to watch her fall, and fuck if I don't want to be the one doing it.

A smug little grin appears on Jax's lips as he runs his fingers through his hair, half embarrassed, half proud.

"Fuck that," Zach barks, reading his expression the same as me. "Fucking own it. You rocked her world and you didn't even get naked. That's a fucking feat. Be proud, man."

"Y-yeah, I guess," he mumbles.

"What about you?" I ask as Zach pulls his hoodie off and throws it behind Jax and out into the hallway to keep clean. He grabs a paintbrush and immediately begins cutting in around the edges of the room.

"What about me?" Jax snaps. "It's not about me, it's about her."

"Not true, man," Zach tells him.

"This is true. And you won't realize it until the first time she wraps those lips—"

"All right, bro. Stop fucking bragging," Zach barks.

"Bragging?" I hiss. "You've been inside her."

"And so could you, if you weren't such a pussy about it. She's been wet for you since I got here. It's only you getting in the way of it happening."

My lips part to argue, but I can't because he's right.

"She tastes so fucking sweet though."

"Now that is something we can fucking agree on."

Jax stands behind us like a freaking statue while we discuss River, his eyes darting between the two of us. I can't decide if he thinks we're completely insane or if he's just being eaten alive with jealousy.

"Don't worry, Jaxy boy. We're gonna make it happen. And you licked your fingers the other day, right?"

His lips part in shock and I have to smother a laugh.

"Next time, man. And there will be a next time."

"Why are you doing all this?"

"Decorating?" I ask naïvely.

"No." He hesitates. "Helping me."

"Every guy deserves a good blowy once in a while,

man. No better way of dealing with stress than watching a girl on her knees, choking on your cock."

"You make it sound so—"

"Dirty?" Zach quips with a smirk.

"Yeah."

"The fucking dirtier the better, you'll see."

"Jax?" I ask, putting an end to this conversation so we can actually get some work done. "You any good with a measure and a saw?"

The three of us fall back on the couch after getting the best part of the wooden flooring down when my cell starts ringing.

"That had better be someone offering to cook us food," Zach complains, wiping his forehead with his arm and leaving a trail of sawdust in its wake.

Pulling my phone out, I find out who it is. "It's Mom."

Zach huffs in annoyance while Jax ignores us in favor of whoever he's messaging. Something tells me it's River, but he hasn't felt the need to share that intel with us yet, and I think we've probably already pushed him hard enough today.

"Hey, Mom. Everything okay?"

"Yeah, fine. Stop worrying, Son," she says, as if it's that fucking easy. "It's the holidays, you're meant to be kicking back and enjoying yourself."

I look around at my current surroundings. Oh yeah, hella relaxing.

"But I need a little favor," she adds.

"Shoot."

"Any chance you could swing by the tree farm and pick one up for the living room?"

"Y-yeah, of course. I've already got the truck, so that's perfect. I'll drop it off a little later, okay?"

"No rush, Son. I know you're busy and I don't like to interrupt your downtime but—"

"Mom, it's fine. Anything for my favorite woman." A smile tugs at my mouth. "Is Kat home with you?" I ask, needing to know someone is keeping an eye on her.

"Yes. We've been binge-watching Hallmark movies." I cringe at the thought alone. "Getting into the Christmas spirit."

"That's great, Mom. Do you need me to grab anything else while I'm out?"

She rattles off a short shopping list, which I try to memorize before we hang up.

"We gotta go out."

"We?" Zach asks.

"We," I confirm. "Come on, lover boy," I say, reaching out to mess up Jax's hair when I pass, but I pause less than an inch from his head as reality hits me. "You should go see her looking like that," I say as a distraction. "Who knows, she might have a thing for hot, sweaty construction men."

Unlike Zach and me, Jax is still fully clothed. I have no idea how he's done it—the bedroom was like a fucking sauna, even with the windows open, and the temperature freezing outside. But the most he went to was pushing his sleeves up, exposing some of his ink.

His eyes flash with desire at my suggestion.

"You've been messaging her all day," I add. "You can't tell me you don't want a rerun of last night."

"I... uh... I think she's busy with Kat."

"Fair enough," I mutter, hating the reminder that the girl I'm lusting over is my kid sister's best friend.

Only thirty minutes later, we've cleaned up, to an extent, and we're heading across town in the truck toward the tree farm.

I told them they could go back to the compound, but they both seemed pretty content with tree shopping, and I wasn't going to argue about having the company. It made me feel less obsessive in my need for River when I knew the two guys sitting right beside me shared the same issues.

We've chosen a tree and grabbed everything that Mom requested from the store before Jax asks a question that makes my step falter.

"Shouldn't we get River a gift while we're here or something?"

Zach and I share a knowing look.

"Don't worry, Jaxy boy. We've got you covered."

"You do?" he asks skeptically. "Should I be concerned?" he asks, looking between the two of us with his brows pinched.

"I dunno. I guess that depends on how much you trust us."

Something dark flickers in his eyes, and I can't help but wonder if he's remembering trusting our advice the other night while he was on his knees for River.

"I do... trust you. I think," he adds lightly.

"Then trust us when we tell you that we've got the most perfect gift lined up. It's going to blow your mind."

"Or River's," Zach quips.

"That too."

"If you wanna go buy her something too, though," I say, "feel free."

He hesitates for a beat before shaking his head and moving toward the exit. "Wouldn't even know where to start."

"Lingerie, Jax. Always fucking lingerie," Zach jokes.

"He just wants to unwrap her." I chuckle, heat licking down my spine at the suggestion.

"Hell yes to that. Who needs anything more than her banging little body?"

Jax stiffens beside me, but my only reaction is to smile, knowing we're going to do everything we can to bring a little pleasure into his life. Hell knows he needs it.

———

"Ah, my heroes," Mom sings as Zach and I manhandle the tree into the house. It looked pretty small at the farm. In Mom's house, not so much.

"Where do you want it, Mrs. Walker?" Jax asks politely as he holds the doors for us.

"Over in the corner. Kat already found the stand up in the attic."

I sense her eyes on me as we maneuver the tree into the living room.

"Kat, get down here. We've got three strapping boys manhandling things in our living room."

"Mom," I balk while Zach bursts out laughing.

"Told you we shouldn't have put our shirts back on. Would have made your mom's day."

"You're her nephew, you sick fuck."

He steps back from the tree and lifts his hoodie, showing everyone who cares about his abs. "Every woman's weakness," he says, pointing at them in case I didn't get the fucking memo already.

"Oh, I miss being young and agile," Mom sighs.

"Mom." I frown. "Really?"

"What?" she argues coyly as footsteps thunder down the stairs. Kat comes to a stop in the doorway, her eyes flicking around the room, taking us all in.

"What the hell have you three been doing?" she asks, focusing on Jax, who looks the worst.

"Working. What have you been doing?" I snap.

She rolls her eyes at me, looking like the brat she is.

"Shame River isn't here. I'm sure she'd enjoy this too," Mom says absently, while the four of us stiffen. "Is she okay? She hasn't been around for a while."

Zach coughs awkwardly before ducking behind the tree, pretending to ensure it's up straight.

"She's been busy, Mom," Kat says, her eyes zeroing in on me.

"Aren't you hanging out with her tonight?" I ask, remembering Jax's words from earlier.

"Uh... no. She said she's busy. Didn't say why, though." She tilts her head to the side like an innocent puppy while her eyes bore into mine. "Mom and I are continuing our binge-fest. Isn't that right, Mom?"

"Yeah, although I think I might be Hallmark'd out. I need something a little more..."

"Action, with a gorgeous hero to save the day?" Kat waggles her brows. "Yeah, me too. So what are you guys doing tonight? Any plans?" she asks, obviously digging for intel on her best friend.

"Nothing exciting. Probably just hanging at the clubhouse," I mutter, turning back toward the tree.

"And you?" she asks, turning her interrogation on Jax.

"Uh... yeah... just hanging out, I guess."

A ripple of awkwardness goes through the air, and I realize that I've never wanted to leave Mom's place as much as I do right now.

Risking a glance over my shoulder, I find Kat with her hands on her hips and a scowl on her face. It makes me wish we did have plans.

Dirty, wicked plans with our girl.

19

RIVER

After three days of radio silence from the guys, I finally text Zach.

Me: Are you avoiding me?

He replies straight away.

Zach: I was waiting for you to reach out...

He has a point. But after the cabin, I wanted space. Even after Jax came to see me, and Ray tried to clear the air, I avoided going to the compound.

Me: Since when do you care what other people want?

Usually he's an act now, think later kind of guy.

Zach: Why do I feel like whatever I say here is going to be the wrong thing? Things got intense at the cabin. We thought you'd probably want some time to figure stuff out.

Before I can text him back, another message comes through.

Zach: But I've missed your pussy. If you

154

want me to come over now and feed it, I'd be more than willing...

Oh. My. God.

I don't know whether to laugh or throw my phone at the wall. He's so freaking dirty and crass. But now I have an ache between my legs.

Damn him.

Despite the flutters in my stomach, there's still a ball of dread that this—me and them—means something different to Zach than it does to me.

Me: It's Christmas Eve. I don't think Ray would appreciate finding you on the doorstep.

Zach: Daddy still giving you shit about me?

My brows furrow.

Me: 1. He's not my daddy. And 2. What is that supposed to mean? Has he said something to you?

Zach: Don't worry about me, Blondie, I can handle the likes of Rhett and Ray.

I want to ask what that means. That he can handle them. But I don't, because it's Christmas Eve. And tomorrow, I'll have to sit around a table with all of them. Zach, Diesel, Jax, and Rhett and Ray.

It's bad enough it's my first Christmas here—my first Christmas without Mom, not that she was ever much use on Christmas Day. But suffering a meal with them all, knowing that Rhett knows about me and Zach, and Ray clearly has suspicions... I'd rather stay at home.

Me: You'll behave tomorrow, right?

Zach: I'll be on my best behavior. Pinky promise.

Nothing about his reply eases the knot in my stomach.

Putting them all in one room together is a disaster waiting to happen.

One I'm stuck right in the middle of.

"**M**erry Christmas." Kat flings her arms around me as Diesel and her mom trail into the clubhouse behind her.

"Merry Christmas." I smile, detangling myself from her arms. "Merry Christmas, Mrs. Walker, I'm so happy you made it."

"Merry Christmas, sweetheart. And how many times do I have to ask you to call me Evelyn." She leans in to give me a kiss. "I'm going to see if I can help with anything. See you two later."

She leaves us alone, making a beeline for the huddle of women setting the makeshift table.

Since Red Ridge hosted Thanksgiving, Ray and Victoria insisted they host today at the Savage Falls compound. It's been a hive of activity since we got here a couple of hours ago.

The old ladies—Quinn's mom Dee, Rosita, and Victoria—have been slaving away all morning, getting the place ready and cooking up a storm. If I didn't have such a pit in my stomach, I'd be salivating at the smells coming from the kitchen. But as it is, I can barely sit still, too anxious for everyone's arrival.

"River." Diesel pulls my attention. "Merry Christmas." The twinkle in his eye makes my heart flutter as we share a secretive smile.

Kat makes a retching sound, lacing her arm through mine and staking her claim. "Go do whatever it is you biker types do," she says with a secretive smile of her own. "River's mine today."

"Kat," I hiss, but Diesel chuckles, amusement dancing in his eyes as he takes off toward where Ray and Crank are talking.

"Did you get them anything?" she whispers, guiding me toward an empty table.

"What? No! I mean, should have I gotten them something? We're not..."

She gives me a pointed look. "You so are. Diesel couldn't wait to get over here. He practically dragged me and Mom out of the house."

"He did?" My chest swells, and it's her turn to chuckle.

"You're in so much trouble, you know."

I frown, and she only laughs harder. "Stop," I implore. "This is going to be hard enough without you making it worse."

Kat holds up her hands and flashes me a wicked grin. "What's Christmas without a little family drama though, am I right?"

"Did somebody say family drama?" Sadie and Quinn appear.

"Nope. We were just talking," I rush out, hoping Kat will drop it.

"Are you okay?" Sadie Ray's eyes narrow with concern.

"Me? Fine. I'm fine."

"You keep saying that..."

So maybe I'd said it once or twice this morning at the house when she and the guys had come over to open gifts. It was loud and busy, and I'd sat quietly on the couch, watching them tease each other. But there was a ripple of tension every time Rhett looked in my direction and Ray caught him watching me.

And now I have to survive dinner with all of them.

Sadie Ray takes a breath, readying herself to say something else, but the doors open and men spill into the clubhouse, laughing and joking, everyone full of holiday cheer.

I find Jax and Zach immediately, surprised to see them sharing a joke. Jax's eyes land on me first. Zach is next, smirking as he looks right at me and leans in to whisper something to Jax.

My stomach curls, tightening with lust and other things I have no right to be thinking surrounded by my family and half the club.

"Trouble," Kat smirks, a knowing glint in her eyes. "So much trouble."

She's right.

I am in deep, deep trouble.

"He's watching you again," Kat whispers, nudging me under the table.

I slam my boot down on her foot, and she yelps under her breath, shooting me a death glare. A saccharine smile tugs at my mouth as I fork another piece of ham into my mouth.

"This is some damn good food," Dane declares.

He, my brother, Sadie and Wes are all sitting at the other end of the table with Ray and Victoria. I've managed to tuck myself on the end, next to Kat. But it hasn't stopped the stares. If Zach is at all bothered by

Rhett's icy gaze set in his direction, he doesn't let on. Just as he doesn't acknowledge Ray's lingering glances.

"You haven't eaten much, sweetheart," Victoria says down the table, motioning to my barely touched plate.

"I... uh, I'm not hungry. Sorry."

"Do you feel okay?"

"I'm fine."

Rhett snorts at that, and all eyes shoot to him.

"Bro," Dane hisses. "Not the time or place."

Rhett visibly stiffens, but Sadie Ray lays a hand on his arm and whispers something to him.

"How was the party the other night?" Zach asks.

And I could kill him.

Dead.

What the hell is he playing at?

"Excuse me?" I barely get the words out over the lump in my throat.

"My bad. I thought D said you and Kat were going to a costume party—"

"Party?" Rhett barks. "What party?"

"Rhett..." Sadie shakes her head, pinning Zach with a hard look.

Jesus, this is turning into a living nightmare.

"It was just a dumb party at Envy," Kat adds with a small shrug. "Nothing to get your panties in a twist over, Savage."

"I'm not sure I like the idea of the two of you at a club, Katrina." Evelyn's brows knit together, and a bolt of guilt goes through me.

"It's not like other clubs, Mom. Styx works there, he's—"

"Stygian?" She gasps. "Now there's a name I haven't heard in a while."

Diesel mutters something under his breath, his expression one of pure thunder. Kat snickers, rolling her eyes. Oh, she knows exactly what buttons she's pressing. But in typical Kat fashion, she doesn't care in the least.

"Well, I guess they're not kids anymore," Ray grunts. "But you're still in high school. There's plenty of time for boys and all of that shit."

Diesel reaches clumsily for his beer, almost choking on his dinner.

"Oh, sweetheart, are you okay?" Evelyn fusses over him, rubbing his back. Zach and a couple of the other guys burst out laughing, and for a moment, the tense mood lifts.

"I don't know about anyone else, but I'm stuffed." Crank's silverware clatters against his clean plate as he leans back in his chair.

A chorus of appreciation ripples down the table, and conversations turn to lighter topics. Dessert. The various gifts people received. Plans for the party tonight.

A party I have no intention of attending.

A room full of drunken bikers and half-naked club whores isn't exactly my idea of fun. Besides, if dinner was any indication, the sooner I can get out of here, the better.

The women begin cleaning away plates and dishes to make way for dessert. Deciding it's a good time to sneak away, I quietly excuse myself and head for the bathrooms.

I half expect Kat or Sadie Ray to follow me, but they don't. And I'm relieved. I just need a second to myself, to calm my racing heart and ease the knot in my stomach. But it's more than that. I'm frustrated. Frustrated that Ray and Rhett still view me as a kid, not a young woman able to make her own choices. Her own decisions. And deep down, I hate that I feel like I'm betraying them by sneaking around with Zach, Diesel, and Jax. But how can I ever tell them, knowing that Rhett already shot Zach?

I grip the counter, inhaling a shaky breath. This is my family, my life, for as wild and messy as it might be. And despite all the tension and awkwardness and hostility between Rhett and Zach, for the first time ever, I feel like I might have found my place in the world.

I just hope my heart can survive the inevitable fallout.

The day goes on and slowly the mood changes. The liquor flows, and more of the single members wander into the clubhouse.

"I think I'm going to go."

"Go?" Kat gawks at me. "But you can't leave. The party is just getting started."

"Exactly why I don't want to stay."

"But you haven't even talked to them." She flicks her head over to where Zach, Diesel, and Jax are sitting at the bar talking and laughing with Crank.

"And say what?" My heart sinks.

I knew that outside of wishing them a Merry Christmas, there wouldn't be a chance to talk to the guys today. But I didn't expect them to act as if I'm not even here.

Since dinner ended and the table was cleared to make room for tonight's festivities, they've barely looked twice at me.

"Hey, what's wrong?" Kat touches my arm and I look back at her.

"Nothing. I guess I just thought..."

"You know they're only giving you space because it's what they expect you to want, given the circumstances."

"Yeah, I know. But I don't... it doesn't matter. It's been a long day. I'm tired. I'm going to see if someone will give me a ride home."

"Are you sure?" Disappointment flickers over her face, but I nod, forcing a smile that doesn't reach my eyes.

"Okay, well text me when you get home. And Riv?"

"Yeah?"

"It'll all work, you know?"

As I grab my jacket and slip out of the party unnoticed, I wish I could believe her.

20

ZACH

"Was all that fucking necessary earlier?" D asks. I don't need him to clarify, I know exactly what he's talking about.

I shrug, not really having any comeback for poking Rhett during dinner. It was a low blow, bringing up the party. But fuck it. River isn't a kid anymore. She's more than capable of making her own decisions. Including bad ones, seeing as she's been hooking up with me.

I get it. If I had a little sister, I wouldn't want her with the likes of me, or any bike riding dicks either. But unfortunately for him, this is River's life. And actually, as far as I can see, it's a hell of a lot better than the one she endured in Colton. So maybe it's not all bad.

"Do you want to get yourself shot again?" he asks, throwing back his whiskey.

"Obviously not. It was just a bit of fun. All of this is just a bit of fun."

My comment drags Jax's eyes up from his cell, and his brows pinch as he stares at me.

"What?"

"Is that all this is to you? A bit of fun?"

"Uh..." My hand lifts, rubbing the back of my neck as I wait for his lips to twitch like he's playing me. "Yeah, I guess."

"Really? She's just a bit of fun?" Hurt crosses his features as my heart starts to race.

I mean, yeah. That's all this is, right? A bit of fun. It's not like I'm the kind of guy she's ever going to picture anything more than a roll around the sack with. D, maybe. He's loyal, steady. Jax... if he can pull his head out of the past, then he'd probably be perfect boyfriend material for her.

But me? Nah. Not a fucking chance.

My lips part to respond but I never get a chance to say anything, because pain explodes across the side of my head. I wheel around toward the person who caused it, my fist pulling back, ready to retaliate.

Just a beat before I throw the punch, I register who is actually standing before me with her hands on her hips and a serious scowl on her face.

"Who the fuck took the batteries out of your vibrator?" I bark, rubbing at the side of my head. Girl's got some strength.

"What's up, Kitty Kat?" D asks his little sister, his voice a little slurred from the drinks the two of us have been putting away all afternoon. Jax is the only sober one. Fuck knows why, although I'm grateful, because one of us needs to drive sometime soon, and it sure as fuck isn't going to be D.

"Don't *Kitty Kat* me, you oblivious douchebag."

Jax's eyes widen at Kat's tone.

"Whoa, say it how it is," I mutter.

"Seriously? Are you three just going to sit there like

everything's all right with the fucking world? Fucking idiots," she mutters to herself.

"Uh... what's—"

"Where's River?" Jax suddenly snaps.

Looking over Kat's shoulder, I find the booth where she was sitting with our girl earlier completely empty. "Kat?"

Her lips peel back as she looks between the three of us, fury written into every single one of her features.

"You don't deserve her. Any of you."

"Where is she?" D growls, suddenly sounding completely sober.

"She left," Kat says, throwing her arms up in defeat. "She left, and none of you motherfuckers even noticed."

"We're trying to give her some space," D argues, getting to his feet.

"Yeah, well, did you ever consider it might be a little too much fucking space? It's Christmas Day, and she's gone home alone. It's her first holiday without her mom. How the hell do you think she's feeling right now?"

"Shit," Jax hisses, rubbing his hand over his face. "We need to go."

"Too fucking right you do," Kat spits. "She shouldn't be alone right now, especially when she's got three fucking boyfriends—"

My stomach knots and my mouth opens before my brain registers the words flowing. "We're not her—"

"Not now, man," D barks, punching me in the shoulder. "Jax, wait. We can't all just fucking walk out. Ray and Rhett have been watching us like hawks all day."

"I don't give a fuck. I'm not letting her think we don't care." He turns to me. "You might not," he snaps, "but I fucking do, and I have no problem with her knowing it."

Jax takes a couple of steps away. "Meet me out by the truck in ten minutes or I'll go without you."

D and I share a look. We've spent days planning River and Jax's Christmas present. There's no fucking way we're letting him head over there without us.

"We'll be there," D confirms.

"Good," Kat seethes. "And you'd all better treat her right. If I hear that you so much as—"

"Yeah, yeah, Walker. We fucking got it." I stand, ready to make a move, but she gets right in my space. It might be intimidating if she didn't have to crane her neck to look up at me. "Problem?" I ask, my brow lifting.

"If you hurt her, Stone, I'll castrate you in your sleep. I don't give a shit if we're related or not. Which, by the way, is fucked up, considering the way you flirted with me in front of her when you first got here."

"All's fair in love and war, Kitty Kat."

"Fuck you, Zach. I swear to God, if my best friend didn't think you had some redeeming qualities, then I'd already have caused you some serious harm."

"That's enough, Katrina," D says, wrapping his arm around her shoulders. "Let's go and get Mom. She needs to get home."

"Did you not just hear a word I said?" she snaps at him.

"You're my cover story. Jesus, Kat."

Together, Kat and D go and collect Aunt Evelyn, and after what looks like a short argument, they finally gather up her stuff and lead her out toward the parking lot.

That just leaves me.

Finishing my drink, I look around the clubhouse at everyone enjoying themselves and try to come up with an excuse for why I don't want to party with them, to get blind drunk, to forget exactly what I'm missing today.

I know River's got it worse, so much fucking worse, but she's not the only one missing people this Christmas. Not even being able to hear my mom's voice has been fucking killer, but one I'm determined not to bring me down. Well, not more than it does any other day, anyway.

———

"So, what's the plan?" I ask, leaning through the two front seats at Jax and D, who were already sitting here, waiting for me after I thanked Ray for his hospitality and told him with a heavy heart that I was missing family and not in the mood for celebrating. Thankfully, he bought the lie, because I'm not sure the truth would have been an easy pill to swallow. Especially after warning me off River only days ago.

"We break the fucking door down if we have to," D spits. "We're getting our girl out of that house and taking her to celebrate Christmas in our own way.

Jax shoots a look at both of us, his brows pulled tight. "Why do I feel like I'm missing something?"

"Because you are. Tough luck though, no time to chat. We've got a girl to abduct," I say as he pulls into Ray's driveway.

"Wait, we can't just—"

"Watch us," D says with a smirk, jumping from the truck at the same time I do, leaving Jax to kill the engine and run to catch up with us.

"Where the fuck did you get that from?" I ask when D shoves a key into the lock of the front door.

Turning to me, he taps his nose. "A magician never reveals his secret, cous."

"Jesus. Are we really—"

"Yes," both D and I bark at Jax before he throws the door open and we all storm into the dark house.

Light flashes from the living room and we immediately all walk that way, coming to an abrupt stop in the living room doorway when our girl comes into view.

"River," Jax breathes, taking another step toward her while I stay put.

Her eyes widen at the sight of us, her small fists clenching in frustration.

She's curled up in the middle of the sectional, watching some sappy Christmas film with tears filling her eyes and—

"What the fuck are you wearing?" I bark.

She looks at the three of us with wide eyes before looking down at herself. "Pajamas. Why, don't you approve?"

"T-they're covered in—"

"Sloths. They're covered in sloths. They were a Christmas present from Sadie," she explains. "You all need to leave. If I wanted to be anywhere near any of you, then I wouldn't have left."

If she managed to say it without her bottom lip trembling, then I might just have believed her with the anger darkening her glassy blue eyes.

"Sure, we'll leave," D states, and she blows out a relieved breath that he's being so reasonable. "But we're not doing it without you."

Surging forward, he grabs her around the waist and

throws her over his shoulder as she kicks, screams and punches in an attempt to stop him.

"Kill the TV, make it look like she was never here. And if anyone asks, pretty girl, you're spending the night with Kat."

"What? No. No. I'm not going with you."

"I think you'll find you are, Blondie," I add, slapping her ass before D marches past me with her. "Shame Sadie didn't buy you anything a little sexier."

Although the sloth-covered bootie shorts are pretty damn sexy. Who knew.

"I didn't dress for you, asshole," she hisses, still thrashing about on D's shoulder.

"Maybe not, but something tells me you're going to be undressing for us very, very soon."

"Unlikely," she snaps. "Diesel," she screams as Jax holds the front door open for him. "Put me down right now."

He ignores her, and before she knows what's happening, I've got her on my lap, her back pinned to my chest as Jax floors the truck out of the driveway and back toward Red Ridge.

Yet still, she fights.

"You're gonna want to stop squirming like that, Blondie, or you're going to find yourself thoroughly fucked before we even get there."

She shudders as my breath tickles down her neck. "Fuck you," she hisses.

"Yeah, that was pretty much the idea."

"I hate you. I hate all of you."

"Now, now. That's not very festive of you, Blondie."

"I don't give a fuck," she sulks. "I don't want—"

Threading my fingers through her hair, I drag her

head back and slam my lips down on hers, both shutting her up and proving one very important point.

She wants this as badly as I do.

The second I push my tongue past her lips, River relaxes in my hold and kisses me back. A smile twitches at my lips as I accept that I was right.

"Our girl fucking loves the fight," I say into our kiss just to prove a point to the assholes in the front. "I bet she's fucking dripping for us, too. Think I should find out?"

21

RIVER

"Don't," I breathe, squirming on Zach's lap as his fingers inch along my thigh, rising higher and higher until he hits the edge of my shorts.

Indignation burns through me, but despite how pissed I am at them, I can't deny the way my skin hums with anticipation.

They came for me.

All of them.

I can't even process what that means—not when Zach's pinky grazes my pussy.

"Zach," Diesel warns, and my eyes collide with his. His gaze is dark, stormy and tortured. My breath catches as Zach hooks my panties aside and pushes a finger inside me. It feels so good, I have to press my lips together to stop the whimper building in my throat from escaping.

All while Diesel watches me, his brows drawn tight, breaths coming in choppy waves as he watches me try to fight my body's reaction to Zach's touch.

"She's fucking soaked, cous," he drawls, licking a path

up the side of my neck as he adds a second finger, stretching me.

Part of me can't believe this is happening. That they kidnapped me from my own damn house and bundled me in the truck to take me to God only knows where. But the other part—the part of me that comes to life in the dark—never wants it to stop.

I grind my hips against Zach's fingers, desperately seeking more friction.

"She's so fucking needy for it." He chuckles against my ear. "Wanna feel her?"

Diesel's eyes flare, his gaze dropping to my legs, right where Zach's fingers are plunging in and out of me.

Do it, I want to challenge him. Because having them both touch me, together... it does things to me.

Things that make me question my sanity. But I don't care.

I don't.

"Touch me," I whisper, a whimper slipping free as Zach starts to massage my clit in lazy, teasing circles.

Diesel meets my hooded gaze again and grits his teeth.

"Shit, man," Zach says. "You're a stronger man than—"

Diesel grabs my thigh, squeezing.

"Go on," Zach encourages. "Feel her. Feel how wet she is for us. For this."

Zach pulls his fingers out and drags my thighs wider, baring me to Diesel. "Fuck," he hisses, running a hand over his face as if he can't quite believe this is happening either.

He reaches for me, sliding two fingers through my wetness.

"Go deep, she likes that." Zach chuckles, still playing with my clit like it's his own personal toy. "You're awfully quiet over there, Jaxy boy. Everything good?"

"I... uh, yeah." Jax grunts, keeping his eye on the road, and Zach chuckles again.

"Don't worry, you'll get yours later."

"Oh God," I cry out, lifting my hips as Diesel pushes two fingers inside of me, deep just like Zach said he should.

"Clench for him, Blondie." Zach collars me around the throat with his big hand. "Show him what he's missing out on. Although if you're lucky, perhaps tonight he'll finally man the fuck up and give you what you want."

"Shit, Stone," Diesel groans, riding me hard with his fingers.

"I'm gonna... oh God..." I bear down on him, clenching my walls so tight I feel everything.

And then the tension snaps, and I moan their names.

Zach... Diesel... Jax.

A maelstrom of sensation rips through me and makes me soar. Their hands. Their hungry gazes. The fact that Jax is sitting right there, driving the truck. Wanting but not touching.

It drives me insane and makes everything so much more.

"Our dirty girl." Zach presses a kiss to my collarbone. "We're gonna have so much fun with you later."

"Suck." Diesel brings his fingers to my lips like an offering, and I draw them into my mouth, tasting my arousal all over him.

"We're almost there," Jax announces, his voice rough against his throat.

"Ready, pretty girl?" Diesel cups my face, his eyes blown with lust.

This isn't my gentle protector. This is the guy who likes to be in control. The guy who keeps a box of toys underneath his bed and enjoys controlling the situation.

"What are you thinking?" he asks.

"I..."

"Here," Jax booms, pulling up outside the cabin.

Diesel's cabin.

Anticipation licks up my spine as he cuts the engine.

"What are we doing here?" I ask, fixing my pajama shorts and running a hand through my untamed hair.

"You'll see," is all Zach says as he taps my thigh and indicates for me to follow Diesel out of the truck. But Diesel doesn't let my feet hit the ground. Instead, he picks me up and I wrap my legs around his waist, my soft laughter filling the night sky.

I was so angry when they stormed my house earlier. Dejected and hurt.

But this...

A girl could get used to this.

The second we step into the cabin, I gasp. It's been transformed. Twinkling lights hang from the beams, casting a warm glow around the room. The dust sheets have all been removed, the mismatched furniture arranged around the fireplace, already piled high with kindling wood. There's even a small tree in the corner, decorated with some scraps of tinsel.

Diesel lowers me to the floor and drops a kiss on my

head. "Merry Christmas, River." He runs his knuckles down my cheek. "I'll get the fire started."

"You did all this... for me?" My hand drifts to my throat, emotion swelling in my chest.

"It was a surprise." Jax says from across the room. "These two fuckers didn't want to tell you but—"

"What he's trying to say, Blondie," Zach stalks toward me, "is that we've been slaving away the last couple of days to get this place into some kind of shape for you—*us*—to have some fun tonight."

"Oh." A shiver runs through me.

"Cat got your tongue?" Zach's hands settle on my hips as he stares down at me.

"I didn't get you a present," I whisper.

"Baby, you are the present. And we're gonna have so much fun unwrapping you." His eyes darken with lust but then flick over my shoulder. "Isn't that right, Jaxy boy?"

There's something in the way he says the words, as if they're a challenge.

"What's going on?" I ask.

"This isn't only about you." Zach says the words onto my lips.

"What do you—"

"You'll see," he drawls before plunging his tongue into my mouth. Claiming me. Owning me until I can't think about anything except Zach and a kiss I think might ruin me for all other kisses.

A hard body moves up behind me, caging me against Zach. I'd know it anywhere.

Diesel.

He pulls the hair off my shoulder and latches his

mouth onto my neck, grazing the skin with his teeth, biting down until I mewl into Zach's mouth.

"Soon." He licks the bite mark, soothing the sting until I'm putty in his hands.

Their hands.

Zach pulls back, letting his eyes drop down my body and back up. "Is it wrong that these ridiculous things are growing on me." He fingers the hem of my sloth pajamas.

"Come on, we have supplies."

Supplies?

That gets my attention, and I follow Diesel over to the breakfast counter. Jax joins us but hovers on the periphery. I hold out my hand, a silent offer.

He doesn't take it, but he does move closer, a faint smile tracing his mouth.

"A drink for the lady." Diesel pulls out a bottle of some kind of wine spritzer and uncaps it.

I eye it curiously. "Are you trying to get me drunk?" My brow lifts playfully.

"Consider it... something to loosen you up." A knowing smirk plays on his lips.

Heat flashes inside me and I shift uncomfortably on the stool.

"Drink up, Blondie. You're gonna need your energy for what we have planned." Zach drags his bottom lip between his teeth, watching me.

Always watching.

"Jax." Diesel pours him a glass of whiskey, double measure.

"I... uh, I don't know."

"Hey, it's okay," I say. "No one's going to make you do anything you don't want to."

"We'll see about that." Zach chuckles darkly.

And there must be something very wrong with me, because the promise in his words stokes the flames already setting me on fire.

"Do you trust us?" Diesel asks and I nod, my throat suddenly dry. "Do you need a safeword?"

"A safeword?" I almost choke over the sentence.

"Yeah. You know, a way of letting us know you need to stop."

"Fuck," Jax hisses, his eyes darting between me and Diesel. "Maybe this isn't such a good idea."

"You want this, don't you? You want to touch her? To feel what it's like?" Zach asks him, and realization slams into me.

This isn't about me at all. Not really.

It's about Jax.

About giving him what he needs.

"Jax, look at me," I demand, a fierce sense of protectiveness rising inside of me. He lifts his face to mine, and some of the worry in his expression melts away. "I want this. I want to help. I want... you. Anyway I can get you."

"Fuck," he hisses again, clenching his hand into a fist. "Fuck."

"Come on, big boy." Zach slaps him on the shoulder. "Take a walk with me." He guides Jax down the hall.

I swallow, my heart crashing against my rib cage.

Is this really happening?

"We thought—"

"Did I say that out loud?" My head whips around to Diesel, and he gives me a small smile. "What?" I ask.

"Do you have any idea how beautiful you are? How precious?" He rounds the counter and runs his thumbs along my jaw. "Are you okay with this?"

"Yes."

"We'll be right there. Every step of the way. If it gets too much—"

"It won't. I want him, Diesel. I want all of you. More than anything. And if this will help him..." My gaze goes to the hall again.

"You're amazing. And one day soon, I'm going to show you." He leans in, capturing my lips in a slow, lazy kiss. "Ready?"

I nod, too overwhelmed to answer. Diesel scoops me off the stool, throws me over his shoulder like a rag doll, and stalks down the hall toward the bedroom.

Inside, Zach and Jax are deep in hushed conversation. They look up the second we enter and a ripple goes through the room, the air taut with tension and anticipation.

Diesel lowers me to the floor and kisses me again. Then a cold mask falls over his expression and my stomach flip flops. "Strip for us," he says in a commanding voice. "Nice and slow. Make it good for Jax."

Zach pushes the man in question into the chair and winks at me. Adrenaline courses through me as their eyes drink me in, soak me up, and sear me to the bone. This is different to the other night when I was in control.

I'm not anymore.

I'm their puppet, but I'm more than willing to let them pull my strings. If it means I get more of them... all of them... I'm in.

All in.

"Don't keep us waiting, Blondie," Zach growls, ripping his t-shirt over his head. My pulse ratchets, my skin burning.

I want this. I want them so much I feel like I might combust.

Slipping my hands under my pajama top, I slowly drag it up my body, giving them a show. Jax sucks in a ragged breath, murmuring to himself, but the longing is evident on his face.

He wants this.

Wants me.

And Zach and Diesel are going to help him take what he wants.

22

DIESEL

My heart thunders in my chest and my mouth waters as she drops her top to the floor at her feet, revealing her perfect tits to us.

My fists curl in frustration. I shouldn't be doing this. The big brother in me still knows how wrong it is. She's the same age as my kid sister, her best fucking friend. And yet, as I stand here watching as she tucks her thumbs into the waistband of her irritatingly cute sloth shorts, the only thing I can think about is tying her to the four-poster bed that now sits in the middle of the room, waiting for her.

She lets the fabric fall to her ankles, her nervous yet hungry eyes shooting between the three of us as if she's expecting us to do something. She's going to be disappointed if that's the case, because there's only one of us who's going to be doing anything anytime soon, and he's currently sitting in the chair, gripping the armrest so tight his knuckles are white.

I'm not worried, though. Our plan is solid, and I know for a fact that he isn't going to be able to resist.

"You're a tease, Blondie," Zach growls as she stands there in just her tiny lace panties.

She sucks in a sharp breath, squaring her shoulders and finding some confidence.

When we first stormed into her house, I wasn't sure if she was going to let this happen. But since Zach pushed his fingers inside her in the truck, she hasn't exactly been arguing about it.

"Oh, you want these off, too?" she asks coyly, running her fingertip along the lace edge.

"You fucking know we do," Jax growls, shocking the shit out of me.

Her eyes find his, and a small, encouraging smile pulls at her lips. My cock jerks in my pants as she pushes her thumbs into the fabric.

'For you,' she mouths at him as the air crackles around us.

"Shit," he hisses when the lace falls to her feet and she steps out of them. "So fucking beautiful, Riv," he mutters, his eyes taking in every inch of her perfect body.

Focusing back on her, I take my time memorizing every one of her curves. "Get on the bed. Slowly."

She swallows nervously and takes a step forward, her breathing erratic and her cheeks and neck flushed with the embarrassment of being bare while we're fully dressed, minus Zach's shirt.

I reach behind me and pull my hoodie off in one swift move. She glances at me appreciatively and I tug my fly open, more than ready to shed it all for her.

Understanding my unspoken demand, she doesn't turn toward the bed until she's right in front of Jax, and when she does, the little temptress bends over, giving him one hell of a view as she crawls on all fours into the center.

"Hot damn, baby," Zach mutters, scrubbing his jaw, his eyes locked on her swollen skin. "Look how needy her cunt is."

"On your back, legs spread, arms above your head."

She shoots me a look over her shoulder and I damn near forget about the plan and drag her to the end of the bed to take her hard and fast in an attempt to sate the need I've been battling with for weeks now.

My teeth grind as I watch her flip onto her back and follow my orders. "Zach," I bark, dragging his attention from her body.

"Shit, yeah," he mutters, taking a step toward the dresser and pulling out the rope we stashed in there, along with a few other things.

He passes half of it to me and we take a side of the bed each, prowling around her like lions circling our prey.

"You need a safeword, pretty girl," I tell her again, dragging my fingertips up her inner arm and watching her shudder from my innocent touch.

"I trust you," she breathes, holding my eyes.

"That's not the point, you need—"

"Come on, baby. Give Daddy D a word," Zach urges, pulling the rope through his fingers.

"Cactus," River blurts.

"Cactus?" Zach asks in amusement. "As in, if you don't stop you'll shove a cactus up our—"

"Enough," I bark, cutting off his teasing almost immediately. "If at any point you need us to stop," I tell River, holding her eyes so she can see how serious I am, "if anything we do gets too much, just say the word, and we'll stop immediately, no questions asked. Right?" I say, looking at Zach and then to Jax, who looks like he's about to combust.

"Got it. But I won't need it. None of you will do anything I can't handle."

"Big words when you have no idea what we're capable of, Blondie."

"I'll take my chances."

Zach looks up at me and I nod. We both make quick work of securing her wrists to the posts on either side of the bed before we mimic the actions with her ankles, leaving her spread-eagled.

"Fuck, the things I could do to you right now," I mutter, rubbing my hand over my face. My cock aches behind the confines of my pants, desperate to finally find its home buried deep inside her.

She squirms on the bed, her chest heaving and her body flushed. "So do it," she begs, seriously testing my restraint.

"One day, pretty girl, I will," I promise her. "But I think it's time we gave Jaxy boy his Christmas gift, don't you?"

Ripping her eyes from mine, she turns to look at Jax. "Jax," she pleads, her brow creasing with concern at the tight expression on his face. "I'm all yours. I can't touch you. Please."

"Shit, Riv," he breathes, pushing to the edge of the seat. "Do you have any idea how incredible you look right now?"

"Show me," she begs. "Show me how much you like it. I'm yours."

His teeth sink into his bottom lip as he pushes to his feet and shoves the long sleeves of his black shirt up his arm, exposing his ink. He prowls closer, his eyes running over every inch of her.

"What do you think, Jaxy boy? Best Christmas gift ever?"

He grunts some kind of agreement, which only increases my curiosity as to what his life was like prior to finding himself a part of the Sinners family.

"Wanna start off slowly?" I ask, nodding toward the open drawer. My mouth waters as I picture all the things I could do to our girl with all the things I'm hiding in here.

He stalks over and reluctantly rips his eyes from River. His gasp of shock rips through the air. "Jesus, D. I-I don't even—"

Picking up an innocent-ish looking feather tickler, I push it into his hand.

"Start slow, build up to the hard stuff. But first..." I grab the bottle of whiskey that's sitting on the top and pour a triple measure into the glass. Add that to what he had in the kitchen, and hopefully, it'll help him push past his limits and discover a whole new world of pleasure.

"She wants it. All of it. And we won't let you hurt her or take it too far. We've got your back, man." I have no idea if it's what he needs to hear, but I remember just how much my encouragement helped the other night, so I intend on continuing.

"Y-yeah. Okay. I got this."

"We know you do, bro. So does she. Look at her," I say, turning back to the girl in question. "She's so desperate for your touch. Look how her hips are grinding into the bed." My fists curl as I watch her hips grind into the mattress with her need.

He swallows thickly before stepping forward. River's eyes follow his movements as he crawls onto the bed between her parted legs.

REAP

The tension in the room is so thick I can barely breathe as we all wait for him to do something. My chest heaves along with hers as I wait, the anticipation almost getting the better of me.

He lifts the tickler, hovering it over her body, hesitating.

"It's okay," she whispers. "Touch me. Please, Jax."

Suddenly, he moves. The tickler goes flying across the room—right along with his inhibitions, apparently—before he falls over her, his hands planted on either side of her head and he captures her lips in a searing kiss.

"Oh shit," Zach breathes, falling into the now vacant chair and shoving his hand into his pants as he watches the show.

Jealousy washes through me as I watch her writhe beneath Jax. My fists curl again, my short nails digging into my palms with my need to throw him across the room and take her myself.

Her moans fill the room as their kiss continues. Red hot desire fills my veins as he takes exactly what I'm desperate for. I close my eyes for a beat, remembering just how she tastes. How her tongue feels sliding against mine.

"Fuck, you're perfect," he tells her when he finally pulls away.

"I need you, Jax. I need—" Her words are cut off and he moves, his lips finding the soft skin of her neck before he slowly descends toward her hard nipples.

He pauses when he's hovering right above one.

"Suck on it, Jax. Taste her. She's so fucking sweet, man," Zach orders, and after a beat, he hesitantly lowers his head.

He flicks her with the tip of his tongue and she jolts against her bindings, proving to him that she's not going

185

anywhere, totally unable to touch him until we release her.

"More," she cries. "Jax, please."

Happy that she's telling the truth, he finally captures her nipple in his mouth as her cries and his deep moan fills the room.

"Hand on the other one," I instruct, my own arm desperate to reach out and do it myself. He follows orders, palming her breasts gently. "She won't break, Jax. Squeeze."

He does, and a loud moan rips through the air that makes my cock jerk.

"Harder," I demand, and he complies while she cries his name. "See. She can take it. She loves it," I urge, moving around the room to get a better view.

Leaning back against the wall, I give in to my need and copy Zach, pushing my hand into my pants and squeezing the base of my cock.

River's eyes find mine briefly. The hunger, the pure carnal need within the blue depths has me pushing my pants over my hips and exposing myself to her.

Her teeth sink into her bottom lip as she watches me stroke myself and Jax continues to experiment with her, making her back arch off the bed.

"Lower, Jax. You want to really taste her, don't you?" Zach growls.

My body burns with need and restraint as Jax begins kissing down her stomach, my hand working my cock faster as I watch her writhe.

"Yes," River hisses when he hits her pubic bone. "Oh my God, Jax. I need your mouth on me. Please."

He looks up at her, their eyes colliding over her

body. Her eyes are dark and desperate, while his still holds uncertainty that she really is okay with this.

When I find out who fucked him up quite this badly, I'm going to put a fucking bullet between his eyes.

Jax's eyes meet mine, and I nod. "Do it, Jax."

"B-but I don't—"

"Listen to her, read her body. She'll tell you."

"Please, Jax. I need—" Her words are cut off as he follows my orders and dives for her.

"Yes, bro. Eat her like you're fucking starving," Zach booms, his own cock now out and being worked almost violently as he watches the show.

"Holy shit," River screams, her hips rolling and her bindings pulling tight.

Jax's body goes rigid and he sits up in horror, his eyes wide and his face pale.

"What the hell?" River barks at him. "Don't stop."

I can't help but bark out a laugh.

"What the fuck are you waiting for?" Zach snaps. "We wanna watch her coming all over your face, bro."

Jax looks down at River once more.

"Please," she begs, her chest heaving and her skin flushed with desire. "I need you to keep going."

But when he still doesn't move, she changes tact.

"Do it, or move and let one of them."

Apparently, that ultimatum was all he needed to hear, because he lowers down again and gets back to work.

23

RIVER

Pleasure races down my spine as Jax licks me. He isn't careful or shy as he spears his tongue inside me, lapping at me, sucking my clit and my folds as if he can't get enough.

"Oh God... God... I'm close..."

I turn my head, pulling on the restraints, heat flashing inside me as my eyes connect with Zach as he jerks himself off.

"She's almost there, man," he says, the muscles in his neck straining. "Put your fingers inside her and fuck her while you suck her clit."

Jax follows his orders with ease, working me with his fingers as he eats me like a man starved. It's all I need to fly off the edge, my body bowing off the bed.

"Jax, oh God..." I cry as I shatter.

"Fuck, she's beautiful when she comes."

I'm aware of Diesel approaching the bed. His knees hit the mattress near my head and he leans over me. "Open."

My lips part and he pushes his dick into my mouth.

"Shit. That feels good. Jax, have a rest. Let Zach get her off now."

"W-what?" I croak around him. But he only goes deeper.

When he pulls out, I suck in a greedy breath. "I want to fuck your mouth, okay?" He runs his thumb over my cheek, painting my lips with his precum.

"And I want to fuck her pussy." Zach appears at the end of the bed, his eyes going to Diesel, who shakes his head.

"Not yet."

"Not even the tip? I need to feel her. Fuck, I need to feel her clenched around me."

"Not. Yet," Diesel growls.

"Fine, Daddy D. You'll have to settle for my tongue then, Blondie." He drops to his knees and pulls my legs over his shoulders, rubbing his nose through my wet folds and breathing me in deeply. My cheeks burn with embarrassment, but it's forgotten almost immediately when he moves against me.

I'm sensitive. Too sensitive. But the second Diesel feeds me his cock and Zach feeds my pussy his tongue, I'm gone... Totally and utterly gone.

They work me in a symphony, playing my body in a way that scares me. How do they... what I need? What I want?

My eyes find Jax in the corner of the room, watching, slowly fisting himself. There isn't even a hint of jealousy in his eyes, only awe and hunger.

"Wanna try something new," Zach murmurs before sliding his hand underneath me. He presses a finger to my ass, and I go stiff.

"Relax, Blondie. You'll enjoy it, I promise." He

chuckles darkly against my clit, sucking it into his mouth as he works the tip inside me, then the knuckle. It burns, and I'm about to yell at him to stop when pleasure blasts through me.

"Ahhh," I cry out.

"Yeah, thought our dirty girl would like it. Wait until it's D filling you there." He gently pumps his finger while eating me with long, slow, measured licks that have me gasping around Diesel's dick.

"Would you like that, pretty girl?" Diesel gazes down at me. "Would you like us both to fuck you one day?"

I nod, drunk on the feel of him. The taste. The feel of both of them as they work me over.

Diesel's thrusts grow harder, more insistent until I feel him swell and he comes down my throat. "Good girl." He runs his knuckles down my cheek, backing away slightly.

Looking at Zach, he says, "Get her there, now."

Anticipation races down my spine, but there isn't time to bask in it as Zach picks up speed, licking and sucking me with such vigor I'm crying—*begging*—for him to stop.

"Not until I get your cum." He breathes the words on me and I whimper, so over-sensitized that pain and pleasure swirl together, making it hard to think.

"Please... *please*..." I don't even know what I'm asking for, but then his tongue swipes my clit. Once, twice, and I shatter again, screaming out as intense waves of pleasure roll through me, wrecking me.

"That's my girl," Zach drawls, licking up every ounce of my release.

He stands, wiping his mouth with the back of his hand. "Now what?" he asks Diesel.

Because he's in control here. This is his show.

And there's something about that fact that makes my blood heat.

Diesel stalks toward Jax and whispers something to him. Jax shakes his head, panic filling his eyes. Diesel grips his shoulder, and they talk in hushed voices.

Zach looms over me, smirking. "Do you have any idea how good you look like this? The things I could do to you."

I smother a moan, straining against the bindings around my wrists. I want to touch him. To touch them. But there's something oddly erotic about being restrained like this. It's not something I imagined I would like, but where the three of them are concerned, I don't think there's anything they could do to me that I wouldn't enjoy.

"Stay right here." Zach winks, heading for Diesel and Jax. The three of them glance my way, varying degrees of lust in their eyes. But the combined heat of their hungry stares electrifies my skin, sending a fresh wave of desire through me.

My body is spent, sated and sore, but I want more.

So much more.

Whatever the guys are discussing, they reach a decision, because Diesel moves toward me. *Prowls* is the only word that fits—a hunter zeroing in on its prey.

"You good?" he asks, and I nod. "Want to stop?"

"N-no."

"Do you trust us?"

"You know I do."

"Zach, untie her arms."

The second I'm free, I rub my wrists, wincing at the ache there.

"Does it hurt?" Jax asks, his eyes blown with raw lust as he takes in my naked body.

"A little," I admit. "But I like it."

"Do you want me?"

"You know I do."

"Pin her wrists," he orders Zach and Diesel, and they circle me like predators.

Kneeling down either side of the bed, they each grab one of my wrists, anchoring me to the mattress. It's different from being bound by rope. More intimate somehow.

Jax drags his dick out of his boxer briefs and jeans and fists himself. "I've dreamed about this so many times. Imagined what it would feel like to bury myself deep in your tight, wet heat." His voice tremors, his expression so dark a kick of fear rolls down my spine.

But this is Jax. He won't hurt me.

Even if he wants to.

Even if he needs to.

"Hold her tight."

"We've got her, bro," Zach drawls. "She's all yours."

"She is, isn't she?"

Jax grips my legs, yanking sharply, stretching my body out before him. A whimper spills from me as he trails his hand up my thighs and cups my sensitive pussy. "I want to fucking ruin you."

"Do your worst," I say, refusing to look away.

This Jax isn't the boy I fell for all those weeks ago. This Jax is someone different. A man trying to outrun his demons. To find a way to destroy them.

He jerks himself harder, thighs pressed into the end of the bed, straining over me. Lowering himself onto me, he slides the tip through my folds, nudging my clit so hard, so viciously, I cry out.

"You want this, don't you?" There's a cruel edge to his words.

"Yes... yes," I pant, overwhelmed, consumed by the intense sensations running through me.

He continues jerking off against my soft flesh. Hard, brutal strokes I feel all the way down to my soul.

Zach and Diesel are quiet beside me, but their touch, the soft brush of their thumbs over my wrists, grounds me.

Suddenly, Jax stills, panting, his jaw clenched so tight it has to hurt. "Tell me you want this." He nuzzles my neck. "Tell me you want me to fuck you, River."

"I want you to fuck me, Jax. So much."

He pulls back and stares down at me as if he can't believe I'm real. But then a stone mask slides over his expression and he collars my throat. "Then take it, my pretty little whore." Without warning, he slams into me so hard, the air punches from my lungs.

His fingers tighten around my neck, my vision darkening with the lack of oxygen as he rides my body with unrelenting punishing strokes. I fracture, my mind and body splintering as an orgasm tears through me, and I think I might be crying as Jax unleashes himself on my body.

"Fuck, Jax. Ease up. You're choking her," Zach hisses.

But he doesn't stop. He keeps fucking me, completely lost to whatever demons haunt him.

"Jax," Diesel's commanding voice cuts through the room. "Stop. Now."

Jax stills, releasing his grip a little and shaking above as he comes back to himself, to the moment as I gasp for air. "Shit, River, I—" He tries to pull away, but I blurt out,

"No, don't stop. I want this. I want you. It's okay, I'm okay..."

He blinks.

Blinks again, hardening inside of me.

"I want this, Jax. I want you."

"Fuck, River." He drops his face to my shoulder and kisses me. "You're incredible... I don't deserve this. You."

"I'm the only one who gets to decide what I do or don't deserve. Now fuck me, Jax. Please."

Something relaxes in him and slowly he begins rocking into me again. It's different this time, more controlled and measured. But just as good. His hand remains flexed around my throat, but he doesn't squeeze, he just leaves it there as if he needs the control, needs to have the ultimate power over me.

"More..." I cry, feeling the build inside me again.

"Fuck..." he roars, sliding his hand under my thigh and spreading me wide. "*Fuck!*"

Jax's entire body locks up as he comes hard.

We're sweaty and breathless, and there isn't a single part of me that doesn't ache, but I'm too spent to care.

"Are you okay?" he asks the second he catches his breath.

"I'm perfect. You're perfect." I tilt my face to kiss him, and my heart swells when he lets me.

He might not be able to let me touch him yet, but I know what happened here tonight is a big deal for him.

For all of us.

"We're going to release you," Diesel says, and I nod.

"It's okay. I won't touch him."

My hands twist into the sheets beneath me as Jax kisses me again, sliding his tongue against mine, whispering sweet nothings onto my lips.

You're amazing.

Perfect.

You're everything I've ever wanted.

My heart is so full, I think it might explode. Jax presses one final kiss to my lips and climbs off me. He takes one last look at me sprawled out before him and shakes his head. "I need some air," he mutters, disappearing.

Panic rises inside of me and Zach catches my eye. "I'll go after him."

Diesel appears with a blanket and lifts me into his arms, wrapping me up tightly as he sits down on the bed with me curled around him.

"How do you feel?" He presses a kiss to my forehead.

"That was... intense. Do you think he's okay?"

"He will be. You gave him a gift tonight, River."

My eyes flutter closed, exhaustion seeping into every part of me. "I'm tired," I murmur.

"Sleep, pretty girl." His lips brush my head again and warmth settles deep in my chest. "I'm here. I'm right here."

24

JAX

The cool air whips around my heated skin as I push out through the front door. I lower down on the step and clench my fists, willing them to stop trembling.

Relief, fear, disgust, lust, all duel within me, making my head spin and my heart ache.

I did it.

I did it, and I didn't hurt her... too much.

"Shit," I hiss, squeezing my eyes closed, remembering just how tight my hold on her throat was.

I knew it was wrong, but until D's deep, demanding voice cut through the air, I couldn't make myself stop.

Pleasure and pain.

Pain and pleasure.

They're a fucked-up mess of the same thing in my head, with a bucket load of violence thrown in for good measure.

But watching them with her, seeing how it can be, how it should be... Fuck. I want it. I want it so fucking bad.

I know I can't have it, though. Not the way I really crave. Because if I were to lose my head, to fall into that pit of darkness within me that *he* crafted all those years ago, and I did something I couldn't come back from? I couldn't... I wouldn't be able to deal with that.

It's why being on the periphery is easier. Watching but not having is safer.

But now I've had her.

Tasted her. Claimed her. Marked her.

And fuck if I don't want it again.

But will she want *me* again? I saw the way her eyes widened in shock as I lost control. I saw the fear that she tried to hide—not that it stopped me.

A shiver of awareness trickles down my spine, telling me that I have company. I'm hardly surprised after what I just showed them, but whoever it is hangs back gives me the space I need to process what just happened.

I did the one thing I never thought I'd be able to do—not without causing some serious damage, anyway. And she wanted it, she begged me for it. Even after...

"Fuck."

What is it about River Savage that manages to cut through all the bullshit of my past and force me to deal with all the baggage I've been carrying around with me for years?

My one and only childhood friend tried. He did whatever he could to try to help me before I skipped town at my first opportunity.

Guilt washes through me as I think about all the messages I've received since I bailed on our meeting a few weeks ago.

All he ever did was try to help me. And in return, I just cut him out of my life.

He's given me all the information I need. He's assured me that my uncle has left town, that after his initial questions about my whereabouts he gave up and decided to get on with his life.

It's exactly what I hoped for but also feared at the same time. If he's not there, where Ant can see him, then where is he? Will I turn a corner one day and walk right into the monster from my past?

I shake the thoughts from my head. The chances of that are so slim they're almost laughable.

I did everything I could when I left to ensure he didn't find me. And if he's not even looking, then I can just pray I never have to see the motherfucker again and begin to believe that this... she... could be my future.

"I know you're there," I say to whoever is loitering. My money is on Zach—something that's only confirmed when he comes to sit beside me.

Looking to my left, I find his eyes. They crinkle with his smile before he clamps his hand on my shoulder.

While River might have been the one to take the biggest risk back there, and I might be eternally grateful for her helping to prove that maybe I'm not the monster I think I am, I owe Zach and D everything for facilitating it.

"Proud of you, man," he says so seriously that I can't help but bark out a laugh.

Thankfully, he sees the insanity in the situation and laughs right along with me.

"Never said that to anyone after watching them give their girl a good fucking, that's for sure," he mutters.

Silence falls between us as the reality of what I just did continues to weigh down on me.

"Talk to me, Jax."

"I hurt her, didn't I?" I whisper, needing to know just how bad it got when everything went black for those few moments.

"Nah. It was nothing she couldn't handle. Pretty sure I've been rougher with her."

"How can... how can you be rough like that on purpose? Aren't you worried you might..."

"There's a very fine line between pleasure and pain, Jax. Something I think you might be more than aware of. You've just got to find where it falls for her. But I can tell you now, that idea you have of sweet little River up in your head? That's not who she is between the sheets. Or up against a wall." His eyes twinkle with amusement. "She's just as freaky as we are, and she loves a little kink. Hell, she just got off with all three of us. There are plenty of women out there who wouldn't be up for that, let alone allowing us to tie them to the bed and be completely at our mercy.

"She trusts you, Jax. And she wants to work with you, give you the space and the time you need to deal with whatever it is that's haunting you. You've just got to find a way to trust yourself."

I blow out a steady breath. "Easier said than done."

"You'll get there. Anything else isn't an option," he says confidently.

"Why are you doing this?" I ask. No one has ever gone to anywhere near this kind of effort for me before, and quite honestly, I'm not even sure what to make of it.

"Other than coming all over my hand while I watch you eat our girl out, you mean?"

"Obviously," I mutter, rolling my eyes.

"Every guy deserves to have a good fuck, Jax. I hate

seeing you missing out on one of the wonders of the world."

I can't help but bark a laugh. "I'm not sure that—"

"You mean to tell me that sliding inside her tight, wet pussy back there wasn't the best fucking thing you've ever felt?" he asks, cutting me off.

I bite down on the inside of my cheek as I think about exactly how it did feel as she dragged me inside her body.

I don't realize I've groaned out loud until Zach laughs.

"Definitely one of the wonders of the world. Play your cards right, Jaxy boy, and you might just get to experience it again before we leave here."

"You think she will?" I ask nervously.

"I fucking know so, man. You heard how loudly she called your name when she came, right? There is most definitely a repeat in your future. You coming back inside? It's fucking Arctic out here." He pushes to his feet and looks down at me.

"Yeah, I'll be there in a bit."

"Sure thing, man. She fucking loved it. Don't allow yourself to think anything else," he says, scrubbing at my hair like an imbecile.

It occurs to me that I've let those motherfuckers touch me more in a few days than I have almost anyone else in my life.

Maybe there is hope for my black and fucked-up soul, after all.

My stomach growls loudly when I finally talk myself into rejoining them in the cabin, and the scent of whatever D is cooking hits my nose.

"That smells insane," I tell him, walking over to where he's stirring something on the stove, looking very domesticated.

"Hungry?" he asks with a smirk as I march over to the bottle of whiskey sitting on the counter beside three glasses.

I pour three generous measures and pass them to both D and Zach with a nod of appreciation for what they did for me tonight. Throwing back the glass, I let the alcohol burn down my throat, warming me from the inside out.

"Where is she?" I ask, not missing the fact that River is nowhere to be seen.

"Having a shower. She had someone's cum running down her thighs," D quips suggestively.

I rub at the back of my neck. "It was a long time coming."

"We should probably be grateful you didn't drown her, huh?" Zach deadpans, much to D's amusement.

"Assholes," I mutter, trying to hide my smile. "Why aren't either of you with her?" I ask, honestly astounded they've left her alone, naked and wet in the shower.

"You're more than welcome to go join her."

I hesitate for a beat, imagining how she might look with rivulets of water racing down her curves.

"Go on," D says. "She's probably wondering why one of us hasn't barged in yet, anyway."

"I-I... uh... I can't shower with—"

"Go see her. No one is expecting anything of you Jax. Least of all River."

My heart races faster with each step I walk toward the en suite attached to D's bedroom. By the time I find the door slightly open and steam billowing out of it, I've almost changed my mind.

But after what I've done tonight, walking into a bathroom shouldn't really faze me.

I knock on the door and wait with my heart in my throat.

"I was wondering if you'd all left," she calls out, her voice a little rougher than I'm used to. I guess screaming our names over and over will do that.

"Hey, it's just me. Is it okay if I—"

"Jax," she breathes, stepping out from behind the new shower curtain D hung a few days ago.

My eyes immediately drop to her body, and I fight to swallow down the desire that bubbles up within me faster than I can control. But it's not her curves that really hold my attention, but the marks.

The bright red marks that wrap around her throat and mar her beautiful, previously flawless skin.

"Shit, Riv. Fuck. *Fuck*." My stomach turns over and I almost run for the toilet to throw up the whiskey that's now sitting heavy like acid inside me.

"Whoa, Jax. Jax," she says, quickly jumping from the shower and coming to stand right in front of me. She reaches out as if she's going to touch me and I instantly jump back, terrified that I'm going to fuck all this up further. "It's okay. I'm okay."

She holds my eyes and remains motionless before me, begging me to calm down.

"I'm so sorry," I whisper.

"You have nothing to be sorry for. You were amazing."

I shake my head, unable to believe her words.

"I wish I could hold you," she says with a sad smile.

My arms twitch at my sides, wishing I could give her exactly that, needing the connection myself but knowing I can't.

"Soon," I promise her. "I'm gonna fix this. For you."

The smile that pulls at her lips makes all the weight I was carrying on my shoulders vanish. "For us," she vows. "I'm here, Jax. And no matter what, I promise that I'll be right here."

I shake my head, lifting my hand and wrapping my fingers gently around the nape of her neck. "You're incredible, Riv."

"So are you. I know you don't believe me right now, but one day you will. I'm going to prove to you that you are worthy of all this and more, Jax."

I dip my head down, pressing my brow to hers and just absorb her strength and belief in me. That is, until a shiver rips through her, reminding me that she's standing naked and the only heat in this place is the fire roaring in the living room.

"Get back in and warm up."

All the air rushes from her lungs as she holds my eyes. "Can you get in with me?" she asks, biting down on her bottom lip.

"Fuck." Hope fills her features as she waits for a response.

"I won't touch you, I swear."

"I can't, Riv, I'm sorry," I whisper so quietly that I'm not sure she'll even be able to hear it over the water pounding into the bathtub behind us.

"That's okay. Stay though, yeah?"

"You want me to watch?" I ask, not quite believing that's what she's suggesting.

"Sure, if you want. Nothing new for you to see now, is there?" She looks over her shoulder before stepping under the water, and I stumble back against the wall, keeping her sinful body in my sights as she lets the jets rush over her.

25

RIVER

I wish we could stay here forever. Just the four of us. No interfering family or overprotective brothers, no club drama to contend with.

After I finished showering, Jax wrapped me in a big, fluffy towel and dried me. We didn't talk about what happened again. There's nothing to say.

I wanted it. I wanted everything he had to give me.

"What are you thinking about, pretty girl?" Diesel asks, taking a long pull on his beer.

The fire is roaring, keeping the frigid air at bay. It's freezing out, but I've never been warmer. And it isn't only the burning kindling. It's them. Every touch or glance burns my skin, stoking the flames inside me.

"Nothing." I smile coyly, biting down on my lip.

"Keep looking at him like that, Blondie, and Daddy D will—"

"Seriously, man. Can you quit it with the Daddy D shit?"

I smother a chuckle. The two of them are like an old married couple, always bickering. Yet the way they support Jax, the fact that they did all this... for him... It's everything.

"So, is anyone going to tell me what really happened with Henry?"

"I thought we'd put that to bed, Blondie?" Zach's eyes narrow.

"No, you just distracted me with all your... your—"

"Orgasms?"

"Zach, man," Diesel groans. "You really want to know this shit, Riv? We did what we needed to do. He's alive. That's all that matters."

"And what if he tells someone? What if—"

"Relax," Zach drawls. "Parsons is a pussy. He isn't going to risk his reputation telling anyone the truth. Besides, it's been over a week. If he'd have told anyone—and he hasn't—we would have heard something by now."

"I still can't believe you went after him. Rhett, I get... but the three of you..." I peer up at them, my cheeks burning.

"Seriously?" Diesel scoffs. "Is it that hard to understand that we would want to hurt someone who had hurt you?"

"I..." Emotion swells inside of me. "I'm still mad at you. All of you." I run my gaze over each of them. Zach only grins as he gets up and heads for the refrigerator, but Jax has the decency to look guilty.

"Henry is connected," I add. "He's—"

"Someone you don't need to worry about. Ever again." Zach appears in front of me. He drops down beside me and pulls me onto his lap. I curl up against his warm body and let out a contented sigh.

"This is nice." I peek up at him.

"Yeah, well, don't get too used to it." A faint smile tugs at his mouth.

Then something occurs to me. "Where does everyone think you are?" I ask.

Kat is covering for me. But the three of them are all missing... that could raise suspicions.

"Stop. Worrying." Zach collars my throat, his thumb rubbing almost tenderly over the red marks that Jax left behind, and tilts my face to his, capturing my lips in a slow, bruising kiss. His tongue sweeps into my mouth, deep and unyielding. Jax and Diesel continue their conversation in the background, as if this is just business as usual. The thought makes laughter bubble in my throat. Zach stills, pulling away and glaring at me. His brow quirks in question, and I fight a smile.

"Care to explain..."

"Just thinking."

"About..." His brow quirks up.

"Things."

Things I don't want to admit. Because while they all came for me tonight, we still haven't really talked about what this is. And part of me is too scared to ask.

But I can't stop myself from falling deeper and deeper into them. I want this, them, the four of us together.

I want it so badly, but I'm terrified that I'm going to end up hurt if one of them decides they can't do this. Can't share me.

A shiver runs through me and Zach notices.

Bringing his mouth to my ear, he whispers, "Something tells me your thoughts are less than pure right now."

I swallow, pressing my lips together to trap a whimper as his hand skims up my thigh.

"You sore?"

"A little."

"How does this feel?" His hand slips under the t-shirt covering my body and finds my panties.

"G-good," I breathe, lifting my hips and chasing his fingers.

"Fuck," Jax rasps, and my eyes find his.

"Wanna give the boys a little show?" Zach asks, hooking two fingers into the damp material and pushing them inside me.

"Go easy on her," Diesel barks.

"Relax. She can handle it, can't you, babe?"

I nod, gasping as he curls his fingers deep.

"Spread your thighs, let them see."

His words command my body, my legs falling open. I'm merely his puppet, their plaything. But I want to please them. To submit and beg.

I want to be theirs.

However they want me.

"Why does it always feel so good?" I murmur, riding Zach's hand as he finger fucks me slow and deep, in no great hurry to get me off.

"Because this," he cups my pussy, "is ours. You're ours, Blondie. This belongs to us."

"Yes... God, yes."

I don't doubt it for a second.

They own my body.

Know exactly how to drive me wild and ruin me.

But it isn't just my body I want to give them.

It's my heart.

And that is a dangerous thing indeed.

I wake to a wall of heat pressed up behind me.

"Morning." Diesel drags me back against his chest. "How did you sleep?" He kisses my shoulder and heat curls in my stomach.

"Hmm." I stretch, the delicious ache in my body a reminder of everything we did last night. "Good, thank you."

"We didn't go too far with you?"

"No. I wanted it, D."

"You're fucking amazing, do you know that? I didn't think..." He trails off.

Rolling over, I gaze up at him. "Hi."

"Hi." He smiles.

"What were you about to say?"

"You caught that, huh?" He drops a kiss on the end of my nose. "I didn't think you would like it."

"It?"

"Come on, Riv, you know what I'm talking about."

"You know... I found it... that box under your bed."

"Fuck," he hisses. "You saw that?"

I nod. "That night we took Kat back to your room when she was drunk. When we..."

"You never said anything."

"I didn't know what to say. Besides, we kind of had a lot of other stuff going on."

"Yeah, I guess we did. But it didn't scare you away."

"No, it didn't." I run my hand up his chest, marveling at how his muscles feel, contracting under my touch. "D, can I ask you something?"

"Anything."

"Why haven't you taken me yet?"

"The truth?"

"Always."

"Part of me still can't reconcile that I get to have this, have you." He brushes the hairs from my eyes and touches his head to mine.

"But you do want to?"

"Want to?" He lets out a sigh of disbelief. "I think about nothing else, pretty girl. But this thing we've got going on is new and intense, and I'm in no rush. I can wait."

"And if I don't want to wait?" I hitch my leg over his hip, pressing closer. He's already hard, long and thick at my stomach.

"River..." My name is a rough whisper against his throat.

"We're all alone, D. And I want you. I want this."

He lets out a pained groan. "We've created a monster."

"Who's a monster?" The bedroom door bursts open and Zach stalks in but quickly draws to a stop. "What is this?" He wags a finger between us.

"We're just talking," Diesel says.

"Talking, huh? Because from where I'm standing, it looks like River is about to climb on your dick and—"

"Zach!" I bury my face in Diesel's shoulder, unable to suppress the laughter rumbling in my chest. The whole thing should be embarrassing, but it isn't.

It feels... right.

"Anyway, I just came to say Jaxy boy has managed to figure out how to turn on the stove and cook breakfast, so if you two are done *talking*, we can eat. Although now that I'm here, I can think of something else I wouldn't mind eating. What do you say, Blondie?"

I peek over at him and poke my tongue out. "She needs a break."

"She?" He lifts an amused brow.

"Yeah, you know. My... pussy."

"Say that again, I didn't hear you."

"Go." Diesel grabs a pillow and launches it at Zach. "Get out of here."

"Daddy D is a grump in the morning. Better try to find a way to cheer him up, Riv. If you know what I'm saying." With a wink, Zach leaves the room, slamming the door behind him.

Diesel lets out an exasperated sigh. "Did that really just happen?"

"He seems happy this morning."

"Something tells me you're having a good effect on him."

"Oh, I don't know about that." I glance away.

"Hey." Diesel cups my face and coaxes me to look at him. "It's you, River. All this is for you."

"I... We should go eat. I'm hungry."

"The girl wants feeding, then let's feed her." Diesel climbs out of bed and pulls on his jeans.

I can barely remember him carrying me to bed last night. After Zach had made me come with his fingers, he lifted me onto his dick and fucked me while I sucked Diesel. By the time they had both finished, I was exhausted. Diesel had scooped me up in his arms and taken me to bed.

"Come on." He offers me his hand and I take it, letting him pull me up. But he doesn't stop there, lifting me up and forcing my legs around his waist.

"D, put me down. I can walk, you know."

"I know, but I like having you close." He nuzzles my neck, and I shriek with surprise.

And I don't tell him, but I like it too.

"Decided not to eat her for breakfast then?" Zach says the second we step into the kitchenette.

"River's hungry."

"I bet she is." He winks again. "Jaxy boy has a sausage you can snack on."

"Dude," Jax grumbles.

Diesel deposits me on a stool and heads to the refrigerator, and it startles me how normal this is. The three of them laughing and joking while Jax makes us breakfast.

A girl could get used to this.

I want to get used to it.

But then Zach says, "We'd better get back once we've eaten. I've already had a text from Stray asking where the fuck I am."

"Me too." Jax gives me a weak smile.

"Oh God, do you think he suspects something?" I ask, and Diesel frowns. "Let's hope he doesn't."

"Yeah, that's the last thing we need," Zach adds.

And just like that, my appetite dies.

I'm in no rush to tell anyone about this—us. But the fact that they're all so horrified about Dane knowing something makes my heart sink.

Would it really be that bad? For people to know there's something between us? A connection I can't and don't want to fight?

I don't expect Rhett or Ray would handle it very well, but it's not their decision.

It's mine.

Except it isn't only mine. It's theirs too, and as I study

the three of them—three guys who have come to mean more to me than I ever expected—part of me wishes I knew what they were thinking.

But maybe I'm not ready for the truth.

Especially if it's not what I want to hear.

26

ZACH

"Stop the car," River demands from the back of the truck not long before the turnoff for the compound.

Obviously, it's not where I'm heading, seeing as she's wearing those weird sloth pajamas. I'm sure that would clue everyone in fast as to where the fuck the four of us have been all night. The pretty hefty hickies I've left all over her neck, and Jax's marks might also give us away.

"What's wrong?" I bark, quickly pulling over and twisting around to look at her sitting beside Jax with their hands entwined.

A smile twitches at my lips at the sight of them. It might not be what I'd be doing if I was allowed to ride back there with her—which I'm pretty sure is the exact reason D threw me the keys and demanded I drive—but it's still a better position than I'm in right now. At least D's torturing himself by sitting up here with me, I guess. He might have blown his load down her throat a handful of times now, but I know he's fucking desperate to get inside her, to finally claim her. What I don't know is why he's holding off when she so clearly wants it too.

River bites down on her bottom lip as if she's already second-guessing her decision to make me stop. Her eyes flick between Jax and D.

"Would... uh... can you two walk back? I think Zach and I need a little time alone."

"Oh, hell yes we do," I sing, more than fucking happy with this turn of events.

"Not for that, horndog," she hisses with a roll of her eyes.

"It could be for that too though, right?"

"Is everything okay?" D asks, his big brother persona rearing its ugly head. Or maybe it's just the daddy side of him. It's hard to tell sometimes.

"Yeah. We've just got a few things to talk about. I'll make sure he behaves."

I scoff at that. "Sure thing, Blondie. I think everyone in this car knows exactly how much you like to submit. Ow," I complain when D's hand whips out faster than I was expecting and slaps me around the head.

"Be fucking nice to her. And for the love of God, if you do get lucky, be gentle," he warns.

"Sure thing, *Daddy*." I smirk.

"Jesus Christ. How the fuck did I get stuck in this thing with you?"

I don't miss the way River tenses at his words. "*Stuck* in this *thing*?" she snaps.

"Shit, I..."

"Chill, man. I'll work my magic. Get you back in her good books."

He ignores me, keeping his eyes on River. "I didn't

mean anything by that, pretty girl. Keep him in check, yeah?"

A reluctant smile pulls at her lips. "Sure."

"Talk to you later?" Jax asks hopefully, capturing her attention.

"Yeah." Leaning in close to him, she whispers something in his ear that makes him tense up at first, but he soon relaxes, wraps his hand around the back of her neck, and claims her lips as if they belong to him.

D elbows me in the arm hard enough to make it go dead, but I don't complain as I watch the two of them.

"Aw, little Jaxy boy is growing up. Aren't you proud, Daddy D?"

This time, I dodge his punch.

"You're a fucking asshole, Stone."

"Naw, you love me really, cous."

Jax finally lets River up for air before they slip out of the car and head down the street toward the compound gates leaving me and River alone.

"Don't tell me you're going to sit back there like you're scared of me? This was your idea, remember?"

"I'm aware."

I watch as River undoes her seat belt and climbs between the front seats in her little sloth shorts.

She moans when I grab a handful of her ass. "We're practically outside the compound, asshole," she hisses, dropping into the seat.

"You were the one who wanted to stop here," I point out.

"Don't make me regret this, Stone," she seethes.

Putting the truck back into drive, I take off before we're spotted by someone. "So what's this about then, Blondie?"

She twists to face me, her arms folded beneath her tempting braless breasts. "Who are you?"

"What?" I ask with a laugh. "You mean, aside from the guy who shows you heaven over and over?"

"I'm being serious, Zach. If that's even your name."

I groan, scrubbing my hand down my face. I knew this was coming. I'm actually surprised she waited this long.

"Everyone is super secretive about it, even after..."

"Your brother shot me?" I offer.

"Yeah. That. I mean, I've put two and two together myself, and I'm assuming I've come up with the right answers. You're a Night Crawler, aren't you?"

My grip on the wheel tightens. "Was, Blondie. I was a Night Crawler." I wince, the name of that stupid fucking gang tasting bitter on my tongue.

"But don't you get blooded in for life or some crap, and the only way out is death?"

"Someone's been doing their homework," I mutter.

"I went to school in Colton for years. They were pretty much all anyone talked about. All the girls wanted to screw the big, bad gangsters and the boys wanted to be one. It was pathetic," she scoffs.

"It's complicated, Riv," I confess. "But yeah, technically I should be dead."

She gasps at how seriously I say that.

"The Crawlers were my life. I was one of those pathetic boys who grew up dreaming of being a part of it. It helped, of course, that my best friend was the boss's son.

"We joined younger than anyone else, did our initiation when we were only fourteen, proved ourselves and took our places. I thought we were made for life."

"What happened?" she asks, leaning closer.

"I fucked up. I did something I couldn't come back from, and I either stuck around and died, or I followed the orders of the person I was trying to protect, left town, and never looked back."

"Your mom?" she asks. "You were protecting your mom, weren't you?"

"Yeah," I admit on a sigh. "For all the good it did. I got out and she's still there in the middle of it in the hope of protecting me from their wrath."

"She loves you, Zach. She's trying to give you a chance."

"What about her, though?" I ask, slamming my hand down on the wheel as my frustration at the whole fucked-up situation grows. "She's stuck there and in bed with the devil."

"Literally?" River asks curiously.

"Yeah. She's paying the price for my crime." My stomach churns. "How the fuck is that fair?"

"I think—although I don't really know, because I don't actually have any experience—that that's what decent parents are meant to do for their kids."

"I don't care, Riv. She doesn't deserve it. Any of it... Especially a fuck-up like me."

"That's bullshit and you know it."

My fingers twist around the wheel, my knuckles turning white with the force of my grip.

"What did you do?" she asks quietly, already suspecting it's bad enough that I'm not going to confess.

"I'm not telling you that, Riv. You might think you've seen me at my worst, but I can assure you, you really haven't."

"I meant what I said, Zach. I'm not scared of you."

"And I meant what I said. You should be," I warn, my voice dropping to a low timbre.

"So..." she continues, ignoring my tone. "You're related to Evelyn somehow."

"She's my dad's sister," I offer.

"And your mom thought it would be safe to hide you here. Didn't either of you think it might be a bit close to home?"

"Keep your friends close and all that," I mutter. "And to answer your first question, my name actually is Zach. Just not Stone."

"So what is it?"

I cut her a look that tells her without words that I'm not giving her that, either. The more she knows about all of this, the more at risk I put her. And I've already got closer to her than I should. When—not if—the day comes that I'm discovered, then there's a chance it won't just be me they go after.

"Going to Colton for my benefit was really stupid, Zach," she hisses, twisting back to sit in the seat properly once more.

"Teaching that motherfucker a lesson for what he did to you was a long time coming. I was gonna do it before I even knew who you were, but... things got in the way."

She chooses to ignore that.

"If they find out you were involved, that the Sinners were involved, they're going to be right on our doorstep. Because of you... Because of me."

"If that happens," and it will eventually, "then I'll go. I never wanted to leave in the first place. I fucking swear to you, Blondie, I won't put you or anyone you care about at risk."

"You already have, Zach. Do you really think the

club, D, Jax, Crank, will just let you go? They're not going—"

She swallows her words, and when I glance over, I find her eyes full of unshed tears.

"Riv."

"Don't," she snaps, batting my hand away when I reach for her. "I'm being stupid."

"Yeah, you are." She rears back in shock. "You shouldn't care about what happens to me, Blondie. I'm a bad person, and I'll get exactly what's coming to me soon enough."

I slow the truck down and turn into Ray's driveway. Thank fuck he's not here. He's probably already at the Red Ridge compound with everyone else, ready for the second day of holiday partying that we're once again missing out on.

"Looks like question time is up," I mutter, looking up at the house.

"So it is," River sighs, looking totally conflicted over everything I just told her. "Zach?" she asks, her stare burning into the side of my face and forcing me to turn toward her.

"Yeah." Our eyes connect, and immediately, the car fills with a heated tension that I can't get enough of.

"Can you promise me something?" I don't reply, because I'm scared she's going to ask something of me that I'm not going to be able to agree to. "Please don't do anything stupid. You can be safe here. The club can keep you safe. Please don't—"

"You worried about me, Blondie?" I reach out, twist my fingers through hers and pull her closer. "I don't make promises I can't keep, Riv. I don't live a nice, easy life, I never have. Blood, death, and violence is all I know."

"For me?" she asks on the off-chance it might be enough.

"I'll see what I can do."

Not wanting to talk anymore, I slam my lips down on hers, kissing her until she's breathless in the hope that she'll forget everything about this conversation.

When I finally let her up for air, she pushes the door open and slides out.

"I'll see you later, yeah?"

"I haven't decided yet," she replies coyly before making her way to the house, those stupid little booty shorts making it really fucking hard not to follow.

The second she's inside, I pull out of the driveway with the intention of heading straight back, but only a few moments later, my cell dings with a message.

I pull it out and stare down at the request from Stray to swing by the store and pick up some more supplies.

"Jesus Christ," I mutter, pressing my foot to the gas as I head back toward a store in Red Ridge.

I grab what I need, and a few extra bits to stash in my room, and I walk out of the store with my hood up and my head down, desperate to put the conversation about my past with River behind me. The holiday has been hard enough without Mom as it is. I don't need to talk about it too.

I'm throwing the bags onto the passenger seat when something flapping under the wiper catches my eye. Leaning around, I pluck it free and hold it up, my stomach plummeting as I instantly recognize the scrawl my name has been written in.

Knocking my hood off, I scan the parking lot, looking for him, but the only people out here are a couple of women chatting and some kids.

"Motherfucker," I hiss.

Opening the folded piece of paper, I hold my breath as I wait to see what he might have left for me.

Y*our girl's pretty.*
    It would be a shame to have an asshole like me anywhere near her...

27

RIVER

"Oh my God," Kat gasps the second she enters my room. "You look like you were mauled by a pack of wild dogs."

"Shh," I hiss. "Victoria is downstairs."

"I hope she didn't see you like this."

"What do you think?" I shoot her a scathing look as I pull the high-collared sweater over my head.

"So I take it you had a good night?" She smirks.

"It was... intense."

"No shit."

"You really want to talk about this?"

"Well yeah, I mean, it's what girlfriends do, isn't it?" Kat gets comfy on my bed, crossing her legs and resting her hands on her knees.

"I really don't know where to start. It was... wild."

"See, I knew it. Wild dogs." She chuckles, and it eases some of the knot in my stomach. It isn't that I don't want to talk to her about the guys. It's that I don't know whether she'll understand.

I'm not even sure I understand it fully yet.

"So is it like a they-all-take-turns scenario, or more like every-hole-is—"

"Oh my God," I splutter, choking on air. "That's—"

"Made you smile, though. It's just sex, babe. Everyone does it. And not everyone likes it vanilla."

"What about you?"

"Oh no you don't. We're talking about you, not me."

"Fine." I pout. "But one day you're going to tell me what happened with Styx."

"We'll see." Another smirk tugs at her mouth. "Now tell me everything."

My cheeks burn as I try to put into words what happened last night. "The guys set things up to try to help Jax..."

"Try to help what— oh... *oh*." Her eyes go wide. "And how was that?"

"A little scary but so good. I didn't think I'd like being restrained like that... having them in complete control of me."

"You're a natural submissive."

"What?"

"You like being dominated." Kat shrugs like it's nothing. Like we're not having a conversation about rough sex and submission.

"I... yeah, I think you're right." I think about how it feels when they make demands of me, pushing me to do things I never imagined myself doing. The way it makes my blood turn molten. "Does that make me weird?"

"Of course it doesn't. We all like what we like, Riv. They wouldn't let anything bad happen to you."

"I can't really explain, but when I'm with them, it feels... right."

She sucks in a sharp breath. "You're catching feelings. Real feelings."

"Well, yeah..."

"Oh, babe." Her lips flatten into a thin line.

My heart sinks. "You think I'm silly for wanting this. Them."

"No, not at all. I just... it's Diesel, Zach, and Jax."

"I know."

God, I know.

But something is changing between us. I felt it last night and again this morning when we were eating breakfast together. Diesel is still hesitant, and Zach acts like it's all just a bit of fun, that it's about helping Jax, but when they look at me, when they touch me, I feel it.

"Just promise you won't fall too deep before you know they all feel the same."

It's already too late, but I don't tell Kat that.

"Anyway, I thought we could go out instead of sitting around talking about all the kinky sex you're having." Kat bursts out laughing at my mortified expression. "You should see your face."

"Stop." I suppress a smile. No matter how awkward the conversation gets, Kat always manages to lighten the mood.

"I'm glad I have you."

"Aw." She grins. "I love you too, babe. Now finish getting ready so we can get out of here"

Kat takes me to a shopping mall just outside of town. It isn't really my favorite thing to do, but it's nice spending some time together away from the club.

We spend the day wandering from store to store, and Kat buys a handful of new outfits with her gift cards from her mom and Diesel.

I'm only browsing until I spot a dark red dress in a little boutique that Kat loves.

"Wow, you have to get it," she says, peering over my shoulder.

"I don't know... it's expensive, and I wouldn't have anywhere to wear it." I finger the price tag, balking at the three figures staring back at me.

"So? A girl doesn't need an excuse to treat herself. And didn't you get some money off Ray and Victoria yesterday?"

I did, but I still can't justify spending the two-hundred and fifty dollars on a dress I'll never wear, no matter how much I love it.

"Yeah, but I want to get some new clothes."

"The dress, River. Buy the dress."

I give it one last, longing look before letting the silky material slip through my fingers. "No. Come on."

"You have better willpower than me." Lacing her arm through mine, Kat tugs me toward the lingerie section. "If you won't buy the dress, at least buy something sexy for the guys."

"Kat." My cheeks flame as I glance at the nearby store assistant.

"Oh, please. I'm sure she's heard it all before. Right, Brenda?" Kat flashes her a grin and the woman blanches. We fall into a fit of laughter as we continue browsing.

It's nice. Normal. It's exactly what I needed after my intense night with the guys.

"Have you heard from them?" she asks as if she can hear my thoughts.

"No."

"And that doesn't bother you?"

"They're probably giving me space."

"Mm-hmm," she murmurs.

"What is that supposed to mean?"

"Well, if it were me..." She waggles her brows.

"Space is good," I reply, but I can't ignore the slight pang in my heart that she might be right.

"Come on, let's go get hot chocolates from the kiosk and sit outside by the tree."

"It's freezing."

"They have those big lamp heaters. You'll be fine. Besides, there's a cute guy who works the counter."

"Of course there is."

We head downstairs and line up for hot chocolates. Kat has whipped cream, marshmallows, and caramel sauce on hers, but I opt for marshmallows only.

"It's really pretty out here," I say as we weave between the little wooden tables to find somewhere to sit.

"Excuse me, miss." A scruffy man steps out from the shadows. "I wondered if you had any spare change. I'd like to get myself one of those hot chocolates."

"Uh, sure."

Kat shoots me a what-the-hell look as I dig around in my purse for five dollars. "Here you go, sir." I hand him the bills, but he snags my wrists and yanks me forward.

"What the—"

227

"Whoa, Mr. I suggest you let her go now or I'll scream."

"Now, now, little lady, I just wanted to thank you. Kindness goes a long way these days."

I try to pull my hand free but his grip tightens, hard enough that I suspect I'll have bruises.

"Seriously, asshole." Kat steps forward. "I'm gonna scream on two. One—"

"Easy." He immediately releases me and backs up. "I meant no harm. You have a good day now." He shuffles off, his tatty trench coat swishing around his legs.

"Okay, that was weird." Kat touches my arms, and I flinch.

"You okay?"

"Y-yeah. I'm fine." I glance back in the direction the man disappeared.

"Asshole left marks." She pulls my wrist but I yank it away, rubbing it gently.

"I'm fine."

"Wait until the guys—"

"We are not telling the guys." I drop onto a chair and sip my hot chocolate.

"And how are you going to explain that?" She motions to the red welt around my wrist.

"It'll be gone in a few hours."

At least, I hope it will be.

We didn't stick around after the incident with the strange man. I wanted Kat to take me home, but she insisted on a detour to the Red Ridge compound. Since Savage Falls hosted

Christmas dinner yesterday, they're having a small get-together for the families. She assured me it would be low-key and not the usual club chaos.

But I was nervous about seeing the guys again in such a public setting. At least Rhett and Ray were nowhere to be seen.

"Thank God." Quinn bounces over to us. "I was beginning to talk to the walls."

"Where's Sadie Ray?"

"The guys had this whole romantic morning planned. Lucky bitch. And Crank couldn't wait to show the guys his new bike. My dad sourced it especially for him. You should have seen his face."

"Men and their toys." Kat rolls her eyes. "Is there food? We didn't get to eat at the mall."

"I think there are some leftovers. You went shopping without me? Rude."

"We needed some much quality girl time, right, babe?" Kat glances at me and I smile. "But it got cut short when this weird—"

"Kat!" I nudge her in the side.

"What? It's Quinn, she won't tell anyone."

"Tell anyone what?" Quinn glances between us. "What's going on?" She motions to an empty booth and we slide into it.

"We got hot chocolates and went to sit outside, but this weird guy grabbed River and—"

"He didn't grab me." Kat pins me with a disapproving look. "Okay, he did. But he was just a homeless guy asking for some spare change."

"He grabbed you? Not cool."

"Right?" Kat nods. "He gave me the creeps."

"Who gave you the creeps?" Crank appears, and I want the leather banquette to swallow me.

"No one," I force a smile, silently praying that Kat keeps her big mouth shut. The last thing I need is the guys finding out.

Not that there's any sign of them.

"Where's D?" Kat asks innocently but casts me a knowing glance.

"He had something to take care of." Crank catches my eye, but I quickly drop my gaze. "Why do I get the feeling I'm missing somethin'?" he adds.

"We were just talking, baby," Quinn purrs. "Girl talk."

He grunts. "I guess I'll leave you to it then."

"Seriously," I snap the second he leaves. "Are you trying to make my life difficult?"

"What?" Kat's expression falls. "I wasn't—"

A commotion over by the door interrupts her, and we all look up to find Diesel, Zach, and Jax entering the clubhouse.

The second they spot me, they falter.

"So it's true then," Quinn whispers.

"What is?" My head whips around to Quinn, and she smirks.

"It's written all over your face, Riv."

"I... Who else knows?"

"Crank suspects. Sadie Ray obviously knows something is going on. Pretty sure Rhett thinks it's just Zach you're... what exactly are you doing with them all?" Her brow lifts playfully, but I feel anything but.

People know.

People are talking about it. Gossiping.

I guess I'd expected it. But it would have been nice not to be the subject of the latest club gossip quite so soon.

"I..." The words get stuck in my throat.

Quinn frowns. "Interesting."

But that's just it. I don't want my life to be interesting to her or anyone else.

"Don't look so worried, babe, I won't tell anyone." She smiles, and this time it's genuine and full of reassurance. But it's too late. My heart is already thundering in my chest like a runaway train.

Because it isn't only Kat and Quinn staring at me. The guys are, too.

And they're heading in my direction.

28

DIESEL

"I fucking knew this was going to happen. This is exactly why we told you to stay in the fucking car," I shout at Zach. "You've brought them right to our fucking door. Put this entire club at risk. Put *River* at risk."

The thought of her getting tangled up in the middle of this sends a violent shiver of fear racing down my spine.

She's already suffered enough, thanks to that cunt Henry and his little friends. There's no way I'm going to allow her to be hurt again. No fucking way.

"I know, all right? I don't need a fucking lecture," Zach spits.

The second I opened my door and found him standing there after dropping River off, my heart jumped into my throat. One look and I knew something was wrong. I just really fucking hoped it wasn't this.

"If you'd have just stayed in the fucking car," I mutter, shoving my hands into my hair and turning my back on them.

"Right, well, if you're just going to stand there having a hissy fit, I'm gonna go and sort it the fuck out."

"What?" Jax barks, jumping up from my couch where he was already sitting when Zach barged in on us. "You can't go to Colton to fix this."

"Why not? It's my shit. I shouldn't have fucking run away from it all in the first place."

"The Crawlers will kill you if you go back," Jax points out, looking more than just a little concerned by that prospect.

I knew their friendship had grown in the past few weeks since Zach has been helping him with his issues, but I still wasn't expecting to see such fear in Jax's expression.

"Maybe they should have just done it before I left. Would have saved all this shit," Zach murmurs.

I step right up to him, slamming my palms into his chest and forcing him to step back.

"What the fuck?" he barks, stepping forward again and getting in my face.

"Don't be so fucking selfish. You're not walking back into that place, so get the fucking idea out of your head," I growl, my chest heaving with anger.

"No one will care. No one really even wants me here."

"That's bullshit and you know it," Jax pipes up, coming to stand shoulder to shoulder with me. "You're one of us now. We're a family. We fucking care."

Zach scoffs, refusing to believe us, which only serves to irritate me further.

"River cares."

A bitter laugh falls from Zach's lips. "River doesn't give a shit about me. She just happens to be fond of the orgasms I can provide. It's you two she wants," he says, pointing between us.

"You're a fucking idiot," I mutter, stalking away from him. "Can we move on from the Zach Stone pity party now? River wants you. She wouldn't have allowed all the things that have happened between you if she didn't. And she would fucking kill us if we let you walk back into that place alone. And I, for one, aren't all that keen on dying anytime soon."

"You just don't want to be taken down by a girl," Zach quips. "If you're going to be so high and mighty about it, maybe we should all go. I'm not sure the club stands much of a chance with the Crawlers, but I'm more than willing to give it a shot."

"We're not dragging the fucking club into a war. We've barely recovered from the last one," I hiss.

"So what, then? We just sit back and wait for the Crawlers to get their hands on River in payback for the shit I caused?"

"What shit did you cause?" Jax asks, still oblivious about the details of Zach's past, just like the rest of the club. It's only Stray, Crank and Savage who know everything after Rhett found out the truth and forced our hands.

"I killed their second. His—" he points at the note now sitting on my bed, "father."

"Oh, so not much then?" Jax asks lightly, although the tight expression on his face tells me how he's really feeling about this.

"What else do you suggest? He might be bluffing," I ask, hopeful.

"He's not." Zach confirms what I already knew deep down.

"We need to talk to Stray and Crank. This is too big to deal with ourselves, especially if he's threatening River."

"We need to make sure all the girls are safe," Jax offers up. "If he's watching us, then he knows they're our weakness."

"We can't drag them into hiding. It'll freak them out. We've only just returned to normal life," I argue, although I completely agree with keeping them all safe. I don't just need to be worrying about River here. I've got Kat to think about as well. If this motherfucker is as brutal as Zach seems to think, then there's no reason why he wouldn't go for her best friend as a way to prove to us that he's more than capable of getting what he wants.

"Then we need to be more creative about it."

"I'm not lying to them," I say. "There are already enough secrets flying around, thanks to Zach."

He looks like he's about to argue but must quickly realize that he doesn't have a leg to stand on.

"Let's go find Stray and Crank and fucking hope they've got some ideas," I mutter, storming past Zach and ripping my door open.

We spend an hour talking in circles with Stray and Crank, who looked just as concerned about this threat as the three of us felt. But we managed to come to a decision. One which will hopefully buy us a little bit of time and keep everyone safe in the meantime.

"I'll head to Savage Falls and talk to Ray and Rhett," Dane says, pushing out from behind his desk. "But I swear to God, if this backfires on our asses and our girls end up in trouble, I'm going to be holding you personally responsible," he spits, pointing directly at Zach.

"Then let me fucking go and deal with it," he argues.

"No," all of us bark in sync.

We might not see eye to eye with everything, but when it comes to club business, one rule overrides all the others. We're family, and we have each other's backs. Always. And that doesn't include sending Zach into the middle of a gang who wants him fucking dead, no matter how new a member of this club he is.

"Get everything sorted for tonight and we'll call Church for tomorrow," Crank demands, following our prez from the room.

Only, he doubles back before he vanishes from our sight. "Your girl's here," he says before finally disappearing.

I look between Zach and Jax. "Not a fucking word to her about this," I warn.

Zach salutes. "Sure thing, Daddy D."

My teeth grind while Jax smirks.

"You're a fucking asshole," I mutter, pushing from the chair.

"You won't be saying that later when she's sucking on your cock like a whore. Speaking of," he quickly adds before I get a chance to say anything, "when are you gonna fuck her, man? She's desperate for it."

"When I'm fucking ready, asshole."

"From where I've been sitting, you're more than ready."

Ignoring his teasing, I turn to Jax. "How are you feeling?"

"I'm good," he lies, rolling his shoulders as if he's trying to release some of the tension pulling at them.

"Did we push too hard last night?" Zach asks, actually sounding serious for once.

"Nah," Jax says, rubbing the back of his neck awkwardly. "I needed it."

"You mean you needed the nut," Zach offers up, ruining his previous concern.

"That too."

"So we're gonna steal her away again tonight and get a rerun, right?"

"Be fucking sensible. Rhett's already put a bullet in your shoulder. Next time it'll be your head."

"He ain't gonna be watching her all fucking night. He's got his own girl to worry about."

"You wanna bet?"

"I'd rather bet that I'm gonna be shooting my load in our girl before the night's out."

"You're a dog," I mutter. "And I need a fucking drink. You're giving me a headache."

There's movement behind me, so I can only assume they're following me.

The second I step into the clubhouse, my eyes find hers. She stares at me, tension crackling between us despite the fact that she's sitting right beside my little sister.

River's gaze rips from mine, looking at the two guys on either side of me, her eyes darkening with desire as if she's remembering another time she's had all our eyes on her.

Fuck. Maybe Zach is right. We're going to have to find a way to get her out from her big brother's watch tonight. I haven't had anywhere near enough time with her yet.

"You two can pack up your shit and meet us over at the cabin later. I'm gonna take River to get what she needs."

"Oh no, you're not—" Zach starts, but I wheel around on him, holding his amused eyes.

"You caused this. Fucking remember that."

"How about you remember that when you've got her alone and she's—"

Twisting his shirt in my fists, I get back in his face once more. "Your mouth is going to get you in some fucking trouble, Stone. Keep it fucking shut."

"Jesus, anyone would think you haven't gotten laid in... wait... you haven't."

"Fuck you," I hiss, throwing him away from me, wishing I'd just taken a swing at him and wiped that smug fucking smirk off his face. "Make yourself fucking useful, Stone. Get us beers."

"Asshole," he hisses as Jax and I stalk toward River, Kat, Quinn and Crank.

"Hey, how's it going?" I ask, my voice lighter than how I really feel.

"Great," my sister sings. "Crank was just telling us about our little impromptu party."

"Yeah?" I ask, looking between our VP and Kat. "You girls all in?" Finally, I risk a look at River.

But exactly as I feared, there's no excitement on her face like the one filling Quinn and Kat's. Instead, her brow is pulled into a tight frown.

"You know we are," Quinn agrees. "Dane's gone to get Sadie, Rhett, and Wes. It'll be great to just hang."

"Do I get to invite a date, seeing as you lot are all coupled up?" Kat asks with a wicked glint in her eyes.

"No," I bark. "You're not dating until you're thirty. And that's if you're lucky."

"Don't even think about pulling the 'you're too young for boys' shit when I know exactly what you've been up to, big brother." Her eyes move from me to River.

"Whatever. I never said you were too young, I just happen to know that you've got shitty taste in guys."

She scoffs, but she knows exactly who I'm talking about.

"Riv," I say, turning to my girl, fighting the all-consuming need that surges through me to pull her onto my lap and claim her right in front of all these motherfuckers.

"Yeah." She smiles innocently, and it makes desire shoot straight to my dick.

Fuck. Maybe Zach had a point about what I wanted from this bit of one-on-one time with her.

"I'm gonna take you home to grab whatever you need."

"Hey, I was gonna take her."

"Consider your service unnecessary," I say to my sister without looking at her.

"You don't just get to steal my friend, douchebag."

"Go home and check on Mom. Make sure she's got everything she needs for a couple of days."

"A couple of days?" River asks, her eyes widening.

"Who knows? We thought it would be nice to just kick back for a bit."

Her eyes narrow on me. "Right. Sure. I guess."

"I've had a hot tub installed on my deck," Crank offers as if it'll squash her suspicions.

"Have you tried it out yet?" Kat asks.

"Hell yeah, we have."

"I think I'll pass, then. Just think of how many of your swimmers are having a party in there."

"Jesus Christ. Let's go before she makes me do something I'll regret," I say, pushing from the chair and waiting for River to join me.

"What?" Kat calls as I start to walk away. "I'm being sensible. I don't want Crank to get me pregnant."

"Seriously?" Quinn hisses before my sister complains as if she's just taken a hit.

"Is everything okay?" River asks, rushing up to my side.

"It will be in about two minutes when I've got you alone, pretty girl."

29

RIVER

Diesel is quiet on the ride to my house.

"Are you sure everything's okay?" I ask.

Something's off, I can sense it. But in typical Sinner fashion, none of the guys will fess up.

"Stop worrying." He squeezes my knee, letting his thumb drift along the curve of my leg. I cover his hand with mine, relishing the heat of his touch and sink back against the seat, closing my eyes.

"Riv?" The ice in his voice makes me startle.

"What's wrong?"

"What the fuck is that?"

My gaze drops to my wrist that's now on full display. Crap. I'd totally forgotten about the bruises.

"Did... we do that?"

"N-no." I yank my hand away and pull my sleeve down. "It's nothing."

"River... you better start talking or I swear to God..."

"Something happened..."

Diesel swerves the truck off the main road and pulls to a stop down a dirt road.

"Was that really necessary?"

"What happened?"

"Kat and I went to the mall earlier."

"The mall? She said she was hanging out at your house."

"You were checking up on me?"

"I... I just wanted to know if you were okay."

"Why?" I frown.

He twists around to face me and slides his hand along my collarbone, burying his fingers into my hair. "Because I care about you, Riv. So fucking much. Now tell me what happened."

"There was a man... He, uh, asked us for some spare change, so I offered him some. But he got quite forceful and grabbed me."

"He put his hands on you?" Fury radiates from Diesel.

"I don't think he wanted to hurt me. He was just—"

"River, he left bruises. Why didn't you call me? Call Zach or Ray? Fuck, why didn't you call for security?"

Pulling out of his hold, I inhale a deep breath. "It was nothing. He was just some creepy homeless guy, D. He probably has mental health issues and—"

"Who else knows about this?"

"Kat... Quinn. But I told her not to tell anyone, because I knew you'd react this way."

"Yeah, well you'd better believe I'll act this way when someone puts their hands on my fucking girl." He lifts his ass off the seat and digs out his cell phone.

"No, D, please, don't tell them. It was nothing. I'm fine, I promise." But he completely ignores me, firing off a text to Zach and Jax, no doubt. Maybe even my brother.

"You know what?" I spit. "Sometimes you really are overbearing, possessive assholes."

His head whips up, but before I can continue my tirade, Diesel pulls me onto his lap until I'm straddling his jean-clad thighs. "Fuck yeah, I am. Because you matter, River. You." His chest heaves as he flexes his hand around the back of my neck.

He leans in, touching his head to mine. "Do you have any idea what you do to me?"

"Show me," I breathe, curling my hands into his cut.

His hands slide down my spine, squeezing my ass and grinding me over him. He's hard and ready, and despite the layers separating us, he feels so good, pushed up against me.

"I don't think I have ever wanted anything as much as I want you, pretty girl." He breathes the words against my lips, sealing them with a kiss. Our tongues meet with desperate urgency, tangling together as he continues to rock me above him.

"Fuck, Riv," he rasps, "I can't wait to get inside you."

"So do it," I whimper, gripping his jaw and kissing him harder.

"Not here, not like this. The first time I take you, I wanna lay you out and take my time. Find all the ways to make your skin flush, to make you scream. Beg me for more."

"God, yes... *yes*." My head falls back as his thrusts turn more insistent.

"Can you feel that? Feel what you do to me?" He trails hot, wet kisses down my jaw, the slope of my neck. "I'm always so fucking hard around you, pretty girl. Imagine me." Thrust. "Imagine me sliding into your pussy, filling you inch by inch, until you're impaled on my cock."

"Diesel, touch me... I need you to touch me."

One of his hands slides between us, dipping under my sweater and up my stomach.

"I want you to get off like this. Riding me. Nothing else. Think you can do that for me?" He squeezes my breast, eliciting a moan from deep inside me.

"Come on, pretty girl. Show me how you'll ride me one day." His fingers dig into the curve of my hip, anchoring us together.

"I'm close..." I moan, pressing my lips together, trying to focus on the sensations rolling through me.

It's just enough, but not nearly how much I want.

My fingers tighten in his cut, pulling us closer as I tilt my hips slightly, grinding against his hard length so I feel every bump and nudge in just the right place.

"Diesel..." I whimper. "D, I'm gonna... God... yes..."

"Yeah, that's it, baby. Take what you need." He caresses my breasts, leaning in to run his nose along my jaw and down the side of my neck.

"Come for me, River. Now." His teeth graze the juncture between my shoulder and neck, and it's enough to make me hurtle off the edge.

Crying out, I bury my face in his shoulder as my orgasm crashes over me.

Diesel cups the back of my neck, forcing me to look at him. "Soon," he growls before slamming his lips down on mine and sealing it with a promise.

By the time we reach Crank's cabin, the party is in full swing. Music pours out of a speaker and the guys have started a fire, the flames licking the dusky sky.

"Do we even want to know?" Zach stalks toward us, wearing a knowing smirk. Jax trails after him.

"So, Blondie, did Daddy D finally give you his big D?"

Rolling my eyes, I say, "I'm going to find the girls. Try to stay out of trouble."

But before I can slip past them, Zach grabs my wrist and pushes my sleeve back. "You should have told us," he says.

"Zach..." I warn.

"Yeah, yeah, don't worry. D already warned us to rein it in. But I don't like knowing some asshole put his hands on you."

"I didn't know you cared so much." The words spill out before I can stop them.

He drops my arm and glowers at me. "What the fuck is that supposed to mean?"

"Nothing. Just... it doesn't matter. I'm going to find Kat."

I hitch my bag up my shoulder and take off toward the cabin. People are already drinking, laughing, and enjoying the beautiful surroundings.

"Finally." Kat spots me and jumps down off the porch and lunges for me. "I thought my brother had kidnapped you or something."

"We weren't that long."

"Long enough." Rhett studies me in that cool, calculating way off his.

"Big brother, I see you're as happy as ever."

He grumbles something under his breath and Sadie Ray nudges his ribs. "Play nice, Savage."

"Yeah, play nice, Savage." Dane appears in a pair of board shorts. "It's a party, and I don't know about anyone else, but I intend on feeling my girl up in the hot tub. Princess, shall we?"

Sadie quirks a brow and shrugs, whipping her t-shirt over her head to reveal a black bikini top.

Kat shoots me an amused grin and I roll my eyes, motioning for her to follow me inside. But Rhett calls after me.

"What?" I meet his steely gaze.

"Come on, Riv. Don't be like that."

"Like what? I'm not—" He gives me a pointed look and I let out a soft sigh. "What do you want, Rhett?"

"I want to know we're okay. That you're okay. Is that too much to ask?"

"I'm fine."

"And you'd tell me, right? If something were going on?"

"Don't do this."

"Do what?"

My eyes shutter and I inhale a shaky breath. "Look Rhett... I love you. You're my brother, my family. But I'm not a kid anymore."

His jaw clenches. "You think I don't know that? I do. I might not like it, but... all I care about is that you're happy, Riv. That's all I want."

"Truly?" I look him dead in the eye. "Do you truly mean that?"

"Of course I do."

My eyes narrow as I give him a sad smile. "We'll see."

"What the fuck is that supposed to mean?"

But I'm already walking away with Kat hot on my heels.

"Oh my God, babe, that was freaking epic."

I don't feel very epic. I feel like I'm going to vomit all over Crank's hardwood floors.

"I think I'm going to puke." I move deeper into the cabin.

"I've got you." Kat grabs my hand and drags me toward the breakfast counter, which has been turned into a makeshift bar, if all the bottles of liquor are anything to go by.

"Here, drink." Kat thrusts a glass into my hand.

"What is it?"

"Just drink it. It'll make you feel better, I promise."

"Said no one ever."

"On three." She lifts her own glass to mine. "One... two... three."

We both down our drinks.

"Atta girl. Another?"

"God, no." I shudder, placing my glass on the counter.

"You know, you did the right thing, standing up to him," she says.

"Did I? Because I can't help but feel like I stoked the fire."

Rhett already suspects enough without me raising his suspicions. But I'm tired of sneaking around and feeling like what I'm doing with the guys is somehow wrong.

I care about them, and I'm pretty sure they all care about me too.

"Hey." Kat touches my arm. "It'll all work out, you'll see. Anyway, I spy three guys all searching the place for you."

"You do—" The words dry on the tip of my tongue as I glance back and see the three of them behind the door.

"So, how are you going to play this?" Kat asks, and I frown.

"What do you mean?"

"Well, are you going to make it easy for them and wait for them to make a move? Or are you going to drive them wild and force their hand?"

"Kat... I'm not sure that's a good idea. Everyone's here. Rhett's here."

"So? I'm not suggesting you let them tie you up and have their way with you in front of him. But a little teasing wouldn't hurt."

"You are so bad," I murmur, eyeing the bottles of liquor.

"Oh, babe, you don't know the half of it." She notices my intention and grins. "A little bit of Dutch courage, I like it."

"Just don't let me do anything stupid." I pour myself another shot and knock it back.

Kat whistles through her teeth, waggling her brows, and says, "Would I ever?"

"**D**ane. Wes. Fuck." Sadie's wanton moan rips through the air, making me shift a little uncomfortably in my seat.

"Fuck," Rhett hisses, his fists clenched so tight his knuckles are white as he watches them.

His need to join them is clearly testing his iron-clad restraint, but I can see from the set of his shoulders, and the way his eyes keep shooting to River, that he's not going to do anything about it. Not with his little sister around.

Her cries for more get louder, allowing images of us being in that hot tub with River to fill my mind. Sadie is hot, there's no denying that. But it isn't the thoughts of her somewhere behind me being savaged by her men making my cock swell in my pants.

A sigh rips past my lips, the heavy weight of reality pressing down on me.

I could have her naked in that hot tub, but I wouldn't be the one making her fall. I probably wouldn't even be able to get in.

I scrub my hand down my face, hating that I constantly feel like I'm letting River down by being so fucking screwed up.

"Savage," Sadie calls, more than a little drunk from the shots she, River, Kat, and Quinn have been doing. "Get that delicious cock of yours over here."

A grunt of annoyance passes his lips before he rubs his palms down his thighs, the bulge in his pants more than obvious. I'm hardly surprised. He's got a prime view from his position on that chair of the goings-on in the hot tub. If the roles were switched and I was watching D and Zach with our girl, I'd be hard as fucking nails. Hell I am, merely thinking about it.

"I'm going to take a piss," I mutter to no one in particular before getting up and stalking away from the fire pit we're sitting around out the back of Crank's place.

As I make my way through the cabin, I can't help but agree that this was a good idea. For tonight, at least, we've got the girls safe under one roof, and they're none the wiser that there's a monster lurking in the shadows, just waiting to strike.

Having said that, I'm not sure keeping it from them is the best idea in the long run.

I know just how much River hates being left out of things. Important things. When she does find out... Well, let's just say I can't see it being a very pleasurable experience for any of us.

I take a piss, hating the tension that pulls across my shoulders as I stand there. Hanging out with friends—my brothers—and my girl shouldn't be this fucking stressful. I should be lounging around like the others, appearing not to give a shit about what's happening outside these walls. But while that concern is there, my fear remains.

Zach seems to have no issue sitting beside River on the couch, stealing any touch he can get away with when he thinks Rhett's not looking. Motherfucker's got a death wish, if you ask me, but whatever. I see the hungry looks D shoots her way, as if the two of them are just biding their time for what's to come. All the while, I sit there terrified about what's next.

Last night was... incredible. But I'm petrified that when we get the chance to do it again, I won't be able to hold back. That I'll take things too far, see red and lose control. That I'll hurt River far worse than she could ever hurt me by touching me, by trying to make me feel good. To fix me.

I fear there is no fixing me.

I'm too fucked up. Too tainted. My soul, too black and tarnished to ever fully give myself over to her.

Twisting around, I stare at myself in the mirror, hating what I find looking back at me. My eyes are dark, the shadows of my past haunting me. I'm exhausted, tense, and downright miserable. But it's fucking ridiculous, seeing as my life is better than it's ever been right now.

Everything from my past is quiet. And I finally, fucking finally have my girl.

But do I?

How long will she really put up with all the barriers and baggage I come with? Not when she could have an easy life with Zach or D. Hell, her life would be easier with literally any other man but me.

A knock on the door startles me, and for a second I panic that I didn't twist the lock. But thankfully, whoever is on the other side doesn't even try it. I don't need anyone seeing the anguish in my features right now. I don't need—

"Jax, it's me," a soft, more than familiar voice calls out. "Are you okay?"

"Shit," I breathe, continuing to stare at myself in the mirror.

My body tenses, but for a whole different reason this time as my cock swells once more.

"Jax, please. I'm—"

Flipping the lock, I pull the door open. But before I get to move, she slips inside the room with me, her back falling against the door and forcing it shut. "Riv, you can't. If Rhett—"

"They left," she says. "His restraint snapped and he all but dragged the three of them from the water and threw them in the truck."

"Damn," I say, rubbing the back of my neck as a smile creeps onto my lips. "I'm sorry I missed that."

River smirks. "Usual Rhett Savage alpha bullshit," she scoffs.

"But he's gone now," I say, taking a step closer to her without even thinking about the move. My need for her right now overrides anything else.

She nods, her eyes dipping down to my lips.

"And the first thing you did was to come and find me?" I ask. "Why?"

Concern fills her eyes, and I hate that she sees the ghosts that haunt mine now almost as much as I can. She lifts her hand and releases her fingers, and a length of soft pink ribbon falls free.

"Riv?" I question, hoping like hell we're on the same page here.

She tilts her chin up and squares her shoulders. "You

need me," she states confidently, much more so than she would if she were sober right now, I'm sure. "So I'm here, offering my... services." She hiccups, and I can't help but laugh at her as my heart pounds steadily in my chest.

This girl... everything about this fucking girl wrecks me.

She's standing here, offering me everything she knows I need to try to get me out of my own head, and I'm so here for it but—

"You deserve more than being tied up in Crank's bathroom, Riv."

"And you deserve more than being haunted by your past every second of the day." She spins around and holds her wrists behind her back in offering to me. "But here we are." She shrugs, waiting for me to jump into action. "I want to feel your lips against mine, Jax. I want to feel the weight of your body against mine. But I won't risk touching you, hurting you."

I stand frozen before her, terrified to allow this to happen but equally desperate for it.

"Please, Jax. I want it to just be us. I want to make you feel good."

"Riv—"

"Please," she begs, looking over her shoulder at me, her eyes wide and full of desire and... love?

Fuck.

Unable to deny her, I pull the ribbon through her fingers and bind her wrists. With my hands on her shoulders, I spin her back around and my lips collide with hers the second they're in reach.

Kissing has never been a trigger for me. Hell, River was the first girl I ever kissed. This... this is ours. My only memory is of us, her. The same as being inside her. But my reaction to everything else, the arousal coursing through my veins... It drags me right back to my past, and it's all too easy to drown in those memories and let them consume me. And it's that darkness I'm terrified of. If I fall into that when I'm alone with her, I could do anything.

Her tongue moves against mine, her kiss as hungry, and I lose myself in her taste, her sweet scent. My palms cup her jaw, my fingers threading into her hair as I gently twist her head to the side to allow me to deepen our kiss.

My head spins with need for my girl as my cock aches behind the confines of my pants.

It's not an unusual issue I've suffered with over the years. River and the guys might think I'm fucked up now, but things have been worse. So much worse. There were times not all that long ago when I couldn't even touch myself.

"Fuck, River," I groan into our kiss. "You have no idea what you do to me, how badly I need you."

She wiggles against me, letting me know that she can feel exactly how badly I need her pressing against her stomach. "Jax?" she asks almost shyly, but the naughty glint in her eye piques my interest.

"Yeah, baby?" I breathe, rubbing my thumb along the fullness of her bottom lip.

"Has anyone... have you ever had... God," she hisses, her embarrassment taking over.

"Hey," I say, dipping down to recapture her eyes. "It's me. You can ask me anything." I might not be able to vocalize the answer, but she can ask.

"I want..." Her tongue sneaks out, hitting the pad of my thumb that's resting against her lip. She shifts forward, capturing it in her mouth as her eyes hold mine, waiting to see how I'll react.

My heart beats wildly in my chest as she ups the ante and circles her tongue around the end of my thumb. And fuck if my cock doesn't jerk as if it's that she's sucking on.

Dragging my digit in deeper, she uses her teeth to lightly graze the skin, and I shamelessly growl in need as I rest my other forearm against the door and watch her.

After a couple of seconds, she releases me.

Her own breathing is ragged, her eyes deep pools of desire. "I want to taste you, Jax. Has anyone ever?"

I shake my head. "N-no, no one has," I confess, feeling like the inadequate child of the group. It's obvious that both D and Zach have experienced a lot already, and here I am, innocent and yet entirely corrupted all at the same time.

"Do you think... I won't touch you. And the second you say stop, I swear to God that I will. I just... I need to know how you taste."

"Fuck, baby. You know how to mess with a guy's head."

Her eyes widen in shock. "No, Jax. That's not what I—"

"I didn't mean it like that. You just make me want all these things I never thought I'd have, and it makes my head spin."

"So..." she prompts, clearly completely on board with this idea.

"How long have you been thinking about sucking my cock, baby?" I ask, unable to stop myself.

A shy smile pulls at her lips as the blush on her cheeks deepens. "A long time," she confesses.

"Okay," I breathe, unable to deny her. "But—"

"I'll stop, I swear."

"I know you will. I trust you. It's me that I don't." I squeeze my eyes shut as I prepare to give her more of my darkened soul. "Touch is one thing. But those few seconds before I come, they're... something else entirely."

"Okay," she breathes, to let me know she's heard me.

"I have no control over it. I fall into this dark place inside me, and I usually don't resurface until I've blown and it's too late. I'm scared of what—"

"I won't let you hurt me, Jax. I can handle the dark."

"Fuck, you utterly wreck me, you know that?"

She smiles, and I'm powerless but to claim those tempting lips once more.

Once I've given myself a good pep talk, I switch our positions, pressing my back against the wall, and I release her. I hold her eyes, silently telling her that it's okay if she wants to back out. She owes me nothing, and I more than understand if this is too much to deal with.

But then, she drops to her knees and it's like the entire world stops spinning. I swear I don't even breathe as she sits there before me, her huge, hungry eyes staring up at me as if I'm some king or something.

It's a fucking heady feeling, one I'm not sure I'll ever get used to.

Reaching for my waistband, I rip the buttons open. River's eyes follow my every move, her breathing becoming more and more erratic by the second.

"You're wet for me, aren't you?" I ask as I tuck my thumbs into my jeans and boxers and shove them down, but I don't push them any lower than necessary, because that would open up a whole new can of worms I'm not ready to deal with.

Her eyes widen and she licks her lips as I wrap my fingers around myself and slowly start stroking.

"Yes," is her simple reply before she shuffles forward, close enough to touch me, if she were able to.

"Holy fuck," I grunt, watching her study me with starving eyes.

"I can only use my mouth. My hands are bound. I won't touch you," she confirms. "But if it's too much, if you need me to stop, I will."

"I know," I choke out, my desperation to know how her tongue is going to feel against me is too much to take.

She nods once before leaning closer and sticking her tongue out. The second her burning flesh connects with mine, my entire body jerks.

"Holy fuck," I grunt when she does it again, my blood beginning to boil in my veins as red hot flames lick at my insides just like River does my cock.

Without realizing it, my fingers thread into her hair as I pull her close with the need to close my eyes and just focus on the sensations—but I can't rip my eyes from her. She's a fucking goddess.

The second my release starts to build, the all too familiar feeling of dread and panic washes through me. It doesn't matter how many times I tell myself that I can let go and enjoy this, there's that little, terrified, abused boy living inside me who just freaks the fuck out.

I grit my teeth until my jaw aches as I fight to stave it off, to enjoy this, to be fucking normal.

But it doesn't matter how much I might want it, how much River might believe I deserve it. That evil beast that was born inside me all those years ago bursts through a beat before I come.

"No," I cry, unaware of anything as pain, disgust, and red hot fear rip through me.

I squeeze my eyes closed, shove my fingers into my hair and curl forward, willing it to dissipate, for reality to set back in. I know I'm not back there, I know my life is different, but it never helps. And I fear I'm never going to be able to get through this and be the man she deserves.

The moment everything starts to settle and I begin to see the light at the end of the very dark tunnel, I blink my eyes open and look for her.

"Fuck," I bark, rushing to tuck myself away and fly over to where she's curled up in the corner where I must have thrown her. "River. Fuck. I'm sorry, I'm—"

"It's okay," she whispers. "I'm okay."

I hold her face in my hands after untying her hands and wipe the stray tears from her lashes. "Nothing about this is okay, River. Nothing."

She holds my eyes for a beat and then says something that makes my heart shatter.

"You did it, Jax. I'm so proud of you."

"You cold?" Diesel asks me as we sit around the fire with the others.

After I managed to convince Jax that I was okay, that what happened wasn't his fault, we returned to the party. He headed straight for Zach, the two of them disappearing outside, while Diesel had made a beeline for me.

He hadn't left my side since.

"A little," I said, fighting a smile when he said, "Crank, man, grab Riv another blanket."

"You grab her a blanket. I kinda have my hands full."

He does, literally. Full of Quinn's ass.

"Is that any way to be a good host, Killian?" She grabs his jaw, kissing him deeply. "I want another one anyway, so I'll grab River one too. Kat, you want?"

"Sure," she slurs, waving her bottle in the air.

Diesel mutters something under his breath and I whisper, "Go easy on her. She's probably feeling left out."

Diesel's eyes snag mine and the world falls away. Until someone clears their throat, and I glance up to find

Crank watching us. I immediately try to move away, but Diesel slides his arm around my waist and anchors me to his side.

"But—"

"Relax, little Savage." Crank winks. "Ain't nobody here goin' to say anything."

I really don't know what to say to that, so I press my lips together.

"He's right, you know." Diesel's fingers run down my spine and his hand fits under my sweater. "It's okay to be like this here."

My eyelashes flutter as I gaze up at him. The liquor from earlier has started to fade, but my blood runs hot for another reason.

The guys talk about the renovations at Diesel's cabin, his plans to overhaul the outside space and create something similar to what Crank has done out here.

Zach and Jax appear, and Zach arches a brow when he spots me nestled into Diesel's side. I'm hardly surprised when he drops down beside me and shuffles right up close, sandwiching me between the two of them.

"What do we have here?" He keeps his voice low, and I'm super aware of Crank, Bones, Tank, and Kat watching us. Although I'm not really sure Kat is watching anything, she's so drunk.

"Hey." I smile at Zach and his brows pinch.

"This is new." His eyes go over my head to Diesel, who shrugs.

"We can trust my guys."

I lean around Zach and ask Jax, "Are you okay?"

"Yeah, I'm good." His eyes darken, but he takes a long pull on his beer, letting his gaze rest on the hypnotic flames.

"I come bearing blankets." Quinn bounds over to me and drops one in my lap with a wink. "Just remember to keep your hands to yourselves." She gives the guys a pointed look, and I bite my fist to stop myself from laughing.

Diesel helps me lay the blanket over my legs, and my heart swells when he takes my hand in his and threads our fingers together.

This is the first time he's ever acknowledged our relationship in public, and I can't help but think it's a step in the right direction.

Until Tank lets out a low whistle. "You must have balls of fucking steel, my man. Savage is not someone I would want to get on the wrong side of. We all heard what he did to Stone."

"Not the time or place, Tank," Crank hisses, pulling Quinn and their extra blanket onto his lap. "In fact, do me a favor and carry Kat to our spare room. She needs to sleep it off."

Sure enough, Kat is almost comatose.

"Ah hell, man, for real?"

"Yup, prospect. Hop to it. And make sure you find her a bucket in case she pukes."

Diesel squeezes my hand, giving me a reassuring smile, and the knot in my stomach eases. But an entirely different sensation sweeps over me when another hand grips my thigh under the blanket.

My eyes snap to Zach, and he smirks.

'Behave,' I mouth.

"With you, Blondie? Never."

"You've sure got your hands full over there, little Savage. I pray to fuckin' God you know what you're all doing."

His words—his warning—sober me up a little, and I lose myself in my thoughts as I watch the flames burn higher and higher, kissing the inky canvas above us.

Diesel's thumb sweeps circles over the curve of my hand while Zach's fingers gently massage my thigh, inching higher and higher. I'm so relaxed and toasty, my eyes start growing heavy.

"Ahh shit, man," Zach murmurs. "We're sending her to sleep."

"It is getting late. Maybe we should call it a night."

"Doesn't sound like a bad idea to me," Crank says. "Unless you wanna ride me under the stars, sunshine."

Zach snorts, but it's drowned out by Quinn's shrieks of protest as she bats Crank's chest.

Thunder cracks overhead, startling us all, and Zach chuckles darkly. "Not afraid of a little storm, are you?" His eyes glint in the moonlight, making him look deadlier than ever.

But I'm not afraid.

"Never," I say with an air of confidence I'm not sure I feel.

"You'll keep an eye on Kat?" Diesel asks Crank, and he nods.

"You know it. I'll make Tank take watch."

"Watch?" I say.

"Figure of speech, babe." Diesel drops a kiss on my head. "Come on, let's get you home." He stands and offers me his hand. But I'm still stuck on the part about getting me home.

Zach taps my leg. "Up you go, Blondie."

Diesel pulls me up, and Zach and Jax join us.

"Thanks for tonight, man," he says to Crank.

"Yeah. Be safe, brother. We'll see you bright and early for breakfast."

"You know it. Come on." He slides his arm around my waist and leads me toward the tree line. "You guys good?" he asks Zach and Jax, and I can't help but feel they're having some secret conversation I'm not a part of.

"What's going on?" I ask.

"Nothing. But we should hurry before the storm hits." Another crash of thunder rumbles in the distance, followed by a crack of lightning overhead.

"Okay, yeah, that sounds like a good idea."

"I knew it." Zach claps his hands. "You are afraid of the storm."

"Am not." I glower at him, pressing into Diesel's side.

"Don't look to Daddy D, Blondie. He won't save you."

Another clash of thunder has me shrieking, and Zach howls with laughter as he lunges for me and picks me up, throwing me over his shoulder.

"Oh my God, Zach, put me down." I hammer my fists against his back as he takes off into the woods.

"Only if you beg."

"Fuck you," I spit, only half joking.

My stomach roils as my body jostles up and down with the force of his movements.

"Your ass looks pretty damn fine in these jeans, Blondie. Although I've got a feeling it looks even better out of them."

The storm turns violent above us, thunder and lightning dueling across the sky. But it's when the heavens open up and big fat drops of rain start hitting me that I really scream.

"Fuck yeah!" Zach lets out a feral holler, the sound of the guys' laughter echoing around us.

"We need to get her to the cabin," Diesel yells.

"Or..." Zach finally stops, lowering me to the ground. Water soaks my clothes, drenching my hair and running down my face. "We could have a little fun."

He reaches for me, but I jerk backward.

"Oh, it's like that, huh?" His eyes dance with desire, hunger and pride. "You gonna run, Blondie?"

"Maybe."

"Better be quick then, because when I catch you, all bets are off." He lunges forward and I spin on my heel and take off, running as fast as I can.

Adrenaline courses through me, my heart careening in my chest as I push harder, muddy water spraying up around me. It's silly, a foolish game of cat and mouse. Especially when I want to be caught. But sometimes, he makes it too easy.

I think I'm clear of him when an arm shoots out and hooks me around the waist, lifting me clean off the ground. A scream rips from my throat but dies in the palm covering my face.

"Run all you want, baby," Zach's gravelly voice makes my stomach curl. "But I'll always fucking catch you."

He spins me around and presses me up against a tree, his hand collaring my throat. Diesel and Jax emerge from the darkness, closing in on us. They're both as drenched as we are, their clothes sticking to their bodies, rivulets of water running down their leather cuts.

"Look what I found." Zach smirks. "The question is, what should we do with her? I imagined fucking her in Crank's hot tub, but I think this is a pretty good alternative."

A shiver goes through me, making my teeth chatter.

And Diesel frowns. "She's cold. We should take this inside."

"Relax, Daddy D. I don't think she minds." Zach's free hand slides to the waistband of my jeans and pops the button. "In fact, I think if I do this..." He pushes his hand inside and dips two fingers inside me. "Fuck, she's soaked."

"You good with this?" Diesel asks, and I nod, lifting my hips, seeking more.

Sitting around the fire, I'd felt sleepy. But I'm wide awake now, and I want this. I want every single experience I can get with them.

Zach curls his fingers deeper and I gasp, his touch bordering on painful. He leans in, sucking my bottom lip between his teeth and biting gently. "I want a taste, and then I want to sink inside you and fuck you raw."

"Yes... God, yes."

Zach drops to his knees and yanks my jeans down. "Help me out," he barks, and Diesel and Jax move closer, helping him lift me enough to get my jeans all the way off. He hitches one of my legs over his shoulder and latches his mouth onto my pussy. It's so intense, so overwhelming, that I almost slip. But strong arms hold me up as Zach eats me, licking and spearing his tongue deep inside me. Rain pelts off us, each blast of icy cold at odds with the heat simmering under my skin. I feel like I'm burning alive.

He maneuvers my other leg over his shoulder so I'm suspended against the tree, pinned in place by his shoulders and the guys. I fist his hair, urging him closer, deeper... needing more. Needing everything he can give me.

"You taste like fucking heaven," he drawls, breathing

the words right onto me, before circling my clit with his tongue.

"Zach... don't stop... God..."

He smirks up at me, a dark, dangerous devil, before diving back, licking me in slow, torturous circles that make me scream his name.

A desperate plea to the gods.

And as my orgasm barrels through me, the thunder and lightning answer.

32

ZACH

Her body tightens as she comes, and I drown in everything that is this incredible woman. She's shy, timid, innocent to the outside, but then with us, she morphs into this little spitfire. A woman who's not ashamed to take what she needs and demand the same of us right along with her.

"Oh God, Zach. I need more," she moans, her eyes flickering open until she finds me still between her thighs.

"I've got you, Blondie," I say right against her pussy, letting the vibration of my voice extend her release.

Another loud clap of thunder booms somewhere around us, the sound of the rain pounding down on the fallen leaves filling my ears as it runs over me.

It might be ice cold, but with River in my arms, I feel none of it. Instead, I just feel the raging fire deep within me, demanding I take her, make her mine.

With the help of D and Jax, we get her back to her feet, and the second she's standing before me, I grasp her chin, claiming her lips and allowing her to taste herself on my tongue.

She moans, sagging back against the tree as our tongues duel and our teeth clash in a hungry and desperate kiss. Her fingers thread into my wet hair, tugging as if she wants to drag me closer before they drop and start roaming over my body, making my muscles bunch wherever she touches.

"Fuck, babe. You drive me crazy," I groan into her kiss.

I know the other two are watching, probably beyond pissed that I've claimed our girl for my own once more, But honestly, I can't find it in myself to care.

They've both already had some time with her this evening. Now, she's mine.

The storm becomes more violent around us as the seconds tick by. The thunder is so loud it makes the ground shake beneath us, and the lightning that follows only a beat later lights up the woodland around us, making it look like we're in some kind of horror movie.

"Zach, man. It's getting worse. We should probably —" D starts, shouting over the pounding rain.

"Nah, I'm going fucking nowhere while I've got my girl trembling in my arms."

"From the cold, you asshat. We're soaked and going to end up with hypothermia. We need to go."

Another earth-shaking clap of thunder sounds out, and River's small hands slide to my chest, pushing slightly.

"He's right, Zach. We shouldn't—" A second loud clap is quickly followed by a bolt of lightning and then what I can only assume is a tree falling.

"Zach," D barks, his voice deeper and more insistent. "Get our fucking girl inside now. I'm not having any of us hurt out here."

"Fine," I hiss, but I'm mostly just annoyed because I know he's right.

Sweeping her feet off the soaked ground, I cradle her against my chest and take off running once more, fully intending on continuing this the second we get inside. Possibly naked and in a warm shower.

Footsteps pound behind us, telling me that they're hot on our heels.

Blinking the rain out of my eyes, I focus on the soft light coming from D's cabin and just keep moving as the storm rages. By the time I approach the building, every single inch of me is soaked through and the cold is starting to seep into my bones.

River's teeth are chattering as she grips onto me for dear life, and I hate that my need for her back there would have stopped me from doing the right thing.

I can't help it. I just lose my head around this woman.

I come to a stop in front of the door and wait for D to slip past so he can unlock it. "It's okay, Riv. We'll strip you off and warm you up. Promise."

Her eyes blaze with fire despite the conditions and D finally opens the door.

The place is almost as cold as outside, making me wish we'd stopped in here first and started a fire. It wasn't hard to predict that it would be where we'd end up once the party was over.

"Strip her," D demands. "Get her out of those wet clothes. And then do your own."

"Who the fuck made you the expert?" I mutter, putting River back on her feet and immediately wrapping my fingers around the bottom of her hoodie, dragging the sopping fabric up her slender body.

"Basic fucking survival skills, Stone. It's not fucking rocket science. Now fucking strip."

"Anyone would think you want to see my cock again, Daddy," I taunt, as I spin River around to look at him, unhooking her bra and dragging it down her arms.

He pauses with his jeans around his knees, his eyes wide and glued to her.

"Look at that, Blondie. Look at the effect you have on Daddy D. Your tits have rendered him useless."

She gasps when my freezing shirt hits her back, but it doesn't stop her head rolling when I cup both her breasts in my hands, pinching her hard nipples between my fingers.

"Look how hot she is for you, Daddy."

His teeth grind and his jaw pops as I keep calling him that. But he has to have figured out by now that I'm not going to stop when he gives me such a killer reaction every time.

"Zach," he growls, quickly losing patience with me.

He manages to finally tug his feet free of the fabric and throws them and his boxers toward the kitchen to deal with later.

"Fine. Get a fire going, and then we can lay her out in front of it. Warm her up real good."

This time when his jaw pops, it's for an entirely different reason. "Do as you're told and you might even get a chance with her."

"Like that, is it?" I mutter, pushing my thumbs into her panties and letting them drop to her feet.

D just rolls his eyes and marches to the fire, not giving two shits that his junk is on full display while he works.

"Just do as he says," River urges, looking back over her shoulder at me.

"Only because you asked so nicely." I wink at her and get to stripping down.

I might give D shit about it, but my clothes are freezing and only getting colder by the second. I'm more than happy to shed them.

River's eyes eat up every bit of skin I reveal until she bites down on her bottom lip when my still hard cock springs free.

"Now," I say, wrapping my hand around it. "Where were we?"

I reach for her, but I'm not fast enough. Strong, inked arms wrap around her and haul her back.

"I'll warm you up, pretty girl," Diesel says with a chuckle. "Unlike some, I can think with my head and not just my dick."

"Yeah, which I bet is getting more than excited at being that close to her ass right now," I sulk.

"Come on, we're going to shower. I'm not having you getting sick."

He looks up, something catching his attention over my shoulder.

"Jax, you need to str—"

"I-I... I can't—"

Spinning around, I find Jax standing behind me in the middle of a puddle of his own making, pure fear on his face.

"They're hard as fuck to get off, man, but it's worth it. I'm warmer already," I half-lie. I'm fucking freezing, but whatever.

"No, it's not that. It's—"

"Come on, man. We've seen your cock more than once—it's decent too, if you need your ego-stroking— what more is there to worry about?"

His throat ripples with a heavy swallow as River's soft, concerned voice fills the air. "Jax, what's wrong?"

He looks between the three of us with his brows pinched together and resignation in his eyes. "You guys go warm her up. I'll go in after."

Silence settles around us, but no one makes any attempt to move or follow his suggestion.

"We're not leaving you, Jax. Not until you tell us what's going on," River says again, ripping herself from D's arms and walking over to him. She trembles, the cold seeping into her bones, but she doesn't step down. She knows he needs her.

She hesitates for a few seconds but obviously reads something I can't in his expression as she reaches for his hands.

His eyes blaze with need for our girl, but it's not enough to swallow the pain. "I can't..." He swallows again. "I—"

She steps a little closer but keeps enough space between them to ensure he's not freaking out. He stares down at her as if she's the only girl in the world, as if we're not standing here watching this interaction, equally as confused by it all.

"I've got some... some scars," he finally confesses, ripping his eyes from River's and casting them toward the floor as if he's ashamed.

"Bro, we've all got scars," I say, pointing out an old knife wound down my side that's now covered in ink before dropping to one on my leg from where I came off my bike not all that long ago.

"Yeah, man. They're pretty unavoidable in the life we live. They're not going to bother us."

It suddenly hits me that in all the weeks I've been

here, I've never seen him shirtless. Not when we've been training or even when we've been playing with River. I was always too distracted to notice. I guess that was his plan. But did he really think he could continue getting away with hiding from us like that? From River?

"Th-they're not like yours. I didn't fall off my bike or lose a fight."

"Okay, so what are they from?" River urges.

He looks at each of us hesitantly before staring back into her eyes and saying two words that sends an arctic chill through the air. "My past."

"Jax," River sighs, pausing as she finds whatever words she wants to say to him. "Your body isn't why I'm standing here right now. Your skin isn't the reason either. It's you, Jax. It's the person you are, it's what's in your heart. I understand you're scared, ashamed even, and I get if today isn't the day you feel you can share this with us. You can go shower first, in private, and steal some of D's dry clothes to wear again. It's totally fine. We're not going to make you do anything you're not ready for. But I need you to know that you can trust me, trust us. Right, guys?" she says, urging us to agree with her. "We're here for you. We want to help you."

Her shoulders drop in defeat when he releases her hands, and her arms fall limply at her sides. Rejection ripples through the room, and I'm half a second from going to her when D steps forward to do exactly that. But right at the last moment, Jax moves, and D halts.

We stand in silence as his fingers curl around the sodden fabric of his hoodie and he lifts slightly. His eyes close as if it's causing him physical pain to do so, and my heart shatters for him, for the little boy hiding within him that was so clearly broken by life.

"River's right, man. You don't have to—" D stops, realizing that it's too late.

The fabric hits the floor as the air crackles around us with anticipation, confusion, and concern.

"Jax, I don't understand," River says. And I have to admit, nor do I. He looks... normal. His arms are inked, like we already knew, but his chest and stomach are clear of anything that might make him react like this.

My brows pinch as I watch him, waiting for him to reveal something we're quite obviously missing. He hangs his head, lifting his hands to his hair for a beat before he sucks in a breath and turns around.

River's gasp cuts through the air like an arrow, and I swear to fucking God that it hits me right in the chest.

"Fuck," D breathes before he can stop himself, whereas I manage to force very different words from my throat.

"Hot as fuck, man. Chicks dig scars."

D cuts me a death glare, and I wonder if maybe humor wasn't the way to handle this situation.

33

RIVER

Emotion wells inside of me, and I have to swallow down the tears burning the backs of my eyes.

Jax's back is a patchwork of scars. Some are round and puckered like... like burn marks that have healed over time, but others are longer, thin silvery welts that look all too like whip marks.

"W-what happened to you?" I barely get the words out of my mouth, my heart shattering for my scarred, broken boy.

I knew Jax's trauma was deep rooted. The way he avoids touch and worries about hurting me all point to severe childhood abuse. But seeing this brings it home.

Diesel steps closer to him. It's a strange scene, the three of us naked, cold, wet and shivering, standing around Jax as he finally shares his truth with us.

"It's okay," I whisper. "Jax, look at me."

He turns slowly, his expression so full of shame and pain that it knocks the wind right out of me.

"Come here."

"I-I can't." He runs a hand down his face, his eyes shuttering as his entire body trembles.

"Yes, you can." Opening my arms to him, I wait, giving him the time and space to decide, even though I want nothing more than to throw my arms around him and never let go. "I'm right here, Jax. I love you."

Someone sucks in a sharp breath, but I don't break eye contact with Jax. Nothing else matters in this moment except for him.

"I love you, and I want to help. Let me help, Jax. Please."

A choked sob bubbles out of him as he stumbles forward, throwing himself into my waiting arms. He anchors his hands behind my back, holding on so tight I can hardly breathe.

I didn't mean to say the words—they just bubbled out —but now they're out there, between us, I realize they're true. They have been for a while. And if it brings him any small measure of relief, then it's worth it.

"Can I hug you?" I ask.

He nods against my shoulder and slowly, cautiously, I lower my hands to his disfigured skin.

"It's okay," I whisper softly. "You're safe now, baby. You're safe." Tears stream down my face as I imagine a young Jax enduring such... such brutality. And to think it was his uncle, someone who was supposed to love and protect him.

Anger swells inside of me like an unforgiving storm, the need to protect Jax, to hurt anyone who would ever dare lay a hand on him burns through me.

"I'm gonna take a shower," Zach says somewhere behind us.

"Go, I'll stay with them," Diesel replies, and I offer him an appreciative nod.

He comes closer, draping a blanket over my shoulders, and the pair of us sink to the floor, still locked together.

Jax flinches and I gently stroke down his spine. "It's just a blanket. Are you cold?"

He doesn't answer, but from the way he's trembling, I'm sure some of it has to be the fact that we all got drenched in the storm.

I reach back, pulling the blanket off me, and pull it over Jax instead. "Is this okay?"

Another small nod, but he won't look at me. He won't lift his face out of the safety of my shoulder.

"I'll be right back," Diesel whispers.

My knees smart from the cold hardwood floor, but I don't want to let Jax go. Instead, I tug him down gently until I'm sitting on my ass and he's curled around me, his head buried in my lap. I stroke his skin, ghosting my fingers over every scar and blemish, trying to erase the pain ingrained in them.

"I hate that this happened to you," I whisper. "But you're safe now, Jax. And you're loved so much. By me, by the club—your real family. Nothing he did to you can touch you here."

Jax sucks in a sharp breath, his hand curving around my thigh, fingers digging into my flesh. But I don't stop him. He needs this.

He needs intimate contact, even if it terrifies him.

Furniture scuffs behind me and Diesel shoves one of the armchairs closer to give me some support. "Should we move him?" he asks, and I shake my head.

"It's fine. You should take a shower and get into some warm clothes. We're okay."

His brows pinch as he drops his concerned gaze to the quiet, trembling guy wrapped around me like a child. "We'll be right down the hall."

"I know. Jax won't hurt me."

I'm not even sure he's aware of what's happening right now, he's so lost to his demons.

With a small nod, Diesel disappears down the hall while I sit with Jax, whispering soothing words to him. Telling him how strong he is.

How brave.

How loved.

⸻

"He's asleep?" Zach appears some time later. My neck and back are stiff from sitting in the same position, but I didn't want to wake Jax. Not when he'd finally drifted into a peaceful sleep.

"Yeah," I whisper.

"Here, let me help." Zach crouches down and gently peels Jax off me so I can wiggle out from under him.

I grab a couple of cushions off the couch and tuck them under his head and pull the blanket up over his body.

"Come here." Zach pulls me into his arms and stares down at me.

"What?" I ask around a yawn.

"You're pretty fucking amazing, you know that, right? What you did for him... and I don't just mean tonight. When I think you can't surprise me anymore, you go and do something else and I..." He trails off, glancing down at the floor.

"Zach?"

278

"You should get showered." His expression hardens, and my heart sinks. Just when I think he's letting down his walls, he slams them back up. "Diesel is done."

"Okay." I let out a soft sigh, backing away from him.

"Wait." He snags my wrist, yanking me into his body. My hand lands on his chest to steady myself, and the air crackles as his gaze darkens.

"Zach, I—"

His mouth crashes down on mine, his hand burying into my damp hair. The kiss isn't sweet or gentle, it's brutal and unyielding. It's Zach's way of keeping me close but keeping me at arm's length all at the same time. I feel his desperation for me as much as I feel his torment over it.

He wants me. He wants this. But he still doesn't want to want it.

"Z-Zach, stop. Stop." I push him away slightly, inhaling a sharp breath.

"Fuck... fuck," he hisses, stepping back and putting some distance between us. "Why can't I let you walk away?"

"Do you really want to?"

"I..."

"It's okay to want this, you know," I say. "To want us." *To want me.* I don't allow those last words to fall from my lips.

"You know who I am, Blondie. There isn't a happy ending in my future."

His words are tiny shards of glass inside my chest. I hate that he holds so little worth for his life.

"I don't believe that."

"Because you're an idealist. A romantic. But there aren't any fairy tale endings here, you know. Not for me."

"So what are you doing, Zach? Why are you here?"

"I... I want to help him." His cold stare drops to Jax's sleeping form.

"And?"

"And I like how good you feel riding my dick."

Disappointment snakes through me. Even now, in a small moment of realness, he still can't own his feelings.

"I'm going to take a shower." I walk away, but his voice gives me pause.

"I can't be who you need, River. Not now, not ever. I can make you scream, make you come so hard you see stars, but that's your lot. If you want hearts and flowers and promises of something real... you have Jax and D for that. But me... I'm just here for the ride."

Pain radiates from my chest at his cold, callous words, but I don't react.

Without looking back at him, I head down the hall. My heart has been through the ringer tonight, but Zach couldn't resist driving the knife a little bit deeper.

He's right, I do have Jax and Diesel, I don't doubt that for a second. But I want him too.

I want all of them.

We're in this together.

At least, I hoped we were.

When I finally leave the sanctuary of Diesel's shower, I'm so exhausted, I can barely get dry and changed into the clean t-shirt Diesel left out for me. There's no sign of him or Zach, so I can only assume they're watching over Jax for me.

Zach's words still weigh heavy on my mind, but I

don't have anything left to give tonight. I'm emotionally drained.

Slipping into Diesel's bed, I burrow under the sheets and close my eyes. Part of me wanted to go and check on Jax, but I don't want to deal with Zach right now.

"River?" Diesel whispers sometime later, and I murmur some intelligible reply.

There's some shuffling and rustling, and then the bed dips beside me and I crack an eye open to find him smiling at me.

"Hey, pretty girl."

"Hey."

"Zach told me what happened. He's an ass."

"He doesn't want this, D. I keep telling myself that he'll come around. That he just needs time... but I—"

"Hey, hey, it'll be okay." He kisses my head. "Zach has a lot of unresolved shit to deal with. He lost everything, Riv, and I think his attitude is more about his fear of losing anything else good in his life than not wanting it."

I give a small shrug.

"He can barely keep his hands off you. Trust me when I say it's more than just sex to him."

"Is it?" I ask.

Even though I feel it sometimes, the intense connection burning between us, he always finds a way to distance himself.

"He took a bullet for you," Diesel chuckles, brushing his lips over mine. "If that doesn't say where his head's at, then I don't know what does." He tucks me closer, running his hand down my spine. "Jax is still sleeping. I think he'll be out for the night."

"I've never wished anyone dead, ever. But I wouldn't

mind someone putting a bullet between Jax's uncle's eyes."

"His uncle? Fuck."

"Yeah. It's bad, D. Really bad. What he went through..."

"Shh. Don't go there, not tonight. He's okay. He'll be okay. And when he's ready, we'll help him. Together."

"You really mean that, don't you?" I lift my eyes to his, hit with a wave of emotion.

"Every word."

"Thank you, D. For being here. For helping him." I nuzzle my cheek against his chest and close my eyes, drifting into a fitful sleep.

I dream of them. Diesel. Jax. And Zach.

At some point, I imagine the bed dipping behind me and a warm body presses up against me.

"I'm sorry, Blondie," Zach whispers, his hand sliding over the curve of my hip. "I... I don't know how to fucking do this, baby."

He presses a kiss against the nape of my neck and my heart flutters.

It feels real.

Too damn real.

"Zach," I murmur, wishing he was really here. That he was finally ready to succumb to what exists between us.

"Shh, baby. I got you." His voice drifts away as I sink deeper into oblivion. "I got you."

34

DIESEL

A groan rumbles up my throat, and I wake to the most incredible feeling of River's ass grinding back against my aching cock.

"Mmm," I moan, snuggling closer to her warm body.

Every inch of me aches to take her, to claim her. But I want it to be right.

I'm aware that makes me sound like a teenage girl, but fuck it. She deserves it.

After the brutal way Zach took her virginity outside a club, it only seems fair that our first time is the thing of fairy tales.

I'm not able to offer her much. I'm a dirty biker who spends his days cussing and knuckle-deep in oil and dirt and dreams of having her chained to my bed at my mercy. But I'm pretty sure I can deliver some romance. I'm pretty fucking confident that I can do a better job than Zach, anyway.

Someone shifting on the other side of the room catches my attention as River seems to have fallen back asleep, her body stilling once more.

"Hey," I breathe when I find Jax sitting in the chair in the corner, the blanket from last night still covering him, and heavy, half-asleep eyes. "How are you doing?"

His eyes move from mine to the girl softly snoring beside me. "She makes it better."

"Yeah," I agree. "She's pretty awesome like that."

A small smile curls at his lips and a little lightness returns to his eyes.

"She meant what she said last night, you know. All of it."

He nods, his Adam's apple bobbing with a swallow.

"Wanna get in here?" I offer, although it damn near kills me to do so.

Longing fills his features, telling me that there is literally nothing he wants more in the world. But sadly, he's also not quite there yet, and regretfully, he shakes his head.

"Diesel," a soft voice moans as a warm hand reaches back for me.

"Morning, pretty girl," I say, turning back to her.

"Is Jax okay?"

Silence fills the room for a beat, but I don't miss the gasp from the man in question that her concern for him was the first thing she thought about.

"Yeah, Riv. I'm good," he whispers.

Pushing up on her elbow, she finds him across the room as Zach groans on her other side, clearly unimpressed with being woken.

Dragging her hand from beneath the sheets, she holds it out for him. "Come join us?" she asks. "I need you close."

He looks torn for a beat, but he quickly decides that

he needs it just as much as she does and he lets the blanket drop as he stands.

"Bro, you stole my underwear?" I ask, staring down at what I know are my boxers.

"Yeah, would you rather I take them off?" He smirks.

"Can't say I'm all too bothered. She might be up for it, though," Zach grumbles, although his eyes remain closed.

As Jax climbs on the bed, I can't help but notice more scars that litter his thighs. These look different again from those that have clearly been inflicted on his back, and my heart aches for the horrors he must have been through.

Flashbacks hit me from the night I tried to patch him up after he was run off the road and ripped up his shoulder pretty bad. I thought he was just being pig-headed at the time, wanting to deal with his own shit. Now, it's really starting to make sense as to why he refused point-blank to strip down any further than to his wifebeater.

Not letting my eyes linger, I look back down at our girl.

"This is nice," she says, locking her fingers with Jax, her other hand squeezing my ass through my boxers.

"Could be better," Zach groans. "D and I could both be inside you right now, getting the day started right."

"Do you ever think of anything other than your cock?" I snap.

"Not often, no. But something tells me that it's the only thing on River's mind right now, seeing as she's surrounded by three hard ones."

"I thought you weren't looking at my cock, Stone," Jax quips.

"I don't need to look to know," he confirms. "We all

know River is naked beneath D's shirt, and I bet she's nice and wet too."

"You're addicted," I quip.

"To River's pussy? Hell yeah, I am."

"To be fair," River says, "he does have an apology to make."

"Fair. And what can I do to make up for being a dick last night, Blondie?"

She thinks for a moment, her teeth sinking into her bottom lip seductively. My cock jerks against her ass as I imagine those pink lips being wrapped around it once more.

"I think we could all do with a coffee. What do you say?" she asks, amusement dancing in her blue eyes.

"Yeah, I could definitely use some caffeine. Jax?"

"Sure thing. Thanks, man. Appreciate it."

"That wasn't exactly what I had in mind," Zach complains.

"Aw, but you want to make me feel better, don't you, baby?" River coos, making me snort a laugh.

"Yeah, I just prefer doing it in other ways. Fucking hell," he mutters, shoving the covers back and throwing his legs over the bed.

He marches across the room and slips into the bathroom, but none of us pay him any mind.

"Jax," River encourages. "I made space for you."

"Nicely played, babe."

"See, I'm not just a pretty face."

"We're more than aware."

Jax takes up Zach's place beside her, keeping a couple of inches between their bodies, although I can tell in his eyes and the hard set of his muscles that he's desperate for more, for the comfort she offered him last night.

The two of them lie motionless, just staring, losing themselves in each other, and I almost excuse myself to go and help Zach with the drinks to give them a moment.

"Don't even think about it," River gasps when I roll away.

"Whatever you say, pretty girl. What do you need, Jax?" I ask, sensing that he's holding something back.

His eyes meet mine over River's shoulder. "I wanna see our girl. All of our girl."

"Your wish is my command."

Without moving her from the bed, I manage to pull my shirt up her body and over her head. "Better?"

He doesn't respond, but the way his eyes blaze as he takes her in says it all. "I don't think I appreciated this as much as I should last night," he murmurs, almost to himself.

River sucks in a breath, her lips parting to respond, but she doesn't get a chance to get any words out because Jax presses two fingers against her lips.

"Zach might have an apology to make, although I'm fairly certain I might have missed what he did, but my thank you is more important. I don't fucking deserve you, River."

She tries to talk again, but this time he silences her with his lips.

Immediately, she leans into him, accepting his kiss. But the second her hand slides from my ass, I capture her wrist, holding it captive behind her so that Jax can take what he needs.

"Oh for fuck's sake," Zach groans when he reemerges from the bathroom and takes in the scene before him. "It's a good thing I like you, Pitbull," he mutters, stalking out of the room for the coffee after a lingering look at the naked girl lying between us.

A low growl rumbles in the back of River's throat, and I can't resist leaning forward and kissing across her shoulder. Her fingers flex, and she quickly realizes that I basically pressed her hand against my cock.

Pulling back, Jax's eyes hold mine and I nod, immediately understanding what he wants.

"Whatever you want, man."

"He didn't say anything," River says, looking between the two of us, her lips swollen from Jax's kiss.

"He doesn't need to, pretty girl. We just know. Up you go," I say, lifting her and slipping beneath her.

I shift us so she's lying back on me, spread her legs wide with my feet, and pin her hands to the bed.

"All yours, Jaxy boy."

"Fuck," he breathes, pushing his hair back from his brow, his eyes shifting over every inch of her, committing it to memory.

"I'm not going anywhere, Jax," she breaths, the erratic movement of her chest giving away just how much she needs whatever he's planning on doing next.

"Good. I'm not sure I'd survive."

Dropping over her, he captures her lips once more in a kiss that makes jealousy knot my stomach and has me wondering why I didn't do that the second she woke.

Before long, he releases her lips and starts painting kisses down her chest until he gets to her nipples.

"Make her cry out loud enough for Zach to hear you," I tell him as a cell phone starts blaring somewhere in the cabin.

"You got it, Daddy," Jax quips, his eyes sparkling with desire.

I roll my eyes at him, pretending to be annoyed, but really I'm just glad he seems to have put the worst parts of last night behind him.

The second he wraps his lips around her, she thrashes against my hold and cries out.

"Motherfucker," Zach barks from the kitchen.

"He deserves it, right?" Jax asks, looking up at River.

"Oh, hell yeah. Even if he didn't, I wouldn't be telling you to stop."

A wicked smile pulls at Jax's lips before I spread her legs wider, inviting him lower. "Fuck, yeah," he grunts, dropping to his front and diving straight for her clit.

"Jax," she screams, her back arching and her ass grinding against my cock once more. "Oh God. *God*, you're good at that," she cries.

"I can't claim it's all the practice like Stone," he mutters, making me laugh before getting back to work.

Another ringtone starts up, but it's just background noise as River starts to lose control.

"I'm gonna release your arms, pretty girl. You gonna be good?"

"Yes," she moans, her head falling back on me as she races toward the finish line. "Oh shit," she screams when I cup both her breasts, pinching and twisting her nipples to add to the pleasure Jax is giving her.

"Come for Jax, pretty girl. Let him show you how grateful he is."

"Yes, yes, yes," she cries as Zach's shadow falls over us, a ringing cell getting louder by the second.

"Oh my God, Jax," River screams, finally falling off the edge.

"Fuck, you're so beautiful," Jax murmurs, sitting back up and wiping his mouth with the back of his hand.

"Something's going on," Zach says, his voice rough with need and his cock trying to bust out of his boxers. "Our cells are blowing up like crazy with calls from Stray and Crank."

"Fuck's sake. Give it here," I ask, holding my hand out.

Swiping the screen, I hit call on Crank's number as Jax gets to his knees and frees his cock, obviously deciding continuing is more important than anything else that's going on. Zach quickly follows as they begin stroking themselves over our girl.

"Wanna taste me, baby?" Zach smirks, hovering over her mouth.

"Fucking really?" I bark with the phone to my ear.

I try to focus. The line crackles before Crank's voice booms. "At fucking last. We've got a problem."

"What's wrong?" I ask, not liking the tone of his voice. River tenses against me, but the horny motherfuckers barely notice as they keep working themselves.

As gently as I can, I slip from beneath her and pad toward the door, dread filling me with every step I take.

"You need to get your asses to the compound."

"We're kind of in the middle of something here," I grit out. "Just tell me what the fuck is—"

"Someone broke in. Hawk and Poker are hurt. Dagger is on his way to the ER. The place is fucking trashed."

"Shit," I hiss, looking over my shoulder. River's eyes are locked on me, a small frown marring her brow, but the other two are too distracted to notice.

Severing our connection, I move farther away before whispering. "Crawlers?"

"I dunno, man. Maybe."

REAP

"Fuck. Fuck," I bark, sensing that I've finally got the attention of the two horny assholes behind me.

"Just fucking get here, yeah? Drop River off at mine. Quinn and Kat are still there. Tank's gonna keep an eye on them."

"I don't fucking like this, man."

He blows out a steady breath. "I know, but what else can we do?"

"Fuck. Yeah, I know. We'll be like... twenty minutes."

I hang up, storm back into the middle of the room and throw my cell on the bed. "Put your cocks away. We've gotta go," I demand, ripping open my closet to find some clothes.

"You're fucking shitting me?" Zach barks, every muscle in his body pulled tight as he chases his release. But the second his eyes meet mine, he stops moving, obviously able to read my thoughts.

"We need to drop Riv at Crank's place. Quinn and Kat are waiting for her. Now," I bark, shoving my feet into a pair of jeans.

"This is fucking bullshit."

"Come on, man. Duty calls," Jax says, climbing from the bed and joining me to borrow some clothes, seeing as ours are still in a damp heap somewhere by the kitchen.

"We'll fucking finish this later, Blondie. You can count on it."

Her eyes burn into my back as she watches us. "You're hiding something, aren't you?" she seethes.

A ripple of unease washes through the room as the three of us look at each other.

"There's been a break-in at the compound," I confess, keeping my suspicions to myself. "We need to go and help sort some shit out."

291

35

RIVER

"Tank..." Quinn says for the third time, but the guy is a closed book, an unmovable rock that won't be cracked.

And she's not the only one it's starting to annoy.

"At least tell us if everyone's okay," I sigh. "Surely, you can do that?"

"Sorry, ladies, but my orders were to stay with you here and wait until someone calls to say otherwise."

"This is bullshit, you know. Someone attacked the club and—"

Tank lets out a frustrated breath. "We don't know what's happening yet. Which is why we need to chill the fuck out and sit tight."

Quinn shoots him a scathing look. "Fine."

"Look, you guys," Kat murmurs, barely picking her head up off the table. "I know it's scary, but Tank is right. Let's just chill out."

"You're a mess. Go back to bed," Quinn snaps, chewing the end of her thumb. She's practically worn a hole in the floor from all her pacing.

"Hey, come on." I go to her and touch her arm. "Let's sit down and put the television on and try to distract ourselves."

Not that I expect it to work.

I haven't been able to stop thinking about the way the guys left in such a hurry. The dark shadows in their eyes. They didn't say anything. They didn't have to. I know exactly where their minds were, because mine was there too.

This has the Night Crawlers written all over it.

They reassured me there would be no blowback for the club, but it's too much of a coincidence. And the timing... the fact that we were at the party here last night and that the guys suggested we come here makes me think they expected something to happen.

Or even worse, they knew it would.

The pit in my stomach quivers as I lead Quinn to the couch. She's pale, dark circles under her eyes.

"Are you okay?" I ask, sensing there's something missing.

"I'm fine. Just pissed that he's keeping us in the dark." She glares at Tank again, but he doesn't react.

"I hate it too, you know. The being kept in the dark, treated like we're not strong enough to handle the truth."

"It's not..." She shakes her head. "It doesn't matter. Hopefully, someone will call soon."

Kat retches, and we both look up just as she bolts up off the chair and stumbles down the hall, hand pressed over mouth.

"Fucking hell," Tank mutters, taking off after her.

Quinn's cell pings and she snatches it up off the table. "Ugh, it's just Sadie."

"Does she know anything yet?"

"Nothing. She's holed up with Dee and Victoria and one of the guys."

I worry my bottom lip. "They'll call. As soon as it's safe, they'll call."

But another thirty minutes pass, and still no one does.

"This is ridiculous." Quinn shoots up. "I'm going over there."

"Hang on, now." Tank steps toward us. He's been sitting over by the breakfast counter since Kat fell asleep after puking her guts up earlier. "You know I can't let you do that."

"Let me? *Let me*? We're not prisoners, Tank, we're—"

The blare of his cell phone is a relief, but it sends a flash of terror through me all the same.

I stand up and reach for Quinn, the two of us holding on to one another as Tank answers. "Hello. Yeah, yeah, they're okay. Well, apart from Kat. She's— yeah, okay." He hangs up and runs a hand over his head. "Crank wants us to head to the compound."

"But everything's okay, right?" I ask.

"I... uh, yeah. I'm sure the guys will fill you in when we get there."

"Thank God," Quinn breathes.

"I'll go get Kat."

"The quicker the better," Tank calls after me. "Crank wants us to hurry."

"Can't you drive faster?" Quinn whines from the back of the truck.

Tank mumbles something under his breath, but Quinn's not paying any attention, frantically texting someone on her cell phone instead.

"Sadie?" I ask, and she shakes her head.

"I'm texting Crank."

"Did he reply?"

"Not yet."

"Hey." I lay my hand on her leg. "They're probably busy cleaning the place up. I'm sure everything is fine."

"How can you be so calm?" She gawks at me.

"I'm not." Not even a little bit. But Quinn seems especially freaked out.

"I hope they're not thinking about locking us down," Kat grumbles. "I can't deal with that again."

"Just how many times do things like this happen?"

Quinn offers me a sympathetic smile. "It's not an everyday thing. But sometimes bad stuff happens, Riv."

Yeah, bad stuff that's all my fault.

I lean my head against the window and close my eyes. It's hard to feel betrayed by them when all they want is to keep me safe and protect me. But I wish they would have told me the truth. This world is still so new to me. I don't want to be a bystander. Not when it concerns people I care about getting hurt.

I smother a sob, and Quinn grabs my hand. "River, what is it?"

"N-nothing. I'm fine, I'm fine."

She pulls me into her side, wrapping her arm around me. "Oh, babe. I'm sorry. Here I am, freaking the hell out, and I didn't stop to ask how you're holding up. You know, this is exactly why I never wanted to end up involved with a biker. This life... It's hard. Messy, scary, and brutal. But you'll never find a bunch of guys more willing to protect the people they care about."

"Shit," Tank says, and we both sit up straight.

"What is it?"

"I think we're being tailed."

"Think or know?" Quinn snaps. "Shit, I'm calling Crank."

"N-no... wait a second, false alarm. They turned off at the last junction."

"Jesus, asshole." Kat punches his shoulder. "Way to scare the crap out of us."

"Sorry, I guess the whole thing's got me on edge. I've never had to babysit two old ladies before."

"Oh, I'm not—"

Quinn chuckles under her breath, pinning me with a knowing look. "I think you'd look cute in a cut," she whispers.

Kat twists around and frowns. "You two are disgusting. That's my brother and my cousins you're mooning over. I need to get new friends." She spins back around and flops against the seat with a huff.

"Love you." I reach over and gently pull a strand of her hair. Kat bats me away but does mumble, "Love you too."

"I'm glad you two found each other. River needs a friend like you in her corner," Quinn says. "A friend who—"

Something slams into the back of the truck, and we all shriek.

"Fuck, fuck, motherfucker." Tank grapples to keep control as the van rear-ends us again.

"Oh my God, Tank, step on it."

"I'm trying, I'm trying."

Quinn has her cell phone out, frantically scrolling—

The phone flies out of her hand as the truck surges forwards and starts to spin, the world whizzing past me as I try to hold onto something, anything.

"Shit, shit, the ravine. Fuck!" Tank screams in desperation as something rams us again. Everything tilts as my life flashes before my eyes. All the things I want to experience and haven't yet.

The things I want to see and do.

Things I want to confess.

"No, no, no!" Kat's cries pierce the air as I try to reach her. Reach anyone. But the world seems to contract, shrinking around me and then exploding in a storm of shattering glass and metal grinding on metal as the truck rolls down the ravine.

My head slams off something, pain splintering through me as my vision grows black. "Q-Quinn? Kat?" I yell, the words ripped from my lungs burning in agony.

Something's wrong. Everything looks and sounds and feels... wrong.

Bang.

Crash.

Thud.

And then silence, my head whipping back one final time and my body crashing into someone as the truck finally settles.

"R-River?" Kat's voices sound distant, like she's under water. Or maybe I am.

"Here, I'm here..."

"Quinn. Do you have eyes on Quinn?" Tank rasps, his voice wet and ragged.

"I..." I inhale a shuddering breath, my ribs smarting as I try to focus. Spots swim across my vision as the inside of the truck, or what's left of the truck, comes into view.

"She's here... I can... Quinn."

Her crumpled form is crushed up against the door, blood trickling down her head. Her panicked eyes collide with mine before they drop to her hand, a hand that's clutching her stomach.

"Quinn?" I yank my eyes back up.

"H-help me, Riv. I need you to help—" She moans in pain.

"Shh, I'm right here. I'm here." Except I'm suspended by my belt, hanging upside down with no clue how to get down and get to her.

Oh God.

"Tank? Can you get free?"

"Fuck, no. I'm stuck, and I'm pretty sure I'm impaled on something."

Kat cries grow louder, and I can't think. I can't think. But Quinn needs me, and Tank is hurt. And something doesn't feel quite right inside me. But I know I have to get to my friends and do something.

Tracing the edge of the seat belt, I manage to locate the buckle and press it, trying to hold on as it slips free. But blistering hot pain slices through my arm and I lose my grip, plummeting toward the ground and smacking my head on something.

"River, oh shit, Riv—"

The voices drown out as blood pools in my ears and everything goes black.

River, Diesel, Jax, and Zach's story concludes in RULE.

DELICIOUSLY DARK ROMANCE

Two angsty romance lovers writing dark heroes and the feisty girls who bring them to their knees.

SIGN UP NOW
To receive news of our releases straight to your inbox.

Want to hang out with us?
Come and join CAITLYN'S DAREDEVILS group on Facebook.

ALSO BY CAITLYN DARE

Rebels at Sterling Prep

Taunt Her

Tame Him

Taint Her

Trust Him

Torment Her

Temper Him

Gravestone Elite

Shattered Legacy

Tarnished Crown

Fractured Reign

Savage Falls Sinners MC

Savage

Sacrifice

Sacred

Sever

Red Ridge Sinners MC

Ruin

Reap

Rule

Dare

Defy

SAVAGE ~ SNEAK PEEK

Chapter One

Sadie

"Sadie Ray, get your ass down here." My dad's gruff voice makes me bristle.

"I'm busy," I yell back, pulling a pillow from behind me and plastering it against my face.

"Don't make me come up there." A growl this time.

A growl that would have most people trembling with fear. But there isn't much about Raymond Dalton, prez of the Savage Falls Sinners MC, that scares me anymore. I've seen my dad broken and bloody, I've seen him almost choke a guy to death for looking at me wrong, and I've seen him shed tears for one of his lost brothers. He might be a giant of a man, all mean-looking tattoos, long dark hair, and menacing eyes, but nobody loves harder than

Ray 'Razor' Dalton, despite what his club name might suggest.

The first thud of his boot against the stairs has me smirking.

The second has me shooting off the bed and darting for my small bathroom.

But before I can make the distance, he barrels into my room like a monster, heaving a deep breath.

"Seriously, Sadie," he grumbles, running a hand over his beard. "I asked you not to pull this shit." Something akin to pain flashes in his eyes, and my bravado slips for a second.

I'm being a brat, I know that, but he deserves it after what he's done—what he's about to do.

"What did you expect, Daddy?" I scowl, folding my arms over my chest for effect.

"Look, sweetheart, I know this isn't easy—"

"Easy? *Easy*?" I balk. "You're moving them in here and expect me to what? Play happy family? I didn't ask for this." I didn't ask for any of it.

He lets out a heavy sigh, tipping his face to the ceiling as if he's silently asking the universe to give him strength. I've seen him do that a lot in my life, as if he doesn't know what to do with me.

I guess sometimes he doesn't.

"I didn't ask for it either, Sadie, girl." He pins me with a pleading look. "But I made a promise to JD."

Guilt snakes through me. Thick and sludgy, it fills me with shame... but then I remember what he did.

What he kept from me for all these years.

Before I can stop myself, I say, "Did JD also ask you to fuck his—"

304

"Don't," he seethes. "Don't talk about things you don't understand."

"Whatever, Dad." I barge around him and storm out of my room, flying down the stairs just as there's a knock.

My blood turns to ice as I glance back at my dad and force the most saccharine smile I can.

"Looks like my new brother and sister are here."

Dad moves around me, and it isn't lost on me that he's practically shielding me from them. But as he opens the door, it occurs to me that maybe he's shielding them from me.

My heart cinches as I drop down on the bottom step, waiting.

I've known for a while that Rhett and River Savage are moving in. They're my dad's best friend's kids. JD Savage. He died way back. Made my dad promise he'd always look out for them and their mom, but I guess that was one promise he couldn't keep.

Julia died a couple of weeks ago after OD'ing.

The whole MC attended her funeral, throwing a huge party after at the compound. If there's anything I've learned growing up as the club's princess, it's that bikers talk when they're drunk. But finding out that my dad planned to move Rhett and River into our house wasn't the only thing I overheard that day.

He'd loved her.

My old man had loved Julia Savage, his dead best friend's wife.

I've always known they were close, but I thought he

was upholding a promise to a friend. I didn't think he was over in Colton, basically creating himself a new family.

I guess it explains a lot. Like why he's so close to Rhett.

Rhett Savage.

God, I hate that blue-eyed, tatted, cocky motherfucker. He's sin wrapped up in muscle and a dirty mouth... and now he's my what? Stepbrother?

The sting of betrayal sits heavy in my chest as I watch Dad welcome River into the house. She's everything I'm not. Slim and petite, with a waterfall of golden hair that falls over her shoulders. I'm all ass and boobs, and I take after my dad with my dark-as-night hair and dark green eyes.

River looks like Princess Barbie, standing there in her floral sundress and jeweled sandals.

"River, meet my daughter, Sadie Ray."

"Hey," she beams, and I flick my hand at her in a lackluster wave.

"Where's Rhett?" Dad cranes his neck to look around her.

"He's getting my things."

"Your things?" His eyes flash with irritation. "I'll go help him. You two girls play nice." He pins me with a warning look, and I narrow my eyes right back.

He ambushed me.

That bastard ambushed me, and I want to hate him for it... I do. But he's my dad. The one guy who's always been there for me, no matter what.

It's not that I resent him finding someone. I don't.

What I resent is him feeling the need to keep it from me.

"I love your hair." River moves closer.

My fingers drift to my wild curls, the flashes of bright pink highlighting them. "Thanks," I mumble.

"I'd never be brave enough to dye mine like that."

"So, you're River. I'm sorry about your mom." I didn't get to say that to her at the funeral, because I didn't realize her mom and my dad had been banging for years.

My chest tightens again.

"I've always wanted a sister." Something etches into her expression, but I'm too busy bristling at the word 'sister' to try to figure out what it is.

"That's... nice." I leap up and shove past her, heading down the hall to the kitchen.

I guess it's *our* kitchen now.

"Come on," I call over my shoulder. "I'll give you the tour."

River follows, gasping when she takes in our big, open-plan kitchen. It's by far the best room in the house. There's a huge oak table, big enough to seat ten burly bikers. It's the heart of the house, and my cousin Quinn and I have spent many a Sunday afternoon with my dad and aunt and our family—the Sinners MC—here. But that's not what catches River's eye. It's the wall of glass that overlooks the small lake.

"Wow," she moves closer, "it's so beautiful." Her eyes widen as she gazes outside, but the sadness never leaves them.

"Right?" I rest my elbows on the counter and watch her. She's not like I imagined, given that her big brother is Rhett Savage.

He's so... bad. And she's so... innocent. They couldn't be more different if they tried.

I don't know what to make of it.

He isn't exactly a talker, and he's always made it

pretty clear he doesn't like me. Which is fine by me; the feeling is entirely mutual. It has absolutely nothing to do with the fact that my dad treats him like the son he always wanted and never had.

Heavy footsteps in the hall draw both our attention, and Dad reappears. He eyes me warily, and I notice he's pulled his long hair into a ponytail. "We put your bags upstairs in your room."

"Thanks, Ray." River smiles, and it's so genuine, so full of gratitude, I want to wipe it right of her pretty little face.

Dammit.

She's like sunshine on a rainy day... and I feel like the thunderstorm circling overhead, about to erupt.

"Where's Rhett?" she asks.

"He's just getting the last of it. I'm surprised you talked him into borrowing a truck. I don't think I've ever seen that kid off his Street Bob."

"He doesn't let me ride his bike."

Of course he doesn't.

I fight the urge to roll my eyes.

"What do you think of the place?" Dad asks, and I swear he looks... nervous.

Razor Dalton doesn't get nervous. Ever.

This is fucked up.

"I love it. This kitchen is amazing. I—"

"I need to..." I thumb to the hall and inch back away from them both. This is too much too soon.

She's staring at Dad—*my* dad—likes he's her real-life hero, and he's acting weird.

I don't like it.

"Sadie Ray, wait—"

But I'm already out of the kitchen, darting down the

hall. Anger burns through me as I grab the stair bannister and swing myself around... slamming straight into a wall of sheer muscle.

"Watch it, princess."

"Get out of my way," I grit out, lifting my chin at Rhett.

A slow smirk spreads over his face. "You ran into me."

"Whatever." I try to barge around him, but he plants his feet wider, crossing his ridiculously big arms over his chest. Even underneath his leather cut, I can see the way his white t-shirt molds to the hard lines of his chest.

"See something you like?"

"Please. I don't date bikers." My brow lifts in annoyance, but he only smirks harder.

"Who said anything about dating?"

Typical Rhett. He thinks he's God's gift to women. He might only be a year older than me, but he acts like he's something. Some*one*.

"Just stay out of my way," I hiss, my hands clenched into fists at my sides.

Amusement flashes in his eyes as he lets them drop lazily down my body, lingering on the low V-neck in my t-shirt.

"Gross. We're practically siblings, and you're looking at me like—"

"Rhett, that you?" Dad calls, his voice like a bucket of ice water over me.

I need to go. Now.

Using Rhett's momentary distraction to my advantage, I shove him—hard—and slip up the stairs, his deep rumble of laughter making my stomach knot.

Without looking back, I turn down the hall but pause when I hear Dad's voice.

"There's a room here for you, you know?"

"Yeah, I know."

"Stay. See how things go..."

"Nah. I like my space, and I have a room at the club."

"Yeah, but come on, son—"

Son. He called him son.

It shouldn't matter... and yet, I feel like I can't breathe.

"I appreciate it, Ray. We both do. But I'm not cut out for family life. Look after River. I'll stop by."

"Damn right you will. Go on," Dad says, "get out of here. I'll see you at the club later."

"Sure thing, old man."

Their laughter drifts up to me, making the knot in my stomach tighten. Rhett loves my dad, I know he does. It's in the way they talk: easy and fluid. It's the respect that shines in Rhett's eyes whenever my dad is around.

They're close.

Real close.

Which is why I've never understood why Rhett Savage acts like he hates me.

DOWNLOAD NOW to continue reading Sadie's, Rhett, Dane and Wes's story.